ENSNARED IN SHADOW

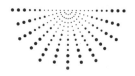

C.C. WOOD

Copyright © 2022 by Crystal W. Wilson

All rights reserved.

No part of this book may be reproduced in any form or by any electronic or mechanical means, including information storage and retrieval systems, without written permission from the author, except for the use of brief quotations in a book review.

PROLOGUE

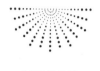

MERRY

I HAD no idea what I was doing.

None.

Okay, so that's partially a lie.

I did know I was packing up my meager belongings and my computer. Then, I was getting the hell out of town.

Where to?

No clue.

I laughed to myself at the little mental rhyme and then shook my head in disgust. I'd been alone for so long that I was beginning to talk to myself, not just out loud, but in my own head. And not in the ordinary way that a person might talk to themselves silently.

No, I had to be amusing.

Or slightly creepy.

As I stuffed the last t-shirt in my suitcase, I glanced around the sterile studio apartment that had been my home for the last six months. There was little more than a bed in one corner, a kitchenette in the opposite corner, and a garage-sale sofa in front of a giant big screen TV from the 1990's that had to weigh a couple hundred pounds. I assumed the owners left it there because it was too heavy to move.

I'd already packed up my small supply of non-perishable food and eaten the last two bananas I had. My clothes and laptop were all ready to go.

The only thing missing was a destination.

But I had to leave. There was an instinctive part of me that was screaming I needed to run as fast and as far as possible. That someone, or *something*, was coming for me and I wanted no part of it.

Considering what had happened to me nearly a year ago, I wasn't going to question that instinct.

Being held hostage by an insane witch with a scary pet vampire that drank life force instead of blood had cured me of any skepticism when it came to sixth senses.

Magic existed. Evil existed.

And both had promised to return for me.

I sure as hell didn't want to be easily found when it did.

As I stared around the crappy apartment, it came to me.

Austin, Texas.

It was as if someone whispered those words in my ear, calling me to a safe haven.

Again, I didn't question the gut feeling that I should head in that direction. Logic had no power against the sort of magic I'd faced.

Seeing as Austin was several states from St. Louis, maybe it would make it even more difficult for Rhiannon to find me when she came back.

And I didn't doubt that she would return. Though she was a powerful witch, I'd dealt with women of her sort before. The kind that were cold inside, cunning, and cruel.

Somehow, they always got their way.

Probably because they didn't care who they destroyed on the path to success.

While I might not have the magic to fight her, she didn't have the technological know-how to track me, which was why she'd kidnapped me in the first place. She'd needed my computer skills.

I made sure to pack every item I owned and donated my single sheet set, blanket, and small collection of mismatched dishes. Every other piece of furniture, cabinetry, and even the walls, had been wiped down from top to bottom. Then, I intended to cleanse the room with burning sage just to be on the safe side.

A year ago, I would have scoffed at the idea of cleansing a room with smoldering dried herbs, but after watching Rhiannon do it on more than one occasion, I wasn't going to discount it any longer.

Once that was done, I would be on my way to Austin.

And, hopefully, to safety.

CHAPTER ONE

MARCUS

SHE'S COMING.

My eyes flew open as the words echoed in my head.

I sat up and threw the blanket off my legs. The room was still dim, but I could see the first watery light of dawn slipping around the edge of the blinds.

Rubbing a hand over my sternum, I leaned over and tried to take a slow, deep breath.

As always, the dreams made my chest feel tight, as though I couldn't take in enough air. Then, there was the headache that accompanied it.

I winced as the first throb hit behind my eyes. I knew Ava would have cuffed me on the back of the head for calling them dreams when, in reality, they were visions. As a powerful sorceress, she would know the difference, I suppose.

But, still, if they happened in my sleep, what else should I call them but dreams?

Mostly they were nightmares that featured the same woman. A woman who'd been trapped and terrified by Rhiannon.

I tried to take comfort that the woman was no longer in danger because Rhiannon had been imprisoned in a magical realm by a deity, the Goddess herself. But from the dreams she shared with me, I doubted that the woman knew.

Rhiannon had wrought so much pain the year before she was caught and sent elsewhere. She'd tried to destroy Macgrath, a man I consider a brother, the one who had turned me into a vampire to save me from death on the battlefield. When that didn't work, she went after his mate, Ava.

Unfortunately, she'd underestimated Ava's powers. And her connections to the Goddess.

In the eleven months since she'd been banished, Ava and Macgrath had worked to heal the damage Rhiannon had caused not only to them, but to others.

Like Caleb.

In her quest for more power, Rhiannon had used ancient magic to create an *animavore*, a soul eater.

Once a normal man, Caleb now required the life force of others to live. Through Rhys, the only other *animavore* in existence, he'd learned to feed without hurting or killing humans and he'd learned to control his power.

Seeing as how Rhys had found his way to Ava just before Rhiannon's reappearance, and met his mate at Ava's shop, I had to believe that it was fated.

Rhiannon had also been the cause of a rift between Macgrath, Callum, and me. The three of us had fought side-by-side for over a thousand years, yet she managed to tear us apart with ridiculous ease.

Those wounds were beginning to heal, but I doubted it would be as quickly or as easily as the ones between Macgrath and Ava.

As the ache behind my eyes began to lessen, I turned my thoughts back toward my dream and the woman.

She'd been in the car, driving through the night.

Coming to Austin.

And, though she didn't realize it, she was coming right to me.

The knowledge was both heady and weighty.

From her nightmares, her memories really, I knew that she no longer felt safe and that she feared Rhiannon's return.

I hadn't told a soul about the dreams. They were too painful. Too intimate.

I not only saw what she did, but I felt her pain, her fear...the utter helplessness.

Also, there was the fact that she was the hacker who'd helped Rhiannon hide her tracks. The computer wizard that Callum couldn't track, no matter how hard he tried.

That was saying something, because not only did his fingers move with preternatural speed, his brain seemed to as well. There were very few hackers who could outdo Callum and he'd been more than a little pissed at his inability to track not only Rhiannon, but the hacker as well.

It also amused me because if he'd had any clue that he'd been chasing a woman, he would have been doubly irritated and even more intrigued.

Despite the tight band of pain that still surrounded my skull, I found myself smiling.

Maybe I could introduce them someday.

My smile faded at the thought. I doubted that would happen. Ever.

The woman in my dreams was coming to Austin and I would likely never meet her. Even if I did, I imagined she would fear me as deeply as she feared Rhiannon and Caleb. If not more.

She was close enough to touch, but still far from my reach.

I jumped at the fist that slammed into my door and bit back a curse.

Consumed with my thoughts, I hadn't heard Callum approach. I hated when he surprised me, which meant he tried to do it as often as possible.

"Ava called. There's a new vamp coming to town today and he's presenting himself to them at nine. She wants us both there."

I sighed and stood. Callum smirked at me when I opened the door. He'd insisted we share a house when we came to Austin. Something about living alone making me intolerable. Or maybe it was insufferable.

"Why does she want *us* there? We have no authority. There are no vampire covens or groups here because of the witches and the wolf pack. They tolerate us because we don't stir up trouble, hunt and kill humans, and we got rid of Rhiannon for them."

Callum crossed his arms over his chest and leaned a shoulder against the jamb. "I brought up all those pertinent details, but Ava said that we were part of her family and this vampire wanted an alliance, which means we all have to be there when they meet so we can make a decision 'together'," he stated, lifting his hands long enough to make the air quotes sign. "I told her that it was six in the bloody morning and I trusted Macgrath to make the best decision, but she wasn't having any of it."

"Well, have fun," I replied, reaching out to shut the door.

Callum straightened and used an arm to keep me from closing him out. "Nu-uh. If I have to go, you have to go. I'm not suffering alone. All for one and one for all."

"For the last time, we're not the Three Musketeers."

"Don't care. If I'm going, you're going."

"No."

Callum lifted a brow and smiled. "So, you want me to tell Ava, the most powerful witch we've ever met, the creator of vampires, that you want your solitude and you're not coming? I'm pretty sure we both know what she'd do then."

I sighed again. "Good point."

In reality, neither of us knew what she would do, and it was better if it stayed that way. If my rotten luck held, she could teleport us both to her shop with a snap of her fingers. The sorceress was beyond powerful and she was the mother of vampires, even if she was a witch rather than a vampire herself.

While she never lorded it over either of us, it wasn't a good idea to underestimate her.

Callum didn't wait for me to say anything else. He tapped the door with a finger. "Be ready to leave at eight. I want to drink some coffee and eat a pastry before we meet the visitor."

"Fine. Workout before or after the meeting?"

He yawned. "After the meeting. I stayed up 'til three in the morning playing Skyrim. I'm gonna take another hour to nap before I get ready."

He'd already turned and walked back down the hall to his room, so he didn't see me roll my eyes.

I glanced back at my bed and considered trying to do the same, but dismissed it. There was no way I could go back to sleep now that I knew she was coming.

I decided to spend an hour on physical conditioning before eating and getting ready to go to Ava's meeting. An extra workout wouldn't hurt me. It would clear the last dregs of my headache away and maybe help me focus on something other than the words that hummed in the corners of my mind.

She's coming.

∼

CALLUM SMIRKED THEN YAWNED as we entered The Magic Bean, the coffee shop-slash-New-Age store that Ava owned. Technically, she carried items for witches, but the word witchcraft was still given a wide berth in the Southern parts of the U.S.

Ava used the term "New Age", which fit in perfectly with the relaxed vibe often found in parts of Austin.

"Oh, man. She made lemon scones," Callum murmured.

I sniffed and closed my eyes in pleasure. Not only had she made lemon scones, she also had snickerdoodles, my absolute favorite.

The perfume of lemon, sugar, vanilla, cinnamon, and coffee entwined to create the siren song of scent. My mouth watered even though I'd eaten eggs, toast, and tomatoes for breakfast just an hour ago.

Before Callum and I could approach the counter and order food, Ava came through the swinging double doors at the back of the shop.

"This way," she said, gesturing toward the back room.

"But...but..." Callum sputtered.

She gave him a stern look. "Get your ass into my office now. You can have a treat later."

9

I'd never seen a grown man pout, but Callum did a damn good impression of one as he followed Ava into the storeroom then further back to her office.

Now that she and Macgrath worked together more often than not, she'd expanded her office so that it held two desks that faced each other and a small four-top table where she could have staff meetings, a private meal, or rendezvous with Macgrath in the middle of the workday.

Don't ask me how I knew the last one because the memories were still a little too vivid and disconcerting.

So vivid and disconcerting that I had to suppress a wince when I saw a plate of scones, another plate of snickerdoodles, an insulated carafe, and coffee cups on top of the table. Considering what I'd witnessed the two of them doing, well, I wasn't sure I wanted to eat anything off that table.

"Don't get crumbs everywhere," Ava admonished Callum as he reached for a scone. "The cleaning staff came through last night and gave the place a thorough once-over." Her eyes met mine and twinkled with amusement.

Oh, yes, she knew exactly why I wasn't reaching for my favorite cookies and she was letting me know that my squeamishness entertained her.

Shit. Now, I had to have one or she'd just give me shit relentlessly about being afraid to eat a cookie because the plate was sitting on the table where she and Macgrath had sex.

I braced myself and grabbed one off the plate. Ava smirked as I bit into it, but I didn't look away.

So what if Macgrath's bare ass had been on this table last week?

"Why do we have to be here again?" Callum asked, his mouth still full of scone.

"First of all," Ava began. "Chew with your mouth closed. Secondly, you're here because, like it or not, you're considered vassals of Macgrath. He is your maker, therefore your ruler."

Callum grunted. "Ruler, my ass," he muttered beneath his breath.

"We know that, but vampires from other areas don't work like that. The Council doesn't work like that."

"There is no Council," I interjected. "Not anymore."

Ava's responding look was dry. "You know better than that. As soon as the fallout settled after Cornelius, a new Council was instated."

"Great, because they were so effective before."

She lifted her hands. "You don't have to tell me. I know. Bureaucracy is as immortal as vampires."

"You still haven't explained why we have to be here," Callum complained before he shoved the rest of the scone in his mouth and reached for a cookie.

"As Magrath's vassals, it's expected that you'll be here as part of his entourage when he's meeting with another vampire leader. I don't want to draw attention to ourselves and create an appearance of weakness."

I nearly choked on my snickerdoodle. I knew for a fact that Ava, and Macgrath for that matter, didn't give a shit about what other people thought of them. Or appearing weak.

Callum hooted, shooting crumbs into the air. "As if either of you give a damn."

Ava stared at him with hard, purple eyes. "What did I tell you about crumbs?"

He chewed quickly and swallowed hard. "Sorry. I'll clean them up before His Lordship gets here."

She gave him the once over. "You might go out back and shake yourself in the alley first because you're a mess." She continued as Callum cursed and looked down at his crumb-covered chest. "And you're right, we don't give a shit about what Andre Dumont or the Council might think. But I don't want to invite speculation or even a possible attack because other vampires and witches think we're weak. I don't want that kind of attention or the headache that goes along with it."

"Okay, that makes sense," Callum muttered. "I'll just, uh, go clean up and grab the handheld vacuum."

He left the office and Ava sighed. She moved to the table and poured out a cup of coffee, which she handed to me.

"How are you doing?" she asked.

I shrugged. "Fine."

Her expression told me that she didn't believe that for a second. "Even with the dreams?"

I frowned at her. I'd never mentioned them. "Are you sneaking into my thoughts?"

"You know better than that. But I see things sometimes. Things that are important to our future."

"And what's so important to our future?" I asked, taking a sip of coffee.

"Her."

It seemed that Ava was actively trying to make me choke this morning. I swallowed the coffee in my mouth and then coughed a little. "Her who?"

"You know exactly who I'm talking about. And she's coming."

I didn't respond. Over the centuries, I'd learned that silence was the best choice when I wasn't sure what to say.

"When the time comes, Marcus, I'll help you." Ava rested a hand on my forearm and squeezed. "Neither of us know the specifics of the future. It's hell to see just enough to know that something is about to happen, but not enough to prevent tragedy."

I laid my hand over hers. She was right. We both had the gift, or curse, of foresight, but it was never enough. Not enough to save the people we cared about. Or prevent horrible things from happening.

Never enough.

"It'll turn out for the best," she murmured. "You'll see."

Her eyes lost focus for a moment and her hand fell away from my arm.

"It seems our guest has arrived," she said, glancing at her watch. "And he's a bit early, too."

I assumed she felt him enter her wards.

She gave Callum a hard look when he re-entered the office and started vacuuming up the crumbs he'd dropped on the floor. "Put your game face on and no fucking around."

He glanced up at her. "I got all the crumbs off and I'd rather not talk to some vampire with a stick up his ass, so I'll stand here and look mean."

"That works."

She turned to me, but I lifted a hand. "I never talk anyway."

Her mouth closed and she nodded. "True enough." When she turned back toward Macgrath, she asked, "Ready?"

"It's your show."

"Just a show," she repeated, glancing at Callum and at me.

Together, Ava and Macgrath left the office and went to meet Andre Dumont.

Callum finished cleaning up and stowed the handheld vacuum. We shared a look and each took a place against opposite walls. Feet apart and hands held together in front of us, we mirrored each other's stances.

While Callum might mouth off, he understood as well as I did the necessity in showing a united front. In presenting an image that would make vampires and other supernatural creatures hesitate before they challenged us.

As the first of Macgrath's lineage, and essentially the first vampires in this realm, vampire politics and machinations were of no interest to us. Getting involved in any sort of political aspirations only meant you'd have to watch your back for the knife that was waiting to slide in.

So, Callum and I would put on the faces of foot soldiers and watch Andre Dumont like a hawk.

Ava and Macgrath returned with a lean vampire behind them. He appeared to have been turned in his mid-thirties. His hair and eyes were black as onyx and he wore a simple white shirt and black pants with plain black shoes.

While his clothes and build seemed casual and non-threatening, the back of my neck prickled. His gaze swept the room, pausing briefly on Callum and then me, and I had the impression he'd committed the placement of each piece of furniture and knickknack to memory.

This was not a vampire to underestimate.

Strangely, there was no presence of power around him, no mantle of age that filled the space. He couldn't be more than a hundred vampire years, probably less.

Yet I wouldn't dare turn my back to him.

Callum and I were warriors, but Andre Dumont was an assassin. He was the shadowed blade; the death blow you would never see strike.

I glanced at Macgrath and knew by the set of his shoulders and the tension in his jaw that he felt the same.

"Mr. Dumont, welcome to Austin," Ava said, interrupting my perusal of the vampire. "This is Callum Donalson and Marcus Vane."

He looked at each of us and nodded, but did not offer his hand. The prickle on the back of my neck intensified and slid like a cold finger down my spine. Under the guise of pouring myself a cup of coffee, I moved closer to the vampire.

"Would you like coffee?" Ava asked, her dark purple eyes shifting from me to Dumont.

"I would. Thank you." His accent was subtle, just the hint of a Southern drawl.

Without waiting to be asked, I poured him a cup and handed it to him, bringing me within arm's reach should he move the wrong way.

Then, Ava ruined it by saying, "Why don't we all sit down and get to know each other a bit?"

The tension coming from Macgrath and Callum increased because it would put her too close to this vampire and whatever ill intentions he could have.

Suddenly, I heard Ava's voice in my head and knew that she was speaking to Macgrath and Callum also.

Will all of you just calm down? He's a young vampire and on his guard. Savannah saw no malevolence in his aura.

Callum, Macgrath, and I looked to each other.

14

For the Goddess's sake, sit down and ease up a bit. I can handle him if necessary. You all know it.

Ava moved to the table and Macgrath somehow managed to beat her there and pull out her chair. She smiled at him and sat, waiting for Andre to take the seat across from her and Macgrath to settle next to her.

I grabbed a stool from the corner and placed it at the end of the table, my body between Dumont and Ava. Callum took the seat next to the vampire, leaving enough space to maneuver if necessary.

"Is this your first time in Austin?" Ava asked Dumont as she poured a cup of coffee for herself and another for Macgrath.

"It is, but I like what I've seen so far."

She smiled, looking as at ease as if she were speaking to a mere human instead of an unfamiliar vampire. "It is a fun place. I can suggest some sights to see if you wish."

Dumont sipped his coffee. "I would appreciate that."

I wanted to tell them to both knock off the bullshit and get to the point, but I knew that wasn't the way things were done amongst vampires. Instead, I drank my own coffee and tried not to glower as the small talk continued.

Finally, Ava asked, "What brought you our way?"

Dumont smiled. "Work, I'm afraid. I'm doing business with some humans here and I didn't want to enter your territory without introducing myself."

It was a lie. That damned tingle on the back of my neck returned.

"Well, it's certainly lovely to meet you," Ava replied. "But I'd prefer the honest answer."

Dumont huffed out a small laugh. "Am I that obvious?"

Ava didn't respond. Instead, she cupped her hands around her coffee and held his gaze.

I felt rather than saw Callum tense his muscles, but Dumont surprised me by speaking rather than attacking.

"If what I've heard of you is true," he said. "Then you know I'm fairly young and my power is still growing. My parish is relatively small so I don't gather much attention from the older vampires in

Louisiana, but I am close to the Texas border, which presents potential problems. For example, last year a powerful sorceress came through town on her way here. I couldn't have fought her, so I found myself in a position to play nice with someone I'd rather not associate with. Again, I've heard things about the four of you and your...entourage and your conflict with this sorceress. It's my understanding that she is no longer a problem, largely due to you."

Dumont paused and studied Ava, waiting for some sort of confirmation.

I had to give it to Macgrath's mate. She had one hell of a poker face. Even though I'd known her for a year now, I had no clue what she was thinking.

"That is true," she stated after a long silence. "Rhiannon Temple is imprisoned and no longer a threat to us or anyone else."

Dumont visibly relaxed. "I have to admit that relieves me."

"This is why you came? To ask about Rhiannon?" Macgrath asked.

"Partially," Dumont said. "I also came to discuss the possibility of an alliance. I realize that I do not have your power or magic," he continued. "But I do have a coven of twenty-five vampires in my parish. We are all young, but that also means we will all grow in strength as the years pass. Should you have need of our aid, we are close enough to be here within a day if necessary. And..." he trailed off.

"If you find yourself facing another sorcerer or sorceress, we have the magic to help you," Ava finished for him.

Dumont nodded. "Yes. I realize that this alliance might not be of much benefit and create risk for you, but we are all long-lived and in twenty or thirty years, we would be a great asset."

Ava cocked her head. "I can see that." Her eyes deepened and grew brighter, the purple becoming almost electric in intensity. "I see a great deal." She paused. "For example, don't your...friends call you Digger?"

Dumont's olive skin paled beneath her perusal and I nearly felt sorry for the poor bastard. I'd been on the receiving end of those eyes and that power before and the weight was almost too heavy for me to bear. I couldn't imagine how it would feel to a vampire so young.

Ava blinked and the brilliant lavender in her eyes faded back to dark indigo. "Your proposal is an interesting one and definitely something I will consider further. However, I know very little about you or your coven. I'm assuming you brought a few of them with you?" she asked.

Dumont nodded, the ashen pallor of his cheeks slowly returning to deep tan. "I have three of mine with me."

"I would like a chance to meet with them." It wasn't a request but a subtle command.

Dumont knew it, too. "Of course. I would be happy to arrange that. You have my cell number, please let me know a time and place of your convenience. I will be here at least two weeks for my business."

Macgrath cocked a brow but didn't say anything. Strange that this vampire was so willing to meet Ava anytime, anywhere. I wondered if it was youth or a cunning scheme to make us feel more relaxed.

"Then I'll be in touch tomorrow," she answered, rising to her feet. "Thank you so much for coming to meet us today." She held out a hand as Dumont stood.

He hesitated for less than a blink, but we all saw it. Still, he was brave enough to take her hand and give it a gentle squeeze.

"I'm honored to meet you, Ms. Amaris." He looked at Macgrath. "And you as well."

Macgrath gave him a respectful nod but didn't hold out a hand. Dumont released Ava's fingers and nodded to Callum and then to me.

"Mr. Donalson. Mr. Vane. I hope I see you again as well."

We both inclined our heads in acceptance but remained silent.

"Come, I'll walk you out." Ava smiled up at him as she came around the table and hooked her arm through his.

After seeing his reaction to her earlier, I no longer worried quite so much about what his plans were. If he'd thought her an easy target when he planned this visit, it was obvious he'd learned otherwise in the last few moments.

Still, I was glad to see Macgrath follow them out of the office, less than two steps behind them.

He would protect his mate at any cost and I imagined that Dumont knew that.

After their footsteps faded, Callum turned to me. "Do you think she knows he's full of shit?"

"Of course she does," I answered with a shrug. "But he's not lying about the alliance. For some reason, he needs us."

"So he's hiding the lie within the truth?"

"Most likely. I think we need to keep an eye on Mr. Dumont while he's in town, Callum. Don't you?"

"Abso-fuckin'-lutely."

Whatever his scheme might be, Andre Dumont was in for an unpleasant surprise if he tried to cause trouble.

A very unpleasant surprise.

CHAPTER TWO

MERRY

I HIT Austin just before sunset. As soon as I saw the city sprawling out next to the highway, something deep inside me relaxed.

All day, I'd been questioning my decision to come, even though I'd promised myself to trust my instincts in the foreseeable future.

But that tension didn't lie.

This was where I belonged. At least for now.

And because I felt that way, I decided to splurge on a nice hotel for the night rather than something cheaper near the highway.

My system was crying out for coffee, so I pulled off the highway at a Starbucks and ordered a cold brew with sweet cream. As I sipped, I searched hotels and found one on South Congress Avenue. The more I looked into the area, the more I liked the sound of it. It seemed fun and a little funky.

Feeling more optimistic than I had since before my ordeal with Rhiannon Temple, I decided to book a room at the South Congress Hotel. A few nights there would give me enough time to find an Airbnb or something a little more long-term. I winced at the price, but I had to believe that it would be worth it.

As if to further prove that my instincts were right, there was an available room for the next week. I booked it for five nights, though I intended to check out early. The price of the room was too steep for me to stay there for a full week, but I wasn't sure how long it might take for me to find a temporary rental.

Satisfied, I carried my iced coffee to the car and pulled up the hotel's address on Google Maps.

An hour later, I settled into the hotel room, surprised at the comfort and spaciousness of the room. It wasn't some sterile suite just like every other one in the rest of the hotel.

I liked it a lot. It reminded me of who I'd been before.

I walked to the window. The woman at the front desk had made sure to give me a window that faced South Congress so I could see the comings and goings. It was dark out but there were still people out, strolling down the sidewalks.

I wanted to do the same. A year ago, I wouldn't have hesitated.

But now I was aware of the creatures that hunted after sunset.

And I was afraid.

I contented myself with watching the people as they walked, laughed, flirted, and argued.

Maybe someday I could join them.

Since I'd been on the run, I'd been working on a way to defend myself from vampires and other supernatural creatures. I'd illegally obtained a police-issue Taser and adapted it to increase the output as much as possible. The only issue was that I didn't want to risk hurting a human by testing it on them. I damn sure didn't want to test it on some random vampire that I came across.

I was stuck. Until I found a way to test it, I could only hope that it would work on a vampire or other preternatural monster.

Then, there was the defense spray I'd mixed up. It contained enough acid to cause major issues for a human. It wouldn't kill a creature that healed as quickly as vampires, but it would definitely hurt them long enough for me to get away. Hopefully, to an extremely fast car.

Again, I had the same issue as the Taser. I had no way to test it. I could only hope it worked when I needed it.

But I had no doubt I would need it in the future.

With a sigh, I got up and moved the chair away from the window. As nice as it was to people-watch, I had to look for an affordable rental. And apply for some freelance programming work while I was at it. I still had a decent nest egg, but I wanted to keep it that way.

Tomorrow morning would be early enough to walk on the sidewalks among all those people.

~

MY FIRST STOP after breakfast wasn't one of the funky shops nearby or even the cool coffee shop down the street. It was the grocery store.

I needed snacks in the worst way because the prices on everything in the hotel minibar made me contemplate the benefits of fasting.

Unfortunately, hangry me didn't last very long.

As I walked through the grocery store, I fought the urge to throw a small mountain of food in my basket. I'd walked to the store and I didn't want to haul fifty pounds of junk food back.

Chips were lightweight. So were gummy bears and Snickers bars. I grabbed a bottle of soda and a small box of Pop-Tarts, too.

I grimaced at my selection of food and decided to at least add some cheese and nut snack packs or something that I could pretend was semi-healthy.

As I walked to the refrigerated section that held the lunch meat, snack packs, and Lunchables, the back of my neck tingled. I slowed my pace and glanced around, aiming for a casual expression.

Then, I saw him about ten feet away, looking at me.

Our eyes met for a brief moment before he looked down at the box of crackers in his hand, but I couldn't stop staring at him.

He wasn't beautiful but he was definitely in "good-looking" territory. His dark brown hair was cut almost brutally short, which drew my attention to the sharp bones of his face. Thick, dark brows slashed over eyes that had pierced mine when our stares collided. His jaw was square and hard.

But his mouth looked soft.

At that moment, my klutz factor kicked in and I caught my elbow

21

on the edge of a small wire basket holding hot dog buns. The legs screeched against the concrete floor and the entire thing tilted.

Oh. Shit.

I watched in horror as the basket crashed to the ground on its side and rolled a few feet to my left.

Right toward the man.

My face burned as I scrambled after the display to stop its motion. I stomped on the urge to look around and see if everyone was staring at me because I was pretty sure they were.

Instead, I carried the rack back to where it had been and picked up the buns that had fallen out when it tipped over. My cheeks were so hot that I was surprised my skin wasn't smoking.

When I straightened, I gasped and nearly knocked the damn thing over again.

Because the dark-haired man was standing right next to me now. I hadn't noticed him coming over in my rush to clean up the mess I'd made.

He dropped two more bags of buns in the basket and smiled at me.

Holy mac and cheese, he had a dimple. Just one.

And now that he was closer, I could see that his eyes were bright blue and even more intense up close.

"I never understood why they put these things in the middle of the aisles," he commented, his voice deep and a little rough. "I manage to bump into one every time I come here."

I swallowed hard and tried to think of a response, but my vocal cords froze in both embarrassment and awe.

Up close, I realized that he was a big man, tall and broad, his shoulders and biceps straining against his t-shirt. And he smelled amazing, fresh and clean but without the heaviness of cologne.

Before I could babble incoherently, he glanced down at my arm and frowned. "You have a scratch there. Are you okay?"

I looked down and saw a long, red welt marring my left forearm. "It's fine," I managed to say, my voice at least an octave higher than usual.

I lifted my head and our eyes met again. This time, there was something about the way the light reflected off his irises that brought that tingle back to my neck.

"Thanks for the help," I said, taking a step back.

"No problem. Are you sure you're okay?"

I nodded. "Yep. Fine. Just need to find my dignity."

Oh, God. What was wrong with me? Why couldn't I talk to people without losing my ability to filter my thoughts before they came out of my mouth?

He smiled at me, the dimple making another appearance. "I'm Marcus."

"Nice to meet you, Marcus. I have to go now. I'm, uh, late."

Then, I scurried away. I swore I could feel his eyes on my back, but I didn't look over my shoulder. I couldn't.

I ditched the idea of healthy snacks and made a beeline for the self-checkout at the front of the store. In less than five minutes, I was back on the street and almost jogging back to the hotel.

The heat in my cheeks didn't begin to fade until I was back inside my room with the door securely locked behind me.

I dropped the grocery bags on the desk and threw myself backward on the bed with a groan.

"What in the hell is wrong with me?" I scrubbed my hands over my face. "I meet a cute guy and lose all ability to speak."

I pressed my palms to my eyes and sighed. I'd always been awkward around men, but things had gotten worse after Rhiannon and her companion had found me. They'd both looked so normal.

In terms of real time, they hadn't held me hostage for very long. Only five days.

But it felt like a lifetime then.

Now, it was nearly impossible for me to trust people.

Rhiannon and Caleb hadn't looked like monsters, but that was exactly what they were. They'd captured me and forced me to do things. And Caleb had fed from me.

Based on lore, I'd assumed vampires fed solely on blood, but he didn't. When he fed from me, I could feel my life seeping away, a year, a month, a minute at a time. It hurt so much. In those excruciating moments, he had the ultimate power over me. Over my life and my death.

I was powerless to stop him from taking my life.

My chest hurt at the memory and I realized I wasn't breathing.

Air rushed out of my mouth with a whoosh and I inhaled—slow, steady, and controlled.

If I didn't handle this now, a panic attack was my next stop and I had to avoid it. I couldn't afford to be weak or vulnerable right now.

This was why I couldn't talk to the gorgeous Marcus with his muscles and bright blue eyes. My mind was still a mess from what had happened last year and I couldn't talk to anyone about it. At best, no one would believe me. At worst, I would end up in a hospital for a psychiatric evaluation.

So, I was on my own.

I was used to it. I'd been alone since my parents died right after I graduated college. I was their only child.

I'd never been a social butterfly, so I didn't have many friends either. Essentially, I'd been alone for most of my adult life.

Sure, I was lonely sometimes, but I'd never understood how isolated I truly was until now.

Tears gathered at the corners of my eyes as I struggled to control my breathing, to keep the panic at bay.

I focused on the next breath. Then, the next. One breath at a time.

It hurt a little less with each inhale.

My current situation was painful, but I wanted to survive more than anything.

I wouldn't stop. I wouldn't give up.

I finally understood that I'd been living half a life for a very long time and I wanted more.

I wanted to savor each day, to enjoy the places and people around me.

I no longer wanted to exist. I wanted to *live*.

As I exhaled on a hiss, I wondered that if instead of running maybe I would be better off figuring out where Rhiannon was and what she was up to. She might be a witch, but she still needed money, food, and shelter to survive. Unless she'd found another programmer like me, I doubted she'd done anything else to hide her assets.

Magic might not leave a paper trail, but money did.

Maybe it was time for me to fight back in my own way.

If I did, maybe I would finally be able to sleep without nightmares.

Or talk to handsome men in grocery stores.

I sat up and took my laptop from the night table next to the bed. I would do a little discreet digging, see what I could find out, and then I would decide what to do next.

I opened my laptop and saw a new message waiting in my inbox with the subject "Job Offer."

Okay, so I would do the digging and deciding after I checked out the email. I needed funds to keep doing what I was doing and I would need more if I chose to fight back.

When I opened the email, I was pleasantly surprised at the offer. One of my previous clients had referred me to Mr. Andre Dumont. The pay was high enough to pique my interest and, based on the details he sent, the job would only take two to four weeks to complete, depending on a few factors that would be determined in the next week.

For the first time in a year, it seemed that destiny was on my side.

I typed out a quick response to his request for an interview, stating that I was available for video chat or telephone interviews, but wouldn't be able to meet face-to-face as I was currently working on a small project in Austin, Texas. It wasn't the complete truth, but saying I was trying to be less of a basket case likely wouldn't net me the gig.

After the email was sent, I settled back against the pillows on the bed with a Snickers bar, a cup of coffee, and started my search for more information on Rhiannon Temple and her current whereabouts.

CHAPTER THREE

MARCUS

MY HEART POUNDED as I watched her walk away from me. It took every ounce of will I possessed to keep my feet still. My instincts urged me to follow her, to tell her that she didn't have to fear me.

I knew who she was. How her mind worked. The depth of her fear. The strength of her spirit.

But I still didn't know her name.

The only thing that kept me in place was the knowledge that she was frightened of me. That was the last thing I wanted.

I waited a few moments, just long enough to leave space between us, and then I followed, abandoning my cart. I wouldn't approach her again. I only wanted to make sure that she made it to her car safely.

I spied her all but throwing her items in bags at the self-checkout and made sure to linger just out of her line of sight.

After she paid, she threw a couple of glances over her shoulder as she walked out the doors and turned left, away from the parking lot.

Frowning, I followed her out of the store. She was practically running with the two plastic bags in her hands. Dammit, she was truly frightened. This was not how I'd imagined our first interaction going.

I let the space between us grow as she continued down the sidewalk. She must be staying close by if she'd walked to the supermarket.

A few moments later, she slowed and went into a building. I took a few more steps until I could read the sign on the side clearly.

South Congress Hotel.

I couldn't believe it. After all these months of seeing her in my sleep, of reliving her nightmares, and feeling her fear, she was incredibly close. Only blocks from The Magic Bean.

I stood on the sidewalk for a few minutes, looking at all the windows on the hotel. I don't know if I expected her to look out or if I just didn't want to leave until I knew she was safe, but I couldn't make my feet move.

"Hey! There you are."

I jolted and whirled around to find Callum standing just behind me. Damn. I'd been so focused on her that he'd managed to sneak up on me. Something he relished in doing, which meant I usually had to stay on my guard.

"What are you doing?" he asked, rocking back and forth on his heels, a smirk on his face.

"Nothing."

He produced an apple from somewhere, probably a pocket, and took a bite. "I haven't startled you like that in a decade, so you were definitely doing something. Maybe thinking too hard."

I closed my eyes for just a moment and rubbed the center of my forehead. "I was distracted. That's all."

Callum crunched on the apple again and said, "Bullshit."

I sidestepped the half-chewed pieces of fruit that he spewed when he spoke. "At least chew that and swallow it before you start talking."

He made an exaggerated face as he did just that, then continued, "I think it has something to do with a certain woman." He smirked again. "The woman of your dreams."

I scowled at him, but didn't speak. I had no idea how he knew all of this. I walked around him and headed back toward The Magic Bean. For all his juvenile jokes and general goofiness, Callum saw a great deal more than I was comfortable with.

I lengthened my stride and ignored him as he fell in step beside me, still smacking that damn apple.

My back teeth clenched as I fought the urge to snatch the fruit from his hand and hurl it as far away as I could. He took another loud, obnoxious bite, made sure to chew it as loudly as possible, and finally swallowed.

"Don't be pissed at me," he said, tossing the core in a trashcan as we passed. "Ava might have mentioned it yesterday when we were at the shop."

Great, now Ava was sharing my private thoughts with Callum and probably Macgrath, too.

"You're following her like a creepy asshole, huh?" he asked when I didn't respond to his statement. "When did that start?"

My molars threatened to crack when they ground together. I picked up speed, but he stayed right with me.

"You might as well talk to me about this because I'm not going away," he said.

I stopped so abruptly that he went a couple of steps before he realized and had to turn around and come back. "There's nothing to talk about. I knew she was coming. I wasn't going to look for her unless I thought she was in immediate danger, but I saw her at the grocery store and I couldn't walk away without talking to her. She's staying at the South Congress Hotel. That's it. There's nothing else to talk about. I'm not going to stalk her or scare her any more than I already have. I won't even see her again unless she needs my help."

He studied me; his expression more serious than usual. "How will you know if she needs help? It's not like she can shoot you a text or call your cell."

"I'll know," I answered.

"But-"

"There's nothing else to talk about, Callum. She's terrified of vampires and witches. And even though she couldn't possibly know what I am, she was scared to death of me. I'm not going to fuck with her head the way Rhiannon did. Or the way Caleb did."

I turned to continue on my way to The Magic Bean, but Callum grabbed my arm with steel fingers.

"Wait, wait, wait. Did you say *Caleb*? Our Caleb? The man Rhiannon turned into an *animavore*? He knows her?"

Damn. Shit. Fuck. This was why I never told anyone anything. When you're privy to someone's deepest fears or darkest secrets, you learn to keep your mouth shut. People deserved basic privacy. I tried my best to control what I saw, to block someone's thoughts, but there were times I couldn't. With my abilities, I thought Ava understood why I remained silent because she had similar talents, but apparently I was wrong.

Callum tightened his grip on my arm. "Marcus, tell me what you know."

"Back when Caleb was under Rhiannon's..." I hesitated, searching for the right word. "When he was under her control, she used him to subdue people. She also used spells, but she preferred to cultivate their fear rather than waste her magic. I've been sharing dreams with this woman for months. I wouldn't even call them dreams. They're nightmares, and Rhiannon and Caleb are in all of them."

"But Caleb wouldn't hurt anyone," Callum argued.

"*Now* he wouldn't, but then he was newly made and had no idea how to control himself. Rhiannon let him feed on this woman nearly every day for a week. She knew what he was doing, and she could feel her life being drained away. She dreams about it nearly every night."

"Shit," Callum murmured.

"I'm connected to this woman, to her pain, but I can't help her. I shouldn't have approached her at all. She's absolutely terrified of supernatural creatures."

He cocked his head to one side as he studied me. "Then why did you talk to her in the store and follow her out?"

Because I couldn't help myself.

I didn't say the words, but they hovered on the tip of my tongue until I realized what he'd said.

"How long, exactly, have you been following me today?" I asked.

"Tone down the stare, dude. After my chat with Ava, I figured I needed to keep an eye on you."

"Why did you think I needed a babysitter?"

"Because I didn't want you to do anything stupid or that might draw attention to us." He paused. "Like following a human out of grocery store and standing on the sidewalk while you stared longingly at her hotel."

I grimaced. "She seemed upset at the store. I just wanted to make sure she made it somewhere safe."

"Uh-huh." Callum nodded, a slow up and down motion that, paired with his uttered agreement, effectively expressed his disbelief and dripped with sarcasm.

"I'm done talking to you about this," I said, slashing my hand through the air. "I know I have to stay away from her. I *will* stay away from her."

With that being said, I turned and continued on my way to The Magic Bean. I couldn't help but notice it was only a few short blocks from the hotel.

It didn't matter. I would stay away from the hotel. I would stay away from her.

It was for the best.

When I entered the store, Harrison Morris, the manager Ava had hired, looked up from the bakery display case he was polishing. Once he saw it was me, he just went back to his polishing without a word.

I didn't mind the dismissal. Harrison struck me as a wolf shifter that only spoke when he felt it was necessary.

Something I could relate to.

Before Ava and Macgrath had found each other again, Harrison had developed an emotional attachment to Ava. I believed that Macgrath would force him out after Rhiannon had been captured, but he hadn't. Probably because Ava wouldn't let him.

Or it could be the fact that Harrison had found another object of his affections. One that was even less likely to return them than Ava had been.

Arien, a witch who had served the Goddess for millennia, stood behind the bar, wiping down the wooden surface. Her willowy body was clad in a gauzy blue sundress that made her bright blue-green eyes seem even more brilliant. Her long black hair was twisted into a simple, thick braid that swung between her shoulder blades.

She smiled at me as I approached the counter.

"Greetings, Marcus. How are you?"

Her voice was low and a bit rough, as though years without use had damaged her vocal cords.

For several years before Rhiannon appeared in Austin, Arien had taken the shape of a cat and served as a guardian to Ava and Savannah. Neither woman had known what Arien truly was, but once she revealed her true identity, Ava insisted that she stay.

Now, Arien worked at The Magic Bean and lived in a rental home that Ava owned.

"I'm well, Arien. How are you?"

"I'm learning how to use the computer," she answered, her tone proud.

Arien had not only spent years as a cat, she was from a completely different realm, one that used magic instead of technology. Learning to utilize technology was an arduous process for her.

"That's great," Callum said, coming up to stand beside me. His hand landed on my shoulder. "Maybe you could teach Marcus here."

I noticed that Harrison's hand stopped moving and his back stiffened as Arien beamed at Callum before shifting her gaze to me.

"I'd be happy to help you learn once I'm proficient," she murmured.

I jabbed Callum in the gut with my elbow, pulling the blow just enough to make it annoying rather than painful. "I appreciate that, Arien, but Callum is exaggerating. I do know how to use the computer. I just prefer not to most of the time."

Arien frowned at me. "Why not? It's a wondrous thing. I'm discovering so much about humans and their mating practices."

I blinked, unable to think of a response.

Unfortunately, Callum beat me to it. "I'm sorry...what?"

Her eyes were wide, a thin ring of bright blue surrounding the jade green of her irises. "The mating practices of humans. How they procreate and have sex for pleasure."

"Uh-"

Arien didn't give him a chance to say anything as she continued, "Though sometimes those men call the women bitches and force them to perform oral sex on them until they gag. I don't think I would like that." She blinked several times, her gaze shifting between the three of us. "Do all men like to do things like that?"

Before Callum could speak, I applied my elbow to his belly again, hard enough to knock the air out of him and prevent him from making the smartass remark I knew was on the tip of his tongue.

"I think you should talk to Ava and Savannah about this," I said.

"But why?" she asked, those eyes guileless. "You are men. You would know better what men prefer during mating."

Callum blocked my elbow before it could make contact again and said, "She has a point."

Harrison growled low in his throat, just loud enough for me to hear.

Did I mention that Arien was the current object of his affection-slash-irritation now that Ava was mated? It was difficult to tell exactly what he felt toward her because some days he acted as though he hated her and other days he couldn't take his eyes off her. We all gave them a wide berth because I had no doubt that anyone near them would be burned when they finally collided.

"No, Arien. Not all men like that. And you should feel free to tell any man that you're involved with if he does something you don't enjoy or like. If he doesn't listen, he's—"

"An asshole," Callum interrupted.

He wasn't wrong.

Harrison chose that moment to speak up. "Where did you find this information on mating practices?" he asked.

Arien turned to him, folding her hands at her waist, the absolute picture of prim innocence. "Something called Pornhub."

Callum made a choking sound and began coughing. "Excuse." *Cough.* "Me." *Cough.*

He stumbled away and into the back room, probably to have his laugh in private.

Even I was biting back a chuckle.

Harrison, however, didn't look amused. He closed his eyes and rubbed the bridge of his nose between his thumb and forefinger.

"What's wrong?" Arien asked, finally picking up on the awkwardness of the moment.

I didn't answer, just looked at Harrison. He lowered his hand, opened his eyes, and stared at me. I shrugged and shook my head.

No way was I explaining this to her. Internet porn wasn't really my thing.

Harrison sighed and shook his head again. Finally, he turned back to Arien. "Those types of websites aren't often realistic. At least from a relationship aspect. There are some people that prefer certain things during sex, but it's usually discussed and agreed upon beforehand. But a lot of those videos are just about sex, not about love."

"Do humans not have sex just for pleasure?" she asked, blinking those wide eyes.

Ruddy color rose in Harrison's cheeks. "Yes, they do. But even then, there's usually a measure of respect and discussion, even if there isn't an emotional attachment." When Arien opened her mouth, he lifted a hand. "I do think you should talk to Ava and Savannah about this because they'll be able to explain things in a way you can understand. Men don't always understand how women think, and they'll be able to help you navigate dating and sex when you're ready to experience them."

"What's dating?" Arien asked.

I cleared my throat. "It's like courting, but without chaperones."

That seemed to explain it to her satisfaction because she nodded and went back to wiping the counter.

Harrison went back to the bakery case, and I decided it was a fine time to go into the back of store and see what Callum was up to.

"I'll see you both later," I said with a small wave of my hand.

"Until then," Arien replied.

I shot Harrison a sympathetic look, but he didn't meet my gaze. I couldn't blame him.

When I went through the doors into the storage area, I found Callum sitting on a stool, wiping his eyes and wheezing.

"Are you still laughing?"

His breath hitched as he answered, "Y-y-yes. That was some funny shit."

"You need to stop flirting with Arien in front of Harrison."

Callum took a couple of deep breaths and got himself under control. "No way. I like being able to hear the wolf grind his teeth. I'm hoping someday tiny pieces of his molars will shoot out of his butt. Maybe it'll dislodge the stick that's planted in there."

"Dear God, Callum."

He got to his feet, his eyes sparkling with mischief and humor. "And, maybe if I keep doing it, he'll finally make his move on her. He never had a chance with Ava, but he does have a chance with her. She watches him when he's not paying attention, which isn't very often. I think she's fascinated with him."

"You could tell him that," I pointed out.

Callum shook his head. "No way. I'm not his keeper. If he wants her, he needs to make an effort." He sighed. "Now, why did we end up here?"

"I wanted coffee, but after that conversation out front, I think I'll just make a cup at home."

He smirked. "You wanted coffee or you just wanted to avoid me and my pointed questions?"

"Both. Are you staying here?"

"Yeah. I told Macgrath I'd take a turn watching that Dumont character and his entourage today. I gotta tell you, I don't trust Dumont, but he's not doing anything other than he said he would. It's making me itchy."

As annoying as Callum could be, I trusted his instincts as much as I trusted my own. If he thought there was something off about Andre Dumont, then there was something off.

"Don't let your guard down," I said.

"I won't."

"Do you want steak for dinner tonight?"

"You're cooking?" he asked.

"Yeah. You want steak or not?"

"Does a dog like to sniff butts?"

I bit back a groan of disgust. "I'll take that as a yes. Text me when you're on your way home and I'll get everything going."

"Sounds great." He waited until I was almost to the back door before he continued, "You're gonna make someone a fantastic wife someday."

For once, I had a pithy parting remark. "Misogyny isn't attractive, Callum. Especially when you run your mouth in front of a woman who can literally turn you into the pig you resemble."

Callum laughed. "It's a good thing Ava isn't in the room then, isn't it?"

I grinned in return. "I don't know. What do you think, Ava?" I shifted my gaze and met Ava's eyes where she stood behind Callum.

He glanced back then jumped like a scalded cat, turning to face her completely. "Oh, shit!"

I chuckled to myself and walked out the back door, but not before I heard Ava say, "I think we need to have a little chat, Callum."

I hoped that if she turned him into a pig, she kept him at her house instead of sending him to mine.

CHAPTER FOUR

MERRY

MY DIGGING into Rhiannon wasn't going as I expected.

It was as if she'd disappeared from the face of the Earth.

I knew that she could do a lot with magic and a decent hacker, but this was on another level. It just wasn't possible, at least not for Rhiannon. Sure, there were some people who could fall completely off the grid, but they tended to stay in one place and live off the land or use only cash.

Rhiannon liked her creature comforts. She wanted nice things, luxurious surroundings, and designer clothes and accessories. She liked money—both having it and spending it.

The bank accounts I'd set up for her were collecting interest. There'd been no deposits, withdrawals, transfers, or debits. The money was just sitting there.

She hadn't touched it.

A chill ran down the back of my neck as I studied the accounts.

I dug deeper, looking for email accounts, possible assumed identities, anything that might point me to her current whereabouts.

There was nothing. Absolutely nothing.

I worked until nearly dark, my anxiety growing with each search and each dead end. I shoved the chair back from the desk and got to my feet. The room did a slow spin and my stomach decided to protest its emptiness.

Shit. I hadn't eaten since this morning.

I was tempted to order delivery but realized that it would take too long. I grabbed my vampire spray and turbo-charged Taser, tucking them into my pockets. I did a quick search on my phone and found a cafe nearby that was still open and had a lot of great reviews. I couldn't stay locked up in my room forever.

Considering their abilities, vampires would just mind control and get an employee to let them in if they really wanted to get to me.

I glanced in the mirror in the bathroom and ran a brush through my hair. Apparently, I'd been running my fingers through it while I was working and it was a mess.

As I got ready, my mind wandered back to the man I saw at the grocery store. Marcus with the gorgeous blue eyes. And the gorgeous other things.

He'd talked to me and I'd run away like a scared child. Even if he'd approached me before Rhiannon kidnapped me, I still would have run away from him.

I wasn't exactly a femme fatale. I usually didn't know a man was attracted to me until he tried to kiss me. Or, if I liked him, I could barely string three words together.

I tended to avoid hot guys because the potential for embarrassment was way too high.

Maybe it was time for me to make some changes there, as well.

My heart rate quickened at the thought and my stomach knotted. Okay, maybe not yet.

For the moment, I would respond when a man I was interested in tried to initiate a basic conversation. As opposed to treating him as though he had a contagious disease.

Who knew? I might run into Marcus again while I was in Austin.

And maybe miniature potbelly pigs would fly past my hotel room window.

I sighed and tossed my hairbrush onto the bathroom counter. I didn't have time for all the "what ifs" in my head. I needed to protect myself first and foremost. Then maybe I could think about men.

As I walked to the restaurant, I kept my head up and looked around, not just to keep an eye out for possible vampires but to enjoy the experience. Last night, I'd wanted to be out here, among the people that strolled along the sidewalks.

Tonight I was here.

Even though it was October, the night air was warm. The sun was going down, filling the sky with streaks of red, orange, and purple. I was tempted to find a bench to sit on, to linger outside and enjoy the gradual changes in the sky until it went dark.

But my stomach reminded me that it had been empty for far too long. Maybe I could enjoy the sunset tomorrow.

I wove my way around the people that lingered on the sidewalk window shopping or chatting with to-go cups of coffee. I noticed the label on them said "The Magic Bean" and decided to stop in there tomorrow for coffee and maybe breakfast if they carried pastries.

Another couple of blocks and I entered the cafe. It was exactly what I expected and needed. Though most of the tables were full, it wasn't loud. Conversations were low and the lights were dim. I didn't relax completely, but the tension headache in my temples faded.

I took my time with dinner, enjoying the atmosphere and the food. I watched the people around me and, for the first time in a long time, immersed myself in a place. I was just finishing the last few bites of my dessert when my phone buzzed.

I clicked on the new email notification and found a message from Mr. Dumont about the job. Destiny was on my side once again because he said he would be in Austin tomorrow for other business and he would like to meet with me and interview me for the job. If things went well, he wanted me to get started right away. He named a place and time and asked if I would be able to make it.

I typed out a quick reply telling him I could and would be there, smiling to myself as I did. The money I would earn from this job would put enough extra padding in my account if I needed to go back on the run.

As I paid my bill, I smiled to myself. Though my short encounter with Rhiannon had derailed me for a year, I already felt more in control and stronger.

But not in control enough to walk back to the hotel without my hand in my pocket, wrapped around the pepper spray.

I refused to feel badly about it. Baby steps were still steps.

THE NEXT MORNING, I didn't have time to go by The Magic Bean before my interview with Mr. Dumont, but I fully intended to drop by after. Hopefully, to celebrate my new job.

I'd gone out to my car the night before and dug through one of the boxes in the trunk that held my extra clothes. Even before I'd essentially gone on the run, I worked from home most of the time and didn't have a lot of dressy clothes. In fact, I only owned two dresses— one black and snug and the other in a deep lavender that edged toward gray and floated around my body. Neither were appropriate for a job interview.

I dug around and found some black pants that were light enough for the warm weather but tailored enough to pass as business wear. I also found a white blouse with vertical black stripes of varying thickness. I didn't remember buying it but figured it was one of those 2 a.m. Amazon purchases that sometimes showed up like little surprises. Again, that was pre-Rhiannon.

I had to settle for simple black sandals to finish the outfit. Maybe they weren't the most professional choice, but they were the closest thing to a dress shoe I owned. I didn't even have heels anymore. Just one pair of tan wedges that I considered tossing but kept because they would go with the lavender dress. As if I would ever have a place to wear it.

I'd ironed the outfit last night before I climbed in bed with my laptop and spent another frustrating hour looking for information on Rhiannon's whereabouts.

I'd given up at midnight because I needed to at least attempt a

C.C. WOOD

good night's sleep. I was a bit nervous about the interview because I hadn't been to one in over a year. Still, I managed to drop into sleep quickly.

And into the hottest, most erotic dream I'd ever experienced.

Strong hands laced with calluses stroked my waist before sliding up to cover my breasts. I shivered when his thumbs rasped over my nipples. My back arched and my head fell back on his shoulder. When I opened my eyes, we were standing in front of the mirror in my hotel room, his broad, tanned body surrounding my smaller, paler form. We were both naked and I could feel the firm length of his cock against my lower back.

I covered his hands with mine, urging him to touch me in the way I liked best. I gasped when he tugged at my nipples as his lips and tongue cruised down the side of my neck.

Then, he lifted his head and I nearly froze.

It was Marcus, the man from the grocery store, and the heat in his eyes made them seem radiant, almost as if they were lit from within. His gaze met mine in the mirror and grew brighter.

"You're beautiful," he said, his voice deeper and rougher than I remembered it. One of his hands left my breast and his palm felt molten as it moved over my abdomen, down and down. I rose up on my tiptoes and chills broke out on my skin as his middle finger slid over my clit and down to my entrance. I inhaled sharply as his finger sank inside me, slow and deep. I arched as other hand cupped my breast and his fingers tugged at my nipple. Fire arced from my nipple to my clit and I shuddered against him. The long hard length of his erection pressed against my back. I wanted to feel him, inside me, around me.

His finger slipped out of me and he began torturing my clit with firm, slow circles, just enough to make every muscle in my abdomen tighten but not enough to take me over the edge.

"Please," I whispered, staring at the image we created in the mirror.

His eyes were even brighter as his mouth trailed over the side of my neck, causing me to shiver.

"Please what?"

40

"I need..." I gasped as he tapped my clit with his finger once before he began circling again. "I need..."

"What do you need?"

"I need to come."

Sharp teeth grazed my throat and the pressure of his other hand at my breast increased, nearly painful against my nipple. I shivered in his arms, my breath coming in short pants as he also increased the pressure his other finger put on my clit.

The tension wound tighter and tighter until it was nearly unbearable. My breath caught in my chest and my hips jerked as the orgasm burst over me. My head fell back against his shoulder as I shuddered against him.

As the last spasm began to fade, I reached back to touch him, to make him feel even a sliver of what I was feeling, and the dream fractured, cracking around the edges with an audible crack.

"What's that?" I asked, my skin cooling rapidly.

Both his hands returned to my waist. "I don't know. I don't even know your name."

I turned toward him, my eyes wandering from his muscular chest and shoulders up to his face and those intensely blue eyes.

Then, I whispered the words I'd wished I'd said back at the grocery store. "I'm Merry."

His hands tightened on my waist. "Why did you run away from me?"

"I was afraid."

"Of me?" He shook his head. "I would never hurt you. Never."

"I was afraid of myself. What I was feeling," I answered.

"What did you feel?"

"Overwhelmed." Feeling more confident in the dream than I did in real life, I reached up and touched his cheek, smiling as he turned his face into my hand. "You call me beautiful, but I think that's what you are."

I learned then that his smile always started in his eyes, warming them and crinkling the corners before his mouth even began to curve. And as his lips moved, that dimple popped out. Before either of us could speak again, there was another audible crack and the dream shattered.

I opened my eyes and stared up at the ceiling, annoyed by the throb in my body and the fatigue that plagued me. Until I glanced at my phone and saw that I'd slept through my alarm by fifteen minutes.

Shit. I'd set it earlier than I needed to be up, but now I would have to rush a little. I almost wished I'd messaged Mr. Dumont back and told him that I could only do a phone or Zoom interview.

It was too late now.

At nine, I put the finishing touches on the small amount of make-up I wore and drank the last of the coffee I'd made in my hotel room. I managed to eat one of the two Pop-Tarts in the package I'd opened, but that was all my nervous stomach could handle.

I walked to the full-length mirror in the main bedroom, ignoring the memory of that erotic dream, and gave my outfit one more quick look. Though it wasn't exactly the professional image I wanted to project, I did look put together. I brushed a few crumbs from my blouse and grabbed my black tote bag. And turned away from the mirror and the image I could still see there of my naked body against Marcus' tanned skin.

According to Google Maps, it should only take me ten minutes to drive to the office building where I was meeting Mr. Dumont, but I wanted to be sure I had plenty of time to find a parking space and take the elevator to the correct floor.

It seemed destiny was still with me because I managed to park, find the building, and get upstairs in less than a half hour. Which meant I had to twiddle my thumbs for another twenty minutes and I would still be fifteen minutes early.

I went to the ladies' room, washed my hands, and touched up my lip gloss before I finally headed to the office suite Mr. Dumont listed and opened the glass door.

The man at the reception desk gave me pause. He wasn't young and not all that friendly. In fact, he looked like his face would crack and fall apart if he tried to smile.

His eyes were so dark that I couldn't differentiate between the pupil and iris. But it was the cold glint in those onyx depths that had my stomach jumping even more than it already was.

"Hi, my name is Merry Clarke. I have an appointment with Mr. Dumont."

He gestured to the chairs against the wall. "Sit."

My eyebrows lifted. It seemed his resting bitch face was an accurate representation of his personality.

He stared back at me, not even blinking, until I turned and walked away from his desk. He waited until I sat down before he picked up the phone on his desk and pressed a few buttons. I couldn't hear what he said, but I didn't need to. I focused on taking deep, slow breaths and tried to be discreet as I pressed a hand against my jumpy stomach.

I would calm down once the interview got started. I hoped.

"Follow me."

I glanced up from my study of the brownish-blue carpet and found the receptionist standing in front of me. Hmmm. Black hair and eyes that matched his black shirt, pants, and shoes. I imagined even his socks and boxers were black.

I bit back the smile that wanted to spread across my face because I didn't want him to think I was laughing at him because he was larger than he appeared when seated behind the desk. His shoulders were broad and his thighs bulged inside his slacks. Not only did he look angry, he was big enough to crush me like a bug.

No laughing or smiling at the large, angry man.

I got to my feet and followed him through a door against the wall behind his desk. He moved quickly and I had to scurry to keep up. I glanced around as we walked down the hall. It was eerily quiet in the office. No ringing phones, no murmur of conversation or hum of printers. I glanced in some of the open office doors and saw that a few of them were completely empty and a couple held desks with computers and phones on top, along with a thick layer of dust. Weird. The place almost seemed abandoned. My stomach sank as I took that in. I hoped that didn't mean Mr. Dumont's business wasn't doing well because I'd been stiffed by clients a couple of times in the past and I really, really didn't want to deal with that again.

I nearly slammed into the man in black's back when he stopped suddenly in front of a closed door.

He shot me another glacial glance but didn't say anything as he opened the door.

"Sorry," I mumbled.

"No problem. Go inside."

It was the most words he'd spoken since I came in and I detected a hint of an accent. Maybe English wasn't his first language and that's why he wasn't very talkative or even overly polite.

"Thanks." I slid past him into the office and hesitated just inside the door.

The door shut behind me with a sharp click and I jumped, twisting to look over my shoulder. Okay, then. That was weird.

Before I settled back down, a man rose from behind the desk and came toward me, holding out a hand and smiling.

"Ms. Clarke, I'm so glad to meet you. Please excuse Marcel's abruptness. He's not our usual receptionist and he's not very happy to be sitting at the desk."

Andre Dumont could have been related to Marcel. His eyes and hair were also so dark that they were black and he had the same olive skin. He was taller and leaner than the other man, but when he smiled, his eyes warmed and he looked natural and friendly.

"No problem," I said, taking his hand.

"I appreciate you taking the time to meet me. I had some business to take care of in Austin and I pushed it up in the schedule so I could catch you before you left the city."

I blinked a few times. That sounded vaguely threatening. Or maybe my paranoia was catching up to me.

"Oh, well, I'm glad we worked it out," I said.

Mr. Dumont's smile widened. "I'm sorry. I worded that poorly. I just purchased this building and I intended to come in next month to meet with the contractor and designer I hired to rehab it, but when you said you were here, it seemed like a sign I should change my schedule."

Okay, so that explained the general mustiness of the building and the empty offices. Some of my discomfort faded.

"I'm glad we were able to meet, too."

"Please, come have a seat," he said, gesturing to the chair opposite of his at the desk. "Would you like some water or coffee?"

"No, thank you." As I'd hoped, my stomach was settling down now that I was face-to-face with Mr. Dumont.

He sat down behind the desk and leaned forward with his fingers laced together. This desk was free of dust, as was the rest of the office. I don't know why I noticed that, but I did.

"Now, let's get down to details. What I need from you is for you to test our current systems for flaws in programming and in security. And, if or when you find any, you outline a protocol to shore up those issues. Implementation will be done in-house, though I would be happy to hire you to consult on that as well, but this contract is solely for diagnostics."

It wasn't exactly the kind of thing I was usually hired to do, but I did have experience with work of this type. It also explained why the pay was higher than usual, too.

I pulled a notebook from my purse. While I loved my computer and all types of technology, when I was taking notes for a job, I preferred paper and pen. Something about the act of writing things down helped me remember them. I was pretty sure I read an article saying that science supported that as fact but I had no idea when or where. Either way, it worked for me, so that's what I did.

Forty-five minutes later, most of my questions were answered and Mr. Dumont got to his feet.

"It was lovely to meet you, Merry. I'm looking forward to working with you."

I rose also and held out my hand. "Thank you, Mr. Dumont. I'm excited about working on this project with you."

He shook his head. "Please call me Andre. Mr. Dumont was my grandfather and he wore sweater vests and bow ties."

I laughed. "He sounds very dapper."

He smiled back at me, his dark eyes sparkling with humor and a touch of mischief. "He was. Now, I'll let you get back to the project you're currently working on. Are you sure that you'll be ready to start on Monday next week?"

Since I still hadn't found anything regarding Rhiannon, I was almost certain I would be free. And if I did happen to come across some information about her, I could pursue it on my own time.

"I'm sure."

"Okay, then. I'll have my assistant get to work on the paperwork and information you'll need. Feel free to contact me or her if you need anything."

"I will. Have a good week."

He walked me out to the lobby of the suite. Marcel was nowhere to be found. Strange.

"I'll speak to you soon, Merry," he said. "Have a good day."

As I walked back toward the elevator even the silence and vacant offices that had creeped me out earlier couldn't deflate my bouncy mood. That was one of the best job interviews I'd ever been on. After my initial nerves had faded, I enjoyed talking to Mr. Dumont. No, Andre. I liked thinking of him as Andre.

I took the elevator downstairs and all but burst out onto the sidewalk into the sunshine. I slid my sunglasses on my nose, tilted my head back toward the sun, and smiled.

It wasn't yet eleven and the single Pop-Tart I'd eaten earlier was long gone. I decided to treat myself to a coffee and pastry at that little coffee shop down the street from my hotel.

I climbed into my car and drove back toward my hotel. I decided not to go upstairs and change before I went to The Magic Bean. I parked in the hotel lot, made sure my car was locked, and headed toward the sidewalk. As I walked, a flash of black caught my eye and I glanced to my right, to the sidewalk on the other side of the street. My eyes scanned the crowd before I faced forward again, my brain taking a moment to decipher what I'd seen.

My feet faltered for a split second before I forced myself to keep going.

The flash of black had been Marcel, the man from Andre's office. And he'd been staring right at me.

The hair on the back of my neck rose and, on instinct, I stuck my hand in my pocket.

My empty pocket.

In my tizzy this morning, I'd left my vampire-strength Taser and pepper spray in my hotel room. I probably shouldn't use it on a human, but I wished I had *something* to use to protect myself. I panted as I walked a bit faster. My first thought was to run back to the hotel, but I didn't want to lead him straight to my room. My private room.

I kept moving toward the coffee shop. Maybe I could slip out the back. Or find someone to help me. I cut my eyes to the left and looked at the reflection in the store window. Maybe he wasn't following me, but had business here.

No, he was still there, keeping pace with me on the other side of the street, his head turned toward me.

I walked faster, almost jogging now, and nearly breathed a sigh of relief as the sign for The Magic Bean came into view.

I heard tires screech and a car horn blow. I turned my head and saw that Marcel was crossing the street with no regard for traffic. He wore black sunglasses, but I knew his gaze was locked on me.

Sucking in a sharp breath, I turned and ran toward the store. I could hear people shouting at him as he crossed the other lane of traffic and knew that if he got his hands on me, I would disappear forever.

I pounded down the sidewalk and jerked the door of the shop open, all but falling inside. Blind with fear, I took two more steps and crashed into a hard body. Hands grasped my elbows to keep me from falling to the floor.

I tilted my head back, gasping for breath, and stared up into familiar blue eyes. The same ones I'd been enamored with in my dream last night.

"Marcus?" I gasped.

"What's wrong?" he asked, his hands pulling me closer. "What happened, Merry?"

The edges of my vision turned grey, then black, narrowing with each beat of my heart. My body felt so heavy, as if my limbs were weighed down with stone. "He's coming," I whispered. "He's coming for me."

"Who? Merry, who is coming for you?"

I shook my head, trying to form coherent words, but my tongue was thick and didn't obey my commands.

My last thought as the darkness closed over my head was that I'd never told Marcus my name, except in a dream.

CHAPTER FIVE

MARCUS

I GATHERED her limp body against mine. Her heart was still beating too fast, but she was breathing easily and her skin was regaining color.

"Marcus, bring her in here."

Ava's voice brought things back into focus. I looked over at Harrison. "She said someone was following her."

He nodded and headed toward the door. I was torn. I wanted to go with him and tear apart the man that frightened Merry, but I also didn't want to leave her.

I wished Callum was here, but he'd taken surveillance duty on Dumont.

I bent and swept one hand behind her legs, lifting her into my arms. Ava opened the swinging doors that led to the back for me and I followed her to her office. I hesitated in front of her couch, thinking of the table incident a couple of weeks ago, and she rolled her eyes.

"What she doesn't know won't hurt her," she muttered.

She arranged a couple of throw pillows on one end and gestured for me to place Merry on the couch. Then, she shooed me back so she could rest a hip on the sofa and lean over the woman I'd been dreaming about for months.

Including an incredible sexy dream last night. One that left me aching when I woke up.

"Is she hurt?"

Ava held a hand over Merry's head, not quite touching, her palm emitting a warm, golden glow. She slowly moved her hand down toward Merry's chest, closing her eyes as she focused her power.

"Ava, is she hurt?" I repeated.

"Zip it," she murmured. "I'm trying to concentrate."

I waited in impatient silence as she finished her scan of Merry's body. Finally, the light from her hand died and she straightened.

"She's fine. I think she fainted from the stress of the situation. Her body is worn out as though she hasn't been sleeping or eating very well."

I frowned as I looked down at Merry's still form. Her brow was puckered as though she could hear what we were saying. I shifted my gaze to Ava. "She's been afraid for a long time."

Ava's indigo eyes were fathomless as she looked back at me. "I'm sure you're right."

"What should we do?"

"Let her rest. Comfort her when she wakes up. And keep her safe."

I wanted to do all those things, but I remembered what Merry said in her dream last night. That she was afraid. Not of me, but of what I made her feel.

"Maybe it's best if you wait with her," I said, taking a step back toward the door.

Ava's eyes narrowed, as though she knew exactly what I was thinking. "Are you sure that's what you want?"

Hell, no, it wasn't what I wanted. I wanted to sit next to Merry and study her face as she slept. To hold her hand when she woke and tell her that everything would be okay, that I would protect her.

"I think it would be best," I finally answered.

Ava's mouth curved in the barest hint of a smile. "I don't agree, but we'll do it your way for now."

I nodded and left the office. Harrison was waiting for me in the back room when I came out.

"Is she all right?" he asked.

"Ava said she's not injured, but she's still unconscious. Did you see anyone?"

Harrison shook his head. "I smelled vampire, but it's not one I'm familiar with. He was long gone by the time I got outside. I tracked him to a parking spot a couple of blocks down, but I missed his car."

The swinging doors between the storeroom and the front of the store opened and Callum appeared, his usual good-natured smile long gone.

"What are you doing here?" I asked. "I thought you were watching Dumont today."

"One of his guys left the office building and I had a gut feeling that I should follow him. Turns out, he was following a woman. A woman that looked a lot like the one you were stalking at the grocery store yesterday."

I scowled at him and ignored the curious look Harrison shot my way. "Did she go to see Dumont?"

Callum shrugged. "I'm not sure. It was an empty office building as far as I could tell, but there were five floors, so I can't be sure."

One of Dumont's guys followed her and scared her half to death. Why else would he have done that if she hadn't had some sort of contact with him?

"It doesn't make any sense," I muttered.

"I know," Callum replied. "By the time I found a parking spot and caught up to him, she was inside the shop. He watched through the front window for a second but took off when he saw Wolf Boy coming out."

Harrison growled in his throat, short and threatening, which made Callum smirk at him.

"He was a fast fucker," Callum continued. "Even with the two of us trying to herd him and flank him, he got away and back to his car. It's almost like he could trace."

My brows lifted. Tracing was essentially teleportation and an ability that came with age for most vampires. Most who had the ability were old, very old, or descendants of vampires with the power. If

Marcel was capable of tracing and he was after Merry, she was in imminent danger.

I turned and sprinted back to Ava's office. Ava was a tough witch and normally I would put my money on her, but if she didn't know he had the ability to trace, he could be inside the shop and on top of her before she could react.

I burst through the office door, Callum and Harrison right behind me, to find Ava sitting in a chair next to the couch, talking to Merry, who was awake.

Merry gasped and scooted back on the couch, staring at the three of us as though we were monsters. Then, she relaxed when her eyes focused on me.

Ava got to her feet and put her hands on her hips as she faced us. "What is wrong with you three?"

"We think the vampire following her can trace," I answered. "I was afraid..." I trailed off, my sentence interrupted by the haughty look Ava shot me.

"Do you really think I wouldn't have wards set to repel that sort of thing, Marcus Vane?" she asked.

"Uh, well, I didn't exactly think about that." I heard Callum and Harrison both take a couple of steps back and cursed them for cowards in my mind.

Ava's stance relaxed and her arms dropped to her sides. "I guess I can't be angry with you for charging to an unneeded rescue. I appreciate it."

She turned toward Merry. "Guys, this is Merry Clarke. Merry, this is Marcus Vane, Callum Donalson, and Harrison Morris. I know they look big and scary but they're really more like annoying adolescent boys."

Oh, yeah, she was still irritated with us for busting into her office.

Merry eyed the three of us with wariness but she relaxed against the pillows on the couch.

"Hello, Merry," Callum said, shoving his way past me. "It's a pleasure to meet you. I can promise that we're harmless as puppies."

She stared at him with wide hazel eyes. Then, she smiled. Just a little. "I don't think I believe that for a minute."

Callum pressed a hand to his chest. "I'm wounded, darlin'."

Ava gave him a shove to his shoulder. "Tone it down."

He sighed and backed away, lifting his hands in surrender. "Yes, ma'am."

Harrison stepped forward. "Hi, Ms. Clarke. It's nice to meet you, even under the circumstances."

The smile widened when she looked at him. But when her gaze shifted to me, it faded.

"Hello, Merry." My throat was dry. What if she looked at me the way she had yesterday—with fear and distrust?

"It's nice to see you again, Marcus."

Ava looked between us. "Have you met before?"

Merry's eyes locked on mine for a protracted moment. Then, she blinked as the connection ended. She cleared her throat and looked up at Ava. "Uh, we ran into each other yesterday at the grocery store."

"Oh, that's...nice," Ava said.

I took a chair from the table and turned it to face Merry before I sat down. I kept several feet of distance between us. I didn't want to intimidate her any more than I already had. "I realize you're not feeling like yourself, but could you tell us what happened before you came into the store?"

A rosy pink flush rose on her neck and cheeks and she lifted her hands to her face. "I feel so ridiculous," she stated. "I think I over-reacted."

Ava moved her chair away from the couch and sat as well. "Why don't you tell us what happened before you came into my shop?"

Merry took a deep breath and ran her finger over the crease in the center of her pants leg. "Well, I had a job interview this morning. I left and headed straight here because I'm staying nearby and I wanted to celebrate with some coffee and a pastry. I, uh, got the job so I was in a good mood." She cleared her throat, glanced up at Ava, and focused on her pant leg again. "I saw something out of the corner of my eye and saw that it was Marcel. He was at the office where I had my job interview. He was watching me and walking on the opposite side of the street, but he was keeping my pace. It...well, it scared me, so I started walking faster. Then, I heard people yelling and horns honking, so I looked over and he was crossing the street, heading straight for me."

She paused and rubbed her eyes. With a sigh, she dropped her hands, her gaze coming to me. "I panicked. I had a bad experience about a year ago and I've had some problems since then."

"Problems?" Ava asked.

Merry shrugged one shoulder. "Bad dreams. Hypervigilance. That sort of thing." She didn't explain how bad the nightmares were. Or the panic attacks that followed them. All things I knew because I was privy to her dreams and had been for months now.

Merry continued. "So I ran." She looked at me again. "I'm sorry I ran into you. And, uh, fainted."

"I'm just glad you're safe," I replied.

The blush returned to her face, chasing away the paleness that had seeped into her skin.

There was a soft knock on the door and Arien stuck her head inside the office. "I brought a mocha latte and a raspberry orange scone for our guest."

Harrison went to the door and held it all the way open for her.

Arien smiled at him and carried the drink and scone to Merry. "I hope you're feeling better." She set the coffee on the table next to the couch and handed the plate with the scone to Merry. "And, if you're not, this will help."

"Thank you," Merry said. She stared down at the plate but didn't touch the scone. "It looks great."

"It tastes even better," Arien stated, her expression serene. "Please try some."

Merry broke off a small corner of the scone and put it in her mouth. After a few moments, she finished the bite and attempted a smile. "It's delicious."

Arien looked at Ava. "Do you need anything else?"

Ava shook her head. "Thank you, Arien."

Arien tilted her head in acknowledgement and left the office.

"Harrison, Callum, will you give us a few minutes?" Ava asked.

Surprisingly, Callum agreed with nothing more than a nod and quick glance at me. Harrison, not surprisingly, didn't say a word either. Once they left, Ava patted Merry's knee. "Go ahead and eat your scone, drink your coffee."

"You're being very kind. I feel so—"

"Merry, Harrison saw the man running after you and went outside to stop him. When the man saw Harrison, he took off. I don't think you overreacted or panicked at all. I think you did exactly what you should have."

Merry set the plate on her lap. "You think so?"

"I do. And I'm glad you did. Otherwise, I wouldn't have had a chance to meet you."

Merry smiled. "I'm glad I had a chance to meet you, too."

"Now, on to more important things. You said you're staying at a hotel nearby?"

"I am, but I'm looking for an extended stay rental. Maybe an Airbnb apartment or house. I'll be here for a little while and the hotel's a little pricey for more than a few nights."

"Well, I may be able to help you with that," Ava said with a smile. "I happen to own several rental properties and I happen to have a vacant one right now. It's just a few blocks away and not far from my own home."

Merry's eyes widened. "Really? How much is the rent?"

Ava named a monthly number that I knew was lower than she usually charged and I bit back a smile. The witch tended to take in strays.

It seemed Merry suspected the price was too low because she asked, "Are you sure that's not the weekly rate?"

Ava laughed. "No, that's the monthly rate. I'm willing to keep it month-to-month if you're not sure how long you'll be here."

"Are you certain it won't be a problem?" Merry pressed.

"I'm sure. You'll be doing me a favor. I just had some repairs and renovations done but I'm not ready to make it available for long-term tenants yet."

Finally, Merry smiled. "That sounds lovely."

"Good," Ava said, clapping her hands together. "Marcus can take you over so you can check the place out and make sure it will fit your needs."

Shit. I should have known she would do that to me.

I could tell that Merry wanted to tell her no, but didn't want to offend her savior. It was up to me to say something.

"Ava, maybe it would be better if you or Savannah—"

"Unfortunately, we have deliveries this afternoon and I'll need her help." Ava turned to Merry. "Marcus is one of the kindest, most honorable men I know. You'll be safe with him and from him. I give you my word."

Merry studied her and I could tell she was weighing both Ava's words and expressions. Finally, she said, "Okay." Then, she reached for her coffee and took a sip before breaking off another piece of the scone.

"May I speak to you a moment, Ava?" I asked.

"Of course. I'll be right back, Merry."

I waited until the office door was shut behind us before I spoke, and even then I whispered.

"Ava, that woman has been traumatized. Not just today, but for several days last year. By Rhiannon and Caleb. She's not comfortable with me. She practically ran away from me yesterday at the grocery store and she wasn't in any danger then. She's too nice and private to tell you all of this, so I'm doing it for her."

Ava patted my arm. "I'm pretty sure she's not the only one who's scared half to death. But you both need to get over it because something is coming. And Macgrath and I will be having a conversation with Andre Dumont about how one of his entourage chased a woman into our store. A human woman. And I couldn't exactly explain all of that to you in front of her."

I sighed because she had a point. She had to say something to Dumont. If she didn't, it made her, and Macgrath, appear weak. Honestly, I didn't want to be there for the discussion either. So, I focused on the other portion of her statements. "What is coming?"

She shrugged. "When I know, you'll know."

"I hate this," I muttered. "I have premonitions just like you do. Why in the hell can't they just be clear and easy to read? Why is it always hints and foreshadowing?"

"I'm sure it's some kind of solar interference or even the Goddess' hand."

"That's comforting."

Her purple eyes brightened as she grinned up at me. "Just be your usual self—strong, silent, but sweet—and you'll grow on her in a matter of hours."

I wanted to sneer at her but I had to smile, too. She always knew what to say to amuse me.

"Fine, I'll take her to the rental house and show her around, but stop trying to throw us together. If she ever realizes what we are, I don't think she'll be calm enough to listen to reason." We were also damn lucky that she hadn't seemed to notice Ava's words about her wards.

Ava cocked her head and narrowed her eyes at me. "I think she's a lot stronger than you think. And I *know* she'll surprise you." She patted my arm again, but this time the gesture felt a little condescending. "Now, I'm going to get you the key and you can take Merry to the house."

She went back into the office and I could hear her talking to Merry, giving her details about the house and how cute the neighborhood was.

And I knew that I was in deep, deep shit.

CHAPTER SIX

MERRY

I KNEW that Ava and Marcus had been discussing me in the hallway and my stomach sank when she came back into the office with a bright smile on her face, chattering away about the house.

Marcus followed her a few moments later, but I couldn't read his expression. He didn't look happy, nor did he look angry. He was just...there.

I tried to study him in a covert fashion, but he caught me staring and attempted a smile. I said "attempted" because it didn't reach his eyes.

He wasn't pleased that he was playing tour guide.

I waited until Ava stopped speaking before I spoke up. "If you'll give me the key and address, I can drive myself over there."

To my surprise, it was Marcus who replied, "I'm not sure that would be a good idea. What if the man is waiting at your car? Or follows you to the house?"

I didn't answer.

"I'm happy to take you."

I glanced up at him and my face must have betrayed my thoughts because he sighed.

"I am," he insisted.

"I promise you that he has no problem taking you to see the rental," Ava stated.

My cheeks flushed because I'd completely forgotten she was in the room. I'd been so focused on Marcus that nothing else existed.

I looked down at the coffee cup in my lap. "Okay. Thank you."

I hated that I was being so passive, but I really didn't want to go alone. I was already worried that Marcel was waiting at my car. That he'd pop out from around a corner between The Magic Bean and the hotel and cart me away before I could so much as scream.

"I, um, need to go by my hotel and change first, if that's okay," I said, glancing up at Marcus.

His stern expression softened and he nodded. "Of course."

I didn't mention that while I was there, I intended to grab my vampire-strength Taser and pepper spray.

Ava took a ring of keys out of her desk drawer and took one off, holding it out to Marcus. "You remember the alarm code, right?"

He nodded.

"There's an alarm?" I asked, my trepidation fading just a bit.

Ava smiled. "All my rental properties are equipped with them now."

Okay, so that was a good thing. Another check mark in the pro column.

I put the cup on top of the empty plate that had held one of the most delicious scones I'd ever eaten and got to my feet.

"Are you ready to go?" I asked Marcus.

"Whenever you are."

Ava came over to me and took my hands. "I'm sorry you had such a scare this morning, but I'm so glad that I got to meet you." She paused. "And that you're going to stay in one of my rentals. I hope you love the house as much as I do."

I squeezed her hands before releasing them. "I'm glad I met you, too. It sounds like a lovely place, so I'm sure I'll love it."

I waved goodbye to Calum, Harrison, and the tall, serene woman who'd brought me coffee and the scone. As Marcus and I emerged from the shop, I caught myself trying to look everywhere at once.

I tried to stop, but my heart was racing and I was breathing too quickly.

"I won't let anything happen to you," Marcus said.

I glanced up at him and found that he was looking around as well, but with calm focus and confidence. Based on his physique and his casual vigilance, I imagined he could handle anything thrown at him.

Despite the fact that I didn't really know him, I believed he would keep me safe.

He ranged himself close to me, as though he intended to step between me and danger. It was a first for me. Most of the men I'd dated were nice guys, but they wouldn't throw themselves in front of a bullet for me. Or fend of men who were following me from job interviews. The most they might do is call 9-1-1 and yell for help. Which wasn't anything to sneeze at, but I had the impression that Marcus could, and would, take any attacker apart with his bare hands.

"We'll take my truck to the house," he stated.

"My car is at the hotel. We can use that."

"We can come back for it."

I glanced up at him. "I'm not sure I'm comfortable with that. Maybe we should take separate cars. I can follow you."

He looked down at me, those blue eyes brighter and deeper in the sunlight. "Does the man following you know what your car looks like?"

Shit. I immediately knew where this was going. "Yes."

"It would be safer in my truck."

The corner of his mouth lifted when I sighed. "Fine."

"I'm a good driver, I promise."

"I'm not worried about that," I muttered.

"Then, what are you worried about?"

I couldn't very well say *I'm afraid of acting like an idiot around you. Like I did yesterday.*

"Nothing, I guess."

I nearly tripped over my feet when his hand brushed my lower back.

"My truck is this way," he murmured, guiding me to an olive-green truck with dark tinted windows and blacked out wheels and trim. It looked muscular, tough, and all business, much like its owner.

I nearly froze again when he opened the passenger door for me and held out his hand to help me inside. The thought of touching him again sent my pulse scrambling, and the old-fashioned gestures—the hand on my back and opening my door for me—threw me for a loop. I appreciated the courtesy, but I hadn't expected it.

"Thanks." My voice was soft because I felt breathless. But he heard me.

"You're welcome."

His fingers were warm and a little rough against mine and he used his opposite hand to boost me into the truck.

I didn't have a chance to babble and embarrass myself because he shut the door and walked around the vehicle.

I pressed my hands to my cheeks and fought the urge to throw the door open and run back toward my hotel. Before I could act on the impulse, he climbed behind the steering wheel and started the truck.

Instead, I said, "We could have walked to the hotel."

Marcus shrugged and checked the mirrors before he pulled into traffic. "I can leave the truck running while we run up to your room so you can change."

"I can go alone."

He didn't even respond out loud. He just looked at me, and I sighed again.

"I'll wait in the hall," he said.

"Okay."

Ten minutes later, I was back in his truck, wearing a pair of wide-legged jeans, a striped t-shirt tucked into the waist, and thick-soled Teva sandals. My Taser and pepper spray were back in my pockets. I no longer felt naked or as helpless as I had earlier.

I paid attention to street names and turns as Marcus drove. I didn't ask him questions, even though I wanted to. The instinct to babble was strong.

It helped that he was so quiet. It wasn't an uncomfortable silence, but I still fought the compulsion to fill it.

Until he pulled up in front of a little cottage that was too adorable for words. It looked like something out of a fairytale. The walls were smooth and white, but dark wooden beams intersected beneath the peaks of the roof. I searched my mind for the term and realized that it was a Tudor-style cottage. The front door was a bright turquoise and there were pots of bright red geraniums and herbs along the sides of the stone steps leading to the tiny porch. Chrysanthemums of purple and yellow were in half barrels along the front of the house on each side of the porch.

It was perfect.

"Based on your face, I'm guessing you like it," Marcus said.

I stopped staring at the house long enough to glance at his face. I realized I was smiling.

"If the inside is half as cute as the outside, I may never leave."

. His eyes twinkled at me and I had a feeling he was biting back a smile.

"Well, let's go see if you like the inside as much."

I opened the door to the truck and as soon as my feet hit the asphalt, there was a man in front of me.

"I'm fine, Marcus. I can climb out of your truck even if it's tall."

When I looked up, I gasped. Because it wasn't Marcus. It was Marcel.

His black eyes burned as he reached for me. I stumbled back, releasing a choked cry, and shoved my hand in my pocket.

Before I could pull the Taser free, Marcus was there. With a vicious snarl, he grabbed the other man and literally *threw him across the street.*

I fell into the open door of the truck, gaping as Marcel rolled a few times and leaped to his feet. In a blink, he was back in front of Marcus. I yelped and moved around toward the end of the truck, unable to believe what I was seeing.

Or in this case, not seeing.

They were moving so fast that their bodies were little more than blurs. Marcel grunted and blood spattered the street just a few inches from my toes. I froze when I looked up and saw Marcus' face, half-turned toward me. His eyes were glowing like icy blue fire and he had fangs.

Oh, my God.

My knees threatened to give out beneath me.

Vampire.

Marcel fell back a few feet and snarled, revealing his own fangs.

They were both vampires.

I wanted to run, probably needed to run, but I knew it would be useless. They were much, much stronger than me and so incredibly fast.

And I had no way of knowing if Marcel had friends on the way.

I had to make a decision.

Did I run away and keep running for the rest of my life? Or did I stand and fight?

I shoved my hands in my pockets and brought out the Taser and the pepper spray. With a flick of my thumb, I powered up the Taser and listened to it hum.

A few seconds later, I saw my chance. They were only a foot from me, eyeing each other warily and looking for a weakness to exploit. Neither of them seemed to notice I was there.

I didn't want to accidentally hit Marcus, so instead of ejecting the prongs I lunged forward and touched them to Marcel's neck, praying the Taser would do its job against the vampire. If nothing else, maybe I could distract him long enough for Marcus to take him down.

The grip vibrated in my hand and I barely heard the faint crackle of electricity over the pounding of my heart in my ears.

For a split second, I thought that I'd been wrong, that it wouldn't work.

But Marcel shuddered and collapsed on the street, his eyes rolling back. Marcus bent to grab him, but he vanished in a crackle of purple lightning and tendrils of black smoke.

Had I killed him?

I nearly dropped the Taser at the thought. I hadn't intended to kill him.

Before I could process the thought, hard, callused hands grasped my arms and hauled me off my feet. The world moved by at a blur as Marcus ran up the front walk and into the house.

"Is he dead?" I asked, my voice catching over the question.

"No, he traced. The bastard."

"Traced?"

"You'd call it teleportation," he answered in an absent tone and opened the front door.

"If he can teleport, he can get in here," I said, looking around wildly.

Wait, what was I doing? I was in the arms of a vampire. Sure, he'd been nice to me so far, but that didn't mean he was trustworthy.

I shoved myself away from him and thumbed my pepper spray spout to the ready position.

Marcus stepped back and lifted both of his hands, palms out. "Whoa."

"Stay back," I said. I didn't want to shock him just in case he was wrong about the whole killing thing. I didn't want to risk killing him unless I had no other choice. I backed up to a corner and kept my eyes on him.

"I'm not going to hurt you, Merry."

I laughed, the sound harsh and nearly hysterical. "Sure. I've heard that before." I chanced a quick glance at the front door to make sure Marcel wasn't there.

"He can't come inside," Marcus stated, his hands still lifted in a gesture of surrender.

"That myth isn't true and I know it," I retorted. "Vampires don't have to be invited."

"They do if the house has been warded by an extremely powerful witch and the mother of all vampires."

I blinked. Okay, that was a new one.

"You're lying."

Marcus shook his head. "Don't say that in front of Ava. You'll hurt her feelings and then she'll feel like she has to prove that she's not only powerful but the mother of all vampires. She'll make Callum call her 'Mommy' or something equally ridiculous."

"What?"

He sighed. "I shouldn't have said that. Please don't mention it to Ava because it'll give her ideas."

I had no idea what he was talking about.

"Look, I swear, *I swear,* that I only want to protect you. I don't want to see you hurt, especially by my hand."

"How can I trust you?" I asked, pressing my back deeper into the corner.

"How can you trust anyone?" he asked. "Sometimes you just have to take the leap."

I wanted to roll my eyes but I couldn't risk taking them off him.

"How about this?" he continued. "You know what I am? You know what I can do?"

I nodded.

"Then, you know I could subvert your will. I could make you do whatever I wanted, right?"

Panic tried to crawl up my throat and I could barely breathe.

"I'm not going to do that, Merry," he said, his voice calm and even. "I haven't even tried, even though I'd really like to call Ava and Callum right now and have them meet us here. Please, please, just let me do that."

I struggled to control my fear and think about what he was saying. He was right. If he wanted to hurt me, he could have done it earlier. Or left me to Marcel. Or...

I narrowed my eyes. "You followed me back to my hotel yesterday, didn't you?"

His jaw tightened and I knew the answer was yes before he finally nodded. "You seemed upset. I waited until you were inside and then I left. That was it. I only wanted to make sure you didn't get hurt."

"Why?" I asked. He'd said that several times today, but he didn't know me.

He hesitated as though he were considering his words carefully. Finally, he answered, "The first time I saw you, I...felt a connection with you. As though I'd seen you before. Or as if I was meant to see you then."

It was my turn to be silent, because I knew exactly what he meant. I'd felt that connection between us, too. It had been there, beneath the flustered feeling and embarrassment, waiting to be acknowledged.

My answer was to slowly lower the pepper spray and Taser.

"Call them. I have a few questions of my own," I said.

Marcus lowered his hands and stepped back to put more distance between us and to make sure that I didn't feel threatened. One of the knots in my stomach loosened. He took care to move slowly as he removed his phone from his back pocket, tapped the screen a few times, and lifted it to his ear.

"I'm going to shut this door, okay?" he said. "No one can come inside, but I don't want them to see either."

I nodded, a short, jerky movement that felt awkward and disjointed.

"Marcel followed us here," he said. "I don't want to move her without back up." He listened to the voice on the other end. "I understand that. Is there someone else?"

After a few more seconds, he sighed. "Fine. Send Harrison. I'll bring her to the store and—" He paused, listening intently. His jaw flexed and I could almost hear his back teeth grinding together. "I don't think that's a good idea." He glanced at me, which made me even more nervous. "She's not going to want to stay with us now that she knows what we are."

I took a small step forward, hoping I would be able to pick up a little of the conversation.

"Here, I'm putting you on speaker so that Merry can hear what you're saying and tell you what she thinks herself."

Marcus lowered the phone and put it on speaker.

"Merry, I know you're upset and scared right now and I don't blame you. I'm also asking you to trust me, even though you barely know me. I want Marcus to take you to the house he shares with Callum. It's outside of the city and I promise you that you'll be safe there."

"I—"

"I realize that you know what we are and I know that's a lot of take in," she continued. "The cottage is warded and safe, but it's obvious that this vampire doesn't intend to leave you alone. It's best if you stay with Marcus and Callum until we can take care of the problem. I give you my word, bound by magic and blood, that neither of them will hurt you."

"People break promises all the time," I pointed out.

"When a witch binds magic and blood to her words, she doesn't break those promises. If she does, she pays in both."

In my mind, I saw the expression on Marcus' face when he fought with Marcel. I remembered the way he put himself between me and the other vampire. And the fact that instead of using his power to force me to drop my weapons and follow his orders, Marcus had used logic and words to convince me.

"I'm tired of running, Ava," I admitted, speaking the words I hadn't dared say out loud before. "I'm tired of being alone."

"You're not alone anymore," she stated. "If you go with Marcus, Macgrath, Callum, and I will meet you at his home. We'll answer any questions you have. And I hope you'll answer a few of mine."

I bit my lip. It was the first time I would be able to talk to someone about Rhiannon and what she had done to me. About Caleb and the nightmare I'd faced while I was trapped with them.

And I didn't have to worry about being thought of as insane.

"Please let us help you, Merry. You don't have to deal with this alone. Not anymore."

I looked up at Marcus and studied his face. He seemed as sincere as Ava.

They were letting me decide, which helped me make the decision.

"Okay. I'll go with Marcus."

Marcus' eyes brightened and for the first time since the insanity began, he smiled at me.

CHAPTER SEVEN

MARCUS

THE WAIT for Harrison seemed interminable. Merry remained silent, her back still to the corner. I hovered by the door and tried to appear harmless. Considering the way she watched me, I didn't think I succeeded.

Thirty minutes later, a car door slammed outside. Merry jumped and her eyes went to the front door. A few moments later, Harrison knocked.

When I opened the door, Merry gasped. Harrison no longer looked as gentle and unassuming as he usually did. His eyes were intense and lighter than usual. The aura of power that he kept locked down shimmered around him, nearly visible in the late morning light. This wasn't the easygoing manager of The Magic Bean. This was the alpha wolf who carried magic in his blood and bones.

Merry must have felt it because she visibly shivered.

"Are either of you hurt?" Harrison asked.

Merry shook her head and I answered, "No."

He nodded once. "Good. We need to go. I left Arien alone at the shop and with everything that's happened today, I need to get back. Are you ready to go?" he asked Merry.

"Yes, but what about my things from the hotel? My car?"

"I can go pick them up for you."

Merry tried to hide her wince, but we both caught it.

"How about if Ava and Savannah pack it up for you and bring it later tonight?" I suggested. "Harrison or Macgrath can drive your car out to the house."

"Okay."

Harrison opened the front door and his head swiveled as he looked around. He inhaled deeply. "We're clear."

Merry hesitated before she came to stand beside me. She wouldn't look directly at me, but at Harrison's back where he stood in the doorway. I hated the fact that she was afraid of me now.

Then, she surprised me by saying, "Thank you for putting yourself between Marcel and me."

I had no idea what to say, but I had to say something. "Anytime."

She glanced up at me then, her skepticism written all over her face.

"I told you that I would protect you. I keep my word."

Merry studied me for several moments. "Against my better judgment, I believe you."

"You should."

Harrison turned back to us. "Merry, you'll walk just behind me. Marcus, stay to her right and close. If they're downwind, I can't smell them, so you'll be between her and anyone who might try to flank us."

Merry shivered at his words. "I don't understand why this is happening," she whispered. "I barely spoke two words to him while I was at the interview."

I remained silent. I had no idea what was happening either, but I had my suspicions based on her nightmares. It wouldn't have surprised me at all if Rhiannon had promised Merry to other vampires, like Dumont, and now he expected to collect. It was something the witch would have done without qualm.

"Let's go."

I kept pace with Merry as we followed Harrison out the front door. He gave me a split second to relock the front door and we were moving again. Harrison helped Merry into the back seat of my truck and I climbed into the front and started the vehicle.

"I'll follow you to your house," Harrison stated before he shut the back door.

"Can I ride up front?" Merry asked from behind me.

"Yes, but you'll have to climb over."

Before I even finished speaking, she was clambering over the console in between the front seats and plopping down in the passenger side.

"Buckle up," I said, checking to make sure that Harrison was right behind me as I put the vehicle in gear.

Though Merry was silent as we drove out of the neighborhood and out of the city, she seemed more relaxed. As the crowd of buildings and cars thinned out, she turned to me. "How far away is your house?"

"Callum and I like our privacy. And it would be damn hard to sneak up on us out here."

Merry shifted. "You don't have neighbors?"

"Our closest neighbors are about a mile away."

She tensed up, just a bit.

I didn't want her to worry about being alone with two strange male vampires. I wasn't like Callum. I didn't know how to lighten a moment, but I had to try.

"Don't worry. I won't let Callum harass you into playing Skyrim with him for twelve hours straight. And I won't let him feed you microwaved burritos and Pop-Tarts for every meal."

It was a miracle, but she smiled at me, wide and bright. "That sounds like my college years all over again, but if I tried to do that now I'd end up needing a chiropractor and a bunch of antacids. So, thanks in advance."

Somehow, I'd said the right thing. "I live to serve."

She laughed. After everything that had happened that day and despite her fears, she was able to not only smile, but laugh.

And she relaxed. The tension in the vehicle vanished.

"So Callum likes to play computer games?"

"Any games. He's got a computer, a PS5, a Nintendo Switch, and he's making noises about getting an Xbox. He's obsessed."

"Do you ever play with him?" she asked.

I had to laugh. "No. I've tried several times, but I'm useless when it comes to technology. I can't figure out what buttons to push when or how often. And he never really tries to teach me, he just beats me over and over again, laughing and gloating the entire time."

"Well, that's not right." She hesitated and cleared her throat before she continued, "I could teach you some stuff. So that the next time he tries to pummel you, you can surprise him with your skill."

I glanced over at her. "I would gladly accept, but I think you'll just get frustrated and give up like Callum did. Then, the two of you can gang up on me and laugh together."

"I won't. I know how frustrating it is. I never had anyone to teach me how to do stuff on my computer and gaming system. I had to learn things for myself. So, I always make an effort to help out noobs."

"Noobs?"

"Newbies."

"Callum just calls me a Luddite."

"Then, won't he be surprised when you give him a run for his money the next time you two play together."

When I exited the highway, Merry's tension returned and she twisted her fingers together. "I know you said that you and Callum lived together, but will your, uh, significant others have any issues with me staying here."

"Significant others?"

Was this her roundabout way of asking if I was single?

"Girlfriends. Boyfriends. Friends with benefits," she explained. "I don't want to cause trouble or end up as a snack."

It was too much to hope that she was softening toward me, seeing me as a man rather than a vampire. No, she was concerned that a female vampire would want to rip her throat out because she was living with us. I tried to squash my disappointment.

"No, we're both single."

She seemed relieved, but probably not for the reason I hoped.

It figured. The first woman I'd felt a connection with in a few centuries and she didn't see me as a man. Only a vampire.

The steering wheel creaked under my hands as my grip tightened.

"What was that?" she asked.

"Nothing." I turned onto a county road. "We'll be at the house in about ten minutes."

"Wow, this is even more secluded than I thought."

"On the upside, you won't hear the neighbors having parties or blasting music in the middle of the night."

"Good point."

I told her a little more about the area as we took two more turns and finally hit the little road that led to the house. It was barely wide enough to be considered two lanes but seeing as there were only two other houses down this way, it wasn't an issue.

"We're here," I said as I slowed to enter the driveway.

"I don't see the house."

"The driveway is nearly a half mile long, so you'll see it in a minute."

The brick ranch house wasn't much to look at but the interior was spacious. It needed some updating, which was why Ava hadn't sold it or rented it out. When Callum and I tried to pay her rent, she insisted we handle the utilities and upkeep and not worry about the rest. She acted as though we were doing her a favor by living in it.

"Wow...it's, well, bigger than I expected," Merry murmured.

I had to smile as I looked at the house. The red brick and cream siding on the eaves made it look dated. The flower beds out front were a mess of weeds and wildflowers.

"I'd love to tell you that the inside is better than the outside, but I'd be lying. It's clean and structurally sound, but the kitchen and bathrooms are definitely a nightmare from the late 80's or early 90's."

"You said it's clean, right? You two aren't going to expect me to scrub bathrooms or vacuum in exchange for room and board, are you?" she asked.

"I don't and I promise to nip that in the bud if Callum suggests it. Which he might because he hates cleaning the toilets. Basically, we clean our own areas like the bedroom and bathrooms that we use. The kitchen is usually handled by whoever didn't make dinner and we split the rest of the stuff like vacuuming, mopping, and dusting, which Callum would never do if I didn't make him."

"Well, I wouldn't mind being on the rotation, but I refuse to take over all cleaning duties. Having a uterus does not make me responsible for housework."

I nearly choked at her words and managed to say, "Will you please say that to Callum at dinner tonight? Preferably not while I'm eating or drinking."

She laughed. "I'll see what I can do."

When she reached for the door handle, I put my hand on her arm. "Let me do a quick look around the house before you get out. Keep the door locked and the truck running. It'll just take a second."

I didn't expect anyone to be there because the wards that Ava set were strong enough to repel nearly any supernatural creature. But it paid to be cautious.

Merry stared at me for a second before she swallowed hard and nodded. "I can do that."

I gave her forearm a gentle squeeze. "I'll be quick and Harrison will wait outside the vehicle in case there's trouble. If anything happens and we go down, don't try to help like you did with Marcel. Just get in the driver's seat and go, as fast as you can." The average vamp could probably keep up with the car, but if she could get away before they could get to it, she had a better shot of escaping unharmed.

"I can't leave you guys," she argued immediately.

"You can and you will. Ava gave you her number, right?"

"Yes, at the store."

"Call her if you have to run and she'll tell you what to do."

Merry opened her mouth to continue arguing, but I shook my head. "You handled things well at the house earlier, but I don't want you to put yourself in danger to help me. Focus on getting away and getting help. It'll take a lot to take Harrison and me out, but it's unlikely we'll die."

"I don't like this," she finally stated.

"I don't think anything will happen. I just want to be prepared. Promise me you'll leave if anything happens."

She stared at me without speaking until I repeated, "Promise me."

Merry sighed. "Fine. I promise."

"Give me a few minutes and then I'll show you the underwhelming interior of the house."

The ghost of a smile crossed her mouth but disappeared far too quickly.

I climbed out of the truck, shut the door, and gestured to Merry to lock it. When the locks clicked, I turned to Harrison, who had parked next to me and walked around while Merry and I were talking.

"I'm going to check around the house. Do you smell anything?" Vampires had finely honed senses, including our olfactory system, but I still had nothing on Harrison's werewolf nose.

He inhaled, turning his head as he took in the air. "No, but I'd feel better after I went around the perimeter."

"Give me a few minutes to look around the house and take her inside, then you're more than welcome to do a perimeter check."

Harrison's head tilted as he studied me. "You like her, don't you?"

"That's irrelevant."

His light brown eyes were oddly intent. "It's not, but I won't argue with you now."

I turned away and made my way around the house, looking for signs that someone had been there. Then, I entered through the back door and checked all the rooms.

No one should have been able to enter due to the warding that Ava had placed on the house, but I still had to check. Wards could be broken. Or someone could sneak through. I'd done it before so I never blindly trusted magic to keep me safe.

The house was empty and there was no sense that someone had been inside since Callum and I had left that morning.

I went back outside into the midday sun and walked to the passenger side of the truck. "All clear," I called to Harrison.

He nodded and loped off in the direction of the trees that lined the edge of the property. His stride was long and smooth, pure wolf.

The door unlocked and I opened it to help Merry out.

"Welcome to our extremely humble abode," I said as I walked her inside.

"Oh, wow," she said, looking around at the living room.

I knew what she saw. A huge brown leather couch that slouched in the middle of the room, facing the huge flat screen TV that Callum had splurged on and mounted to the wall.

The coffee table was old, scratched, and stood a little crooked. The end tables had been salvaged from a garage sale. Probably sometime in the 1970's. The true color of the wood was indiscernible beneath years that had accumulated on the surface.

The tile floor was beige and clean because I'd mopped it myself the day before I saw Merry at the grocery store.

"The couch looks comfy and, um, big," she finally said.

I snorted. "It is comfy and large. It's also ugly, but we were more concerned with function than looks."

I saw another ghostly smile cross her face and disappear as quickly as it arrived.

"The kitchen is straight back. I'll take you in there in a minute and show you where everything is."

"Including the frozen burritos and Pop-Tarts, right?" she asked.

"Naturally."

This time, her smile was clearly visible.

"But, first, I'm going to show you to the two extra bedrooms so you can pick the one you want." I paused. "I'm going to warn you that they're as ugly as the rest of the house, but the beds are new and comfortable and we have a great water heater so you can take as many long, hot showers as you like."

"If you have decent internet service, then it sounds perfect, no matter how it looks," she said.

"Considering how much time Callum spends gaming, you can be assured we have great service. Follow me," I said.

I walked down the hall and gestured to the door to my left. "That's my room. Callum's is at the end of the hall. I gave him the biggest room since he's got his computer set up in there." I turned the knob on the door directly to my right, the spare room right across from mine. "This is one of the spare bedrooms. The bed is bigger in this one. The bathroom is shared between the two spare rooms, but since we don't have any other guests, you'll have it to yourself."

She peeked inside and her eyes widened. I didn't blame her. The bed was a king-size and had a canopy frame. There were no drapes because the ones that came with the bed fell apart in the washer. Apparently, they were dry-clean only.

"Here, let me show you the other one and you can decide," I said.

Merry was silent as she followed me into the next room and this time she couldn't hide her wince.

"Yeah, I know it's bad," I admitted. "As I said, we don't usually have guests and if we do, they're men who don't care about anything but having a bed."

"I see," she murmured.

I didn't see how she couldn't. The comforter on the bed was an assault on the eyes with reds, yellows, and oranges swirled across its length. The walls were painted dark blue. It was a mess.

"We could go buy another comforter tomorrow if you want," I offered, a little embarrassed that Callum and I hadn't done anything to make this room more inhabitable in the year we'd lived in the house.

"No, no, that's okay. I'll take the other room. I wouldn't mind having a bigger bed."

"Okay. Well, the offer stands for that room too if you don't like the bedding or if it's uncomfortable. I've never slept in there, so I have no idea if the sheets are like sandpaper or not."

"I'm sure it'll be fine," she said, her voice faint.

I immediately decided to order new sheets and blankets from Amazon and use same-day or one day delivery. She hadn't asked to be here and I wanted her to be comfortable while she was.

"Let me show you the kitchen and the garage before you decide to take your chances at a hotel."

Her mouth curved up just a bit. "It's fine. As long as I have a semi-comfortable bed, snacks, and great Wi-Fi, I'm good."

Relief rushed through me. But I was still going to take a moment to lie down on her bed and test its comfort. I'd get another damn mattress for her if I had to, even if she didn't complain.

Harrison knocked on the door and came in as we walked into the kitchen. "All clear," he said.

"Great. Want some water or something?" I asked.

He seemed surprised by my question and blinked before he answered, "Some cold water would be great. It's hot for October." He looked around the living room and smirked. "This looks like one of the houses students rent near campus."

"Harrison is working on his PhD," I explained to Merry. "He doesn't hang out on college campuses to pick up co-eds or anything."

She laughed. "Good to know."

I got a bottle of water out of the fridge. "Want a glass?" I asked Harrison.

He shook his head but snorted when I tossed the bottle to him.

"I'm sorry. I'm not being a good host. Do you want anything?" I asked Merry.

"Water would be good. Though you might not want to throw it at me. I'm a little clumsy so it'll probably end up on the living room floor."

"I like you more," I said. "So I wouldn't do that."

She and Harrison both smiled and I could see that she relaxed even more.

I got two more water bottles out of the fridge and handed her one.

"It's nearly lunch time. How about I make something?" I looked at Harrison. "Are you staying?"

He shook his head and drained the rest of his water. "No, I have to get back to the shop. Arien is alone there."

"Thank you for your help."

He studied me. "No problem. Call me if you run into any more problems."

"I will."

Something passed between us and I knew we'd turned a corner. We were on the same side and maybe friends rather than wary allies.

"I'll see you soon," he said finally. He turned to Merry and took a card out of his pocket. "If you need anything or you get tired of Callum's insanity, call me and I'll come save you."

She laughed a little and took the card. "Thank you. That's...sweet."

"You say that now, but I've dealt with him nearly every day for a year. You may decide that I'm the lesser evil."

Her smile widened. "Thank you, Harrison."

And just like that, I didn't like him quite so much. "Be careful on your way back to the Bean," I said. "Let me get you another bottle of water for the road."

Harrison's smirk returned when I took another water from the fridge and threw it at him. This time a lot harder and faster.

Merry gasped as the bottle whizzed through the air and landed in Harrison's palm with a thump.

"Thanks," he said. He winked at Merry and sauntered out the front door.

"Um...did he make you mad?" she asked.

"Not really, but we like to give each other a hard time."

"Okay, so it's a guy thing. I get it."

"Do you want to watch TV or take a nap while I cook lunch?" I asked.

"Can I hang out in here?"

That pleased me a great deal. "Of course."

Maybe things between us weren't as hopeless as I feared.

Then, I saw her hand rest on her pocket where she carried the stunner she'd used on Marcel earlier. My stomach knotted.

Maybe I was in denial.

CHAPTER EIGHT

MERRY

THE AFTERNOON TOOK on a surreal quality.

I sat in Marcus' ugly kitchen and watched as he whipped up a frittata and a salad for our lunch. It was as good as something I would have gotten at a restaurant on South Congress or anywhere else.

He was quiet but not in an awkward way. He didn't smile a lot, but he didn't seem angry either.

I couldn't quite decide what I thought of him. My first instinct was to like him, but I wasn't sure if that was because I thought he was gorgeous or because I had a sex dream about him. Or because he was genuinely a nice guy.

I couldn't let myself like him. Because he was a vampire. He was dangerous to me. To any human.

With that tug-of-war going on inside me, I tried to relax and focus on the facts, the aspects of him I could plainly see. Things about him that were concrete rather than my beliefs based on my experience with Rhiannon and Caleb. I couldn't think of him the way I did them because he wasn't like them.

First, he hadn't hurt me the first time we met, even though he could. Though the same could be said for just about any man I met.

Second, he'd protected me from Marcel, even though he didn't know me. Not something every stranger would do for me.

Third, he offered me a safe place to stay. Indefinitely. That was kindness I wouldn't expect from many people who barely knew me.

If he was a human man, I'd still be cautious about how much I trusted him, but not as skittish as I was right now.

"Come to any conclusions?" Marcus asked.

"What?" I blinked and focused on him.

"You were thinking hard over there, so I wondered if you'd come to any conclusions," he repeated.

"Maybe," I answered. "I'm still examining the facts."

"Facts are important."

I studied him and wondered if he was making fun of me, but his eyes were kind.

"And are the facts in your possession helping you determine anything?"

"Yes," I answered, shoving my plate away.

He glanced down at it. "You didn't eat much."

"I'm stressed out," I admitted. "And when I'm stressed, I can't eat."

"I can make you something else."

"This was delicious," I said. "I wouldn't be able to eat anything else either."

"If you're sure."

"I am. Thanks, though."

He rose and took both of our plates to the sink.

I got to my feet as well. "I can do the dishes."

"I'll take you up on that another time," he said. "I think you should relax right now."

"I'm not sure what I can do to relax," I admitted.

"We have a bunch of streaming services. We could watch something. Anything you want," he said.

"Anything?" I asked.

"Anything," he confirmed.

And that was how we ended up watching One Punch Man, the dubbed version because reading the subtitles gave me a headache.

"Okay, explain this to me again," Marcus said. "He's a superhero...for fun?"

After the first episode, I'd caved and asked Marcus if he had any popcorn. I wasn't very hungry but any kind of TV binge required snacks.

I finished munching on my current bite of popcorn and said, "Yes. Saitama trained every day for three years and now he's the strongest man in the world."

"What sort of training did he do?"

"Watch and see," I said.

"Just tell me," he insisted.

I glanced over at him and took another handful of popcorn. "You're one of those, aren't you?"

He frowned at me. "One of those what?"

"Those people who can't just watch and wait to see if their questions are answered. You probably snoop for possible Christmas presents, too."

"I would never snoop. And I can wait."

"Okay," I said, putting more popcorn in my mouth.

He turned back toward the TV and watched in silence.

This lasted for approximately five minutes, which was four minutes longer than I thought it would.

"Just tell me," he finally mumbled.

I grinned and looked toward him. "He did a hundred sit-ups, a hundred push-ups, a hundred squats, and a 10K run every single day for three years."

"That's all?" Marcus asked.

My eyebrows rose. "Are you saying you could do that?"

I couldn't help myself. I glanced down at his chest and arms and then back up to his face. I mean, he looked like he worked out. A lot. But still, that wasn't an easy workout for most people.

Marcus actually smiled. I hadn't been counting, per se, but I was pretty sure this was only the third time he'd smiled at me.

"I could."

I shot him a narrow-eyed glance. "You realize that I can't just take your word for it, right?"

"Tomorrow morning, I'll prove it."

"What's wrong with today?" I challenged. I immediately cringed internally. Shit. What was wrong with me?

His eyes sparkled with humor. "I worked out today already. My days of two physical training sessions are over now that I'm a civilian."

"You were in the military?"

His gaze flattened and I could almost see him shutting down. "Of a sort. A long, long time ago."

Okay, so that topic was off limits. "Tomorrow morning, then."

"I'll wake you up at five."

I nearly choked on my popcorn. "F-f-five? In the morning?"

He leaned forward, concerned. "Hey, are you okay?"

I nodded and waved a hand. By the time I got the cough under control, my eyes were streaming.

Before I could speak, Marcus put my water bottle in my hand. "Here, drink a few sips until you feel better."

Finally, I was able to say something else. "You get up at five a.m. to work out very often?"

"Every day."

"Every..." I stopped to clear my throat. "Every day?"

"Yes."

"Um, any way I could talk you into taking a video for me? I'm not exactly a morning person."

"Nope," he said, shaking his head. "If you want proof, you'll have to see it in person."

"Shit," I sighed. "Never mind. I don't want proof that badly."

I ignored the way the corners of his mouth curved up for a split second before he suppressed the smile. "Well, just let me know if you change your mind."

"Fat chance," I muttered beneath my breath before I took another sip of water.

Marcus straightened and got to his feet in one smooth motion. His expression was tight, scary. I would be running like hell if he looked at me that way. He moved to the front window and glanced outside.

Whatever he saw must have been expected because his stance

relaxed.

"It's Ava, Macgrath, and Callum," he said.

Marcus moved to the front door and opened it to let them in.

Ava and the man who must have been Macgrath both looked tense and annoyed. Callum seemed as laid back and somewhat goofy as he'd been earlier. I wondered if it was his default setting. A sort of defense mechanism to keep people from looking too closely at what he was hiding.

"Hey, there, Merry!" Callum said, sauntering over to the couch to plop down next to me. "Fancy meeting you here."

Everyone else shot him exasperated looks.

"What?" he asked.

"They're wondering if you're as oblivious as you seem," I answered, even though I knew the question was rhetorical. "I know you're not." I patted his knee. "Now, scoot over. You're about to squash me."

Callum studied me with eyes that were abruptly laser bright and scalpel sharp. It was as if a switch had been flipped and a completely different person was looking at me. The hair at the base of my neck lifted and a shiver ran from the crown of my head all the way down my spine.

"And you're very observant," he murmured.

"Um, yes, I am. Do I need to run away as fast as I can?"

"Callum, quit scaring her," Marcus said. His voice wasn't loud but it rang with command.

As quickly as it appeared, the expression on his face morphed back to its usual smirk. "Sorry if I scared you. It always surprises me when people see more than I want them to."

"Uh, I'll keep that in mind the next time I look at you," I replied, trying to move away from him. Unfortunately, the arm of the couch was right behind my hip and I had nowhere to go.

Callum's gaze softened. "I really did scare you, huh? I'm sorry. I wasn't trying to."

"I'll accept your apology if you give me some space," I said.

He shifted over to the opposite side of the couch and slouched against the back, stretching his legs out in front of him.

"How did it go with Dumont?" Marcus asked. He was glaring at Callum, but Ava must have understood he was asking her because she was the one who answered.

"Marcel is returning home. He is young and sometimes his blood-lust still gets the best of him."

Marcus' head snapped around so he could look at her. "And you believe that complete crock of bullshit? Young vampires can't usually trace unless they're a direct descendent of a very powerful master. Dumont isn't that old or powerful."

I felt my eyebrows lift. He was practically snarling. That was definitely scary. And reminded me a little of the werewolf shifter romances I sometimes read on my phone. But I wasn't sure if it was in a good way or a bad way.

Ava shrugged and glanced at Macgrath.

"Of course we didn't," he said. "But, as Marcel is his vassal and Dumont has promised to discipline him and send him home. Since he didn't hurt you, only scared you, we can't ask for more. At least according to the laws laid out by the Vampire Council." Macgrath sneered as he continued, "Which is exactly why I hate the damn Council in the first place. Complete waste of blood."

Ava came over to the coffee table and sat down on it, facing me. "I'm sorry, Merry. I hate that we can't take any action against him, but we're not in a position to take on the Council. Not yet."

"But Marcel is leaving town?" I asked.

Ava nodded. "He's going back to Louisiana."

I supposed that was better than nothing. But Ava was right. Marcel hadn't hurt me. He hadn't done more than terrify me about out of my wits.

Jeez, that sounded much worse in my head than it did when Ava said it.

It scared me all over again and irritated the hell out of me at the same time.

"Great, so he acts like an asshole, gets a slap on the damn wrist, and gets to go home like a bad little boy. Meanwhile, I'll probably be having nightmares about him for the next six months!" I had no idea that I was going to say all that. Nor that I was going to leap to my feet so I could pace around the living room. I whirled toward Macgrath. "Does that sound right to you?"

He crossed his arms over his chest and I was suddenly aware of how huge he was. He was great looking and resembled Marcus and Callum more than I would have expected, but he was also a lot bigger than me. More than a lot.

Maybe I shouldn't be mouthing off to him because I was pretty sure he could pound me to dust with one fist.

"No, it doesn't sound right to me, but Ava wouldn't let me behead him."

Okay. Wow. Not what I was expecting.

I blinked a few times. I had no idea how to respond.

Finally, I settled for, "Maybe that would be a little excessive."

He shrugged. "That's what she said."

I wasn't sure if his surly attitude made me feel better or fear for my safety.

Ava sighed and elbowed him. "Stop with your scary barbarian attitude. She doesn't know you well enough to understand that it's just an act."

He lifted an eyebrow at her. "Who said it's an act?"

She jabbed him in the side with her elbow and he dropped his arms from across his chest. His face...changed. His jaw relaxed and his eyes sparkled with humor and affection. He even smiled.

And just like that, he looked like a handsome man in love rather than a warrior who'd decapitate me and drink coffee from my skull.

"Who would you rather have on your side?" he asked, looking at me. "The guy who carries a sword and destroys your enemies or the guy who pats your head and tells you it's all going to be okay?"

"Good point," I murmured.

Macgrath evaded another elbow jab from Ava. "Hey, she's not scared of me anymore. Stop tickling me with your elbow."

Ava scowled at him. "I'm about to tickle you with something a lot more painful."

"So I should be safe to go back to the hotel, right?" I asked. "If

85

Marcel is leaving town?"

The vampires and witch in the room shared a look, one that spoke volumes.

"Is there something else I should know?"

Ava glanced at the men, who suddenly found very interesting things on the walls, ceiling, and out the windows. She sighed.

"There's a few things you should know," she said. "I know you understand that Marcel is a vampire. Well, so is his boss, Andre Dumont. He's in town to form an alliance with us. And now we've basically shown him that you're under our protection, that you're valuable to us. As a human, he'll consider you a weak link and go after you the moment you're alone again."

"But I don't even know you. Any of you!" I exclaimed, lifting my arms. "It's ridiculous that he would think I'm important to you."

"As far as I'm concerned, any human who might be in danger because they've had contact with me is important," Ava said. "And I like what I know of you so far. I don't want to see you become a vampire snack."

I flinched at her words, curling my arms around my waist.

Ava paused and studied me. "Have you encountered vampires before?" she asked, her voice gentle.

"Yes," I whispered. "A vampire and the, uh, witch who created him. But he didn't drink my blood. He..." My throat was suddenly tight. "He..." I shook my head. "I can't truly describe it but it felt like he was sucking away my life, my ability to breathe and for my heart to beat. But somehow, she was worse. So much worse. She made me do things, made me help her."

I couldn't speak anymore because my vocal cords felt frozen, so I just kept shaking my head and hugging myself. I thought about going back to the hotel and my skin chilled. I found I could speak after all.

"I can't go through that again," I said. "I can't be at the mercy of someone without mercy."

"Then, it's settled," Ava said. "You'll stay here with Marcus and Callum for a while. At least until Dumont returns home and we know you'll be safe on your own."

The anxiety was growing, swelling, taking over my thoughts and turning them into pure panic. I couldn't catch my breath. I tried to fill my lungs but they seized as if in the grip of a giant.

Suddenly, Marcus was right in front of me, his wild blue eyes filling my vision, glowing with a faint light. His hands cupped my cheeks, his palms so hot they were nearly unbearable against my frigid skin. "One easy breath, Merry. In and out, nice and slow."

I focused on his eyes, the heat of his fingers, and the low rumble of his voice. Then, I was able to breathe.

I filled my lungs with air and released it, once, twice, before I spoke. "You're not using vampire mind tricks on me, are you?" I asked.

"No, I promise I'm not," he answered.

"Then why are your eyes glowing?"

He blinked and the light faded. "It happens sometimes when I sense heightened emotion."

"You mean blind panic?"

"Fear, anger, sadness, joy, any intense emotion can bring it out."

From the short distance away, I could see every nuance of his expression. He was sincere.

"Okay." I inhaled and exhaled again. "I'm okay now," I stated.

Marcus nodded and released my face before he took a couple of steps back.

I kept my eyes on him. "I know Ava said I could stay with you, but I need to know—are you okay with that?"

My question seemed to take him aback. "Of course, otherwise I wouldn't have brought you here."

"Yes, but that was with the expectation of a short stay. Now, it looks like I might be here for...a while."

He shrugged. "You're better company than Callum."

The vampire in question snorted. "And she'll be better company than you, especially if she likes to game."

I turned to Callum. "Are you sure you don't mind either?"

He grinned at me. "I don't know you well, but I like what I know so far. Plus, you're a lot prettier than my stoic roommate over there. It'll be a bonus."

"You'll let me know when you're ready for me to leave?"

Callum waved a hand. "Don't hold your breath. I've been with that one for centuries and I haven't kicked him out yet."

"Okay, since that's settled," Ava said. "Macgrath will go get your bags out of the car. Your car is parked next to Marcus' vehicle. You might consider putting it in the garage, just in case." This, she said to Marcus.

"No problem," he said.

Ava came over to me and took both of my hands in hers. "I'll come out and see you tomorrow. Or you can have Marcus or Callum bring you to the shop if you're desperate to get away from all this testosterone."

"I can't thank you enough for helping me."

She smiled and squeezed my hands. "Don't thank me yet. You haven't been stuck with these two for a full twenty-four hours yet. You may be calling me to complain tomorrow night."

"I guess we'll see," I answered.

Ava released my hands and pointed at Callum. "Be on your best behavior, please. She's a nice woman and doesn't need to deal with your shit."

"Who me?" Callum asked, his hand pressed to his chest, aghast.

Ava rolled her eyes and turned to Marcus. "And you. Don't be your usual antisocial self."

Unlike Callum, he nodded. "Of course not."

Ava merely sighed and spoke to me. "If you get bored, don't hesitate to force him to hang out with you, take you somewhere, or call me. Do you still have your Taser?"

I nodded.

"Then, feel free to use it on Callum if he gets too annoying."

"Hey!"

I had to smile. Despite knowing what they all were and that they could kill me with no effort, I wasn't afraid of them anymore. They were going out of their way to help me and to keep me safe.

I only hoped my instincts in this case were right.

And that I wouldn't regret this later.

CHAPTER NINE

MARCUS

AFTER DINNER, Merry disappeared into her room to unpack and set up her computer. She mentioned having to find work since she wouldn't be doing the job Dumont hired her to do.

When Ava and Macgrath left, she grew quiet, thoughtful. I no longer sensed fear from her, but she was stressed. Anxious.

Even Callum's attempts at humor didn't pull her out of herself.

"You should go talk to her," Callum murmured to me as we cleaned up the kitchen. "I know you want to."

"And how do you know that?" I asked, ignoring his suggestion.

"Because you keep looking over your shoulder toward the hallway."

I shrugged and focused on washing the dishes. "She needs time to acclimate to us. She doesn't need me in her face all the time."

"She likes you, you know," he said after few seconds of silence.

"No, she just doesn't fear me anymore. That's not the same thing."

"Well, she likes to look at your...everything when you're not paying attention."

"Looking isn't the same as liking," I grumbled, scrubbing the pan in my hand a little harder.

"It's a start."

"Are you going to speculate about Merry's thoughts and feelings or dry the damn dishes?" I asked.

Callum stopped speaking and picked up the towel and the pan I'd just rinsed.

I couldn't stop thinking about what he said.

Or the dream that I'd shared with Merry after we met.

But as I told Callum, looking and appreciating the view wasn't the same as having a deeper emotion. For some reason, I wanted Merry to regard me with something more than attraction, deeper than enjoying what I looked like.

At nine, I gave up trying to watch television. Callum had closed himself up in his room after he helped me clean the kitchen, stating he was going to play some computer game. I wanted to hang out in the living room in case Merry emerged from her room, but her door remained shut.

I should have realized it wouldn't be that simple.

I should have reinforced my mental shields. But it didn't occur to me before I got in bed.

I knew immediately I was dreaming, even though I was still in my room. But I wasn't alone in my narrow bed.

Slender hands cupped my shoulders as I rolled over onto my back. She rolled with me until her body sprawled over mine.

"Strange," she whispered.

"What's strange?"

"This is my second dream about you and I barely know you."

"You have to know someone well to dream about them?"

Merry smiled down at me. "I guess not." Her hand cupped my face and she swept her thumb over my bottom lip. "It's just strange that I'm having sexy dreams about a vampire, especially when I'm not sure if I can trust him."

My hands tightened on her waist. "You can trust me."

"Maybe, but even the untrustworthy would say that."

"Merry—"

She kissed me, just a light brush of lips against mine, and I lost my train of thought. Unlike the last dream, she was clothed. Her shirt was thin and light blue with delicate, skinny straps, and she wore matching shorts.

I completely forgot about clothing when her lips opened over mine and her tongue brushed against my mouth.

She settled against me, her body molding to mine, and the rest of the world, the fact that this was a dream, vanished.

Her hands moved over my chest and down. As her fingers slipped just under the edge of my shorts, something moved in the darkness of my room.

A figure.

I clasped a hand over her wrist. "Wait."

"What's wrong?"

"Someone's here."

Her body went rigid against mine. "Who?"

I stared into the shadows, but all I could make out was the faint shape of a man in the corner of the room. "I don't know. They're watching."

A thud echoed and the room vibrated.

"What was that?" she asked, fear creeping into her voice.

"I don't know."

I didn't have the power or skills that Ava possessed, but I knew how to reach out for another mind. I focused on the shadow as another pounding noise came and the bed shuddered beneath us. I reached out, aiming for the mind that I could sense on the edges of the dream, but it recoiled.

I had the impression of desperation, shock, and frustration before a huge boom resonated and the dream splintered and exploded around me.

I opened my eyes and stared up at the dark ceiling in my bedroom. My skin was still hot and my dick ached, but I was alone on the bed.

Merry.

I sat up and grabbed a t-shirt out of the dresser. Before I could rethink my decision, I pulled the cotton over my head as I opened my door. Moving silently, I went across the hall to Merry's room and cracked the door open.

She lay curled on her side, the blankets pulled up to her neck. There was no movement or anything to indicate that she'd been dreaming or that I'd woken her.

I waited a moment, casting out my mind and searching for the presence I'd sensed in my dream earlier.

Nothing. There was no one there. No trace of the shadow.

I pulled the door shut, careful not to make a sound, and turned to go back to my room. A large form stood to my left and, without thinking, I shot out a fist, catching Callum right in the face.

"Ow—"

I grabbed the back of his head with one hand and slapped my other over his mouth. "Quiet or you'll wake up Merry."

"Mphuncker," he mumbled.

I jerked my head toward the living room and released him. He followed me into the kitchen.

"What the fuck, Marcus?"

"Right back at you, Callum," I retorted. "We have a guest and you shouldn't be wandering around at night, trying to sneak up on either one of us."

"I wasn't trying to sneak up on you. I heard you get up and wondered if something was wrong. I figured you heard me, too."

I hadn't. I didn't want to admit that my guard had been lowered so much that I hadn't even noticed him approach. But I wouldn't lie, either.

"I was distracted," I finally said.

Callum started to smirk, but it quickly faded when he realized I was serious.

"Shit."

"I don't know what's wrong with me."

"You don't?" he asked. "Because I think it's obvious."

"Then, please enlighten me."

He went to the fridge and took out a bottle of water. "You aren't just attracted to her. You don't just like her. You have deeper feelings than that." He cracked the top on the bottle and took a deep drink.

"Deeper than what? Than a crush? Than a fling?"

"You're falling in love with her," he answered.

I couldn't argue because he was right. For months, I'd been dreaming about her. Most of them were her nightmares, but there were a few from the past. Memories of her childhood, her college years, and times before she'd been traumatized by Rhiannon. I may not have spent much time with her in person, but I'd spent months with her mind and her thoughts as she slept.

"It doesn't matter," I stated. "Whether I meant to connect with her the way I have or not, I've invaded her dreams, her thoughts. Essentially, her privacy. It wouldn't be right for me to pursue her." I moved past him to the fridge for a water of my own. "And then there's Caleb. When she finds out about him and the fact that he's part of our group, she will never trust us again. She'll never trust *me* again."

"You can't know that," he argued.

"I can because I've read her thoughts in her dreams, remember?"

"Shit," he repeated.

We drank our water in the silence. I'd left the light over the stove on in case Merry woke up and needed a drink or snack in the middle of the night. It was the only illumination in the room.

"You have two choices," he stated.

"Oh, really. What are they?"

"You can brood and watch her with calf eyes until she walks out of your life. Or..."

He paused, likely for dramatic effect, and it was annoying.

"Or what, Callum?"

"You could prove to her that you're different. I think she already understands that we're different, but she senses you on another level. An animal level." His voice dropped as he said it, almost a growl, and I rolled my eyes. "So, it's both a good thing and a bad thing for you because she's attracted and super aware, but that also makes her more nervous than she already is."

"There's a much bigger problem than any of this," I stated. "Someone is watching her."

Callum straightened, his head swiveling. "What the fuck, man?

Why didn't you lead with that? Did you check the perimeter? Why didn't our wards or alarms go off?"

I shook my head. "Not that kind of watching. Whoever is observing her has connected to her the way I have. Or the way Ava would. But they're extremely skilled. Tonight was the first night that I even caught a glimpse of them and I've been in her dreams for months."

I heard a gasp from the mouth of the kitchen and closed my eyes. What the hell was wrong with me tonight? First, Callum was able to sneak up on me and now Merry had managed to come out of her room without either of us realizing it.

When I opened my eyes and looked at her, Merry's face was nearly white, even in the dim, yellow glow of the stove light. Her eyes were nearly black in the shadows but my vision was acute enough to see the accusation in them.

"You've seen my dreams?" Her voice was soft, frighteningly so. She wasn't just upset. She was beyond angry.

"Yes."

"*All* my dreams? Even tonight?"

I nodded.

"What in the hell is wrong with you?" she asked. Then, she raised a hand. "No, don't bother trying to answer that. There's no explanation that would be worth a damn. No excuse for that kind of...of violation."

She was right. There was nothing I could say, no way I could explain. At least not in a forgivable way. The fact that I had no choice in where my talents took me wouldn't matter to her. I'd lied to her. It might have been by omission, but it was still a lie.

"First thing in the morning, I'm calling Ava," she said.

"I understand," I said. "Callum can take you to her tonight if you want."

"I can?" Callum asked. When he saw my stare, he turned the question into a statement. "I can."

"No, Ava needs to sleep. The morning will be early enough." Her dark eyes bored into me. "Stay away from me. And stay out of my head."

With that, she turned away and her footsteps seemed to echo as she marched down the short hall to the guest room. The door slammed, the sound as sharp and painful as a bullet.

"Look, Marcus, let me talk to her—"

I lifted a hand. "I told you that it was useless. It's even more useless now. Just let it go. It's for the best."

"You don't—"

"Good night, Callum."

I tried to walk past him, to brush off anything he might have to say. We'd been brothers in arms for so long, he knew when to push and when to back down.

For all his joking and ridiculous behavior, he knew when to stop.

At least, that's what I believed.

He lunged forward and grabbed my arm, jerking me back. "No, you don't get to walk away and shut down. Not this time. You're going to listen to what I have to say."

I jerked at my arm, but he held fast.

"Dammit, Marcus, you're going to listen to me if I have to beat it through your thick skull first."

I stopped trying to pull away and leaned into him instead. "This isn't something I can joke my way out of. That woman was innocent and did nothing to deserve what happened to her. Rhiannon violated her mind and now she feels I did the same. She's right to feel that way. And now someone else is watching her and it's not me."

"She's reasonable. If you only explained that you have no control over who you connect with, I'm—"

I'd had enough. I twisted my forearm out of his hold and shoved him away. Both of our water bottles hit the floor. He flew back against the cabinets with a clatter, knocking over a bowl of fruit and the crock of kitchen utensils next to it.

"Just shut up," I said.

I tried to keep my voice down, but Callum didn't seem to have my same concern.

"What the fuck, Marcus?" he roared as he straightened.

"You just don't know when to stop, do you, Callum? You have to keep pushing and pushing until someone snaps. Does it entertain you? Is it funny that I'm twisted up in knots over Merry and I can't do anything about it?"

"You can!"

"No, I can't!" I finally snapped and roared right back at him. "Why can't *you* understand that? I will not do anything else to make her feel out of control of her own life! She needs to feel safe and she isn't. Not while she's being stalked in her dreams." I shoved him again when he got too close to me.

"You're not stalking her. You can't help the connection. You're doing everything you can to make her safe."

"I'm not talking about me, asshole! I'm talking about whoever is waiting in the shadows of her dreams. She doesn't even know they're there. I've been trying to explain it to you but you're too fucking thick to understand, it seems."

With that, it was on, as Ava would say. Callum rounded on me and caught me in the jaw with a left cross. He always did have a sneaky left. Which he usually followed up with a right kick to the knee or a right elbow to the jaw.

I dodged the kick and countered with an elbow of my own. Callum twisted and looped an arm around my neck, locking me into a chokehold.

"Seriously, what the fuck, man?" he asked.

I threw another elbow in his gut, which made him grunt, but he didn't relax his grip. I tried stomping on his bare foot, but he expected that, too.

Finally, I bit his arm.

"Aw, son of a fucking bitch!" he yelped, finally releasing me and shoving me away.

I fell face-first into the fridge and whirled around in a crouch, my hands lifted to protect my head and a snarl on my lips.

And I immediately locked eyes with Merry.

As soon as I rose from my crouch, Callum caught on and glanced behind him as well. I knew from the expression on his face that he'd known exactly how long she'd been standing there. The manipulative shithead wanted her to hear everything, whether I was willing to try and convince her or not.

As her eyes tracked between the two of us, I decided I was done for the night. I couldn't deal with Callum's bullshit anymore and I couldn't answer the questions I saw in her eyes.

I took the coward's way out.

I walked to the back door and out into the night.

CHAPTER TEN

MERRY

I STARED at the back door, trying to process everything I'd just seen and heard.

"I'm sorry, Merry," Callum said. He actually looked contrite as opposed to mischievous, which seemed to be his default expression.

"You're bleeding." I picked my way around the apples, oranges, and peaches on the floor to the paper towel roll and ripped one off. After I dampened it, I walked over to Callum and started dabbing around the injury. Only to realize that the wounds had already healed. I envied that a little, but the whole drinking blood and losing my humanity thing wasn't worth it.

"Thanks." He took the paper towel from me. "I'm already good as new. Physically, at least."

"What were you fighting about?" I asked. "Neither of you seems like the type to randomly beat the crap out of each other."

"I think you heard exactly what we were arguing about," he answered.

"Fine, I heard. But I don't understand. Marcus was right—he violated my privacy. My thoughts. My feelings. All things that should only be shared when *I want* to share them."

Callum sighed and tossed the wet paper towel into the trashcan. "If he'd had a choice, I would agree, but he didn't. He doesn't."

I gave him my best hard stare.

"He's like a radio receiver. If someone, uh, broadcasts the right signal, he picks it up. He doesn't have a choice. He can mostly block it out when he's awake, but if he's asleep..."

"I'm not sure I believe that," I replied, crossing my arms over my chest.

"Okay, then, do you believe this? You're not the first person he's connected with and not even the first one who needed help or protection. But you are the first that he's found before it was too late."

"I came to Austin, he didn't come to me," I pointed out.

"It was only a matter of time. He's been getting quieter and more grim with each passing day. I wanted to tell him to do something about whatever was making him so unhappy but telling Marcus what to do doesn't work well. Once he's decided the best course of action, that's it. There is no arguing. No negotiating. His mind is made up. If I'd realized this was all about you, I would have found you myself."

Okay, that wasn't creepy or anything. I blinked a few times and refocused on what he'd said. "And what do you mean by too late?"

Callum crouched down and righted the bowl that once held the fruit. He started piling apples, peaches, and oranges inside. Unable to stand there and watch him clean up without doing anything, I squatted across from him and started helping.

"A few years ago," he paused. "Okay, so it was more like fifteen or twenty years because time feels different to us, there was a young man. He wasn't much more than a boy, only nineteen. He had...talents of the same vein of Ava and Marcus. He was still human, but a vampire was courting him. One who didn't have the same attitude towards humans that we do."

"Now you've lost me again," I said, putting the last orange in the bowl. "I don't even understand what that means. I mean, I know what courting means in the romantic sense, but I'm guessing it doesn't mean the same thing in vampire-speak. And then there's attitude towards humans. Isn't the very definition of vampirism that you lose your humanity, therefore you don't have the same thoughts and feelings anymore?"

Callum carried the bowl to the counter and set it aside. "Let me address the humanity thing first because, wow, that's a lot. When you become a vampire, you don't become some emotionless monster with no empathy and uncontrollable murderous impulses. We think and feel the same way we did as humans. We love, we laugh, and we argue —the same as humans. If someone is a shitty person before they turn, they're still shitty. The only difference is that now they can kill you with very little effort and use their ability to control minds to avoid the consequences. Vampirism doesn't change who we are at our core. It just makes us capable of being the best or worst of ourselves. I realize you don't know Marcus and that this is difficult to believe, but he has always been first, and foremost, a protector. He took up weapons to defend our village when we were attacked. He was the first to stand between danger and those who were too weak to protect themselves. We've been brothers-in-arms for over a thousand years and that aspect of him remains his strongest and most unshakeable. Only now he has the physical and mental abilities to best nearly any enemy."

He took a deep breath before he continued, "And it's because of that characteristic that the story I'm about to tell you is so painful for Marcus. It's something he doesn't talk about, not even with me, but I think you need to know because you'll understand so much more then." He glanced at the clock in the microwave. "How about I make us a cup of coffee while I tell you the story?"

"Fine," I agreed. Anything to get him to go on with the story because, even if it wasn't the complete truth, I wanted to hear. Damn, Callum knew exactly what he was doing. He knew how to hook someone into listening to his story.

He moved around the kitchen and made two cups of coffee as he spoke, "This boy, Tomas, lived in Spain and his family was very religious and conservative. They refused to acknowledge his gifts and vigorously encouraged him to repress them as much as possible." He added creamer to one cup, stirred it, and brought it to me. As he set it on the table in front of me, he continued, "And by vigorously encouraged, I mean they beat him, sometimes only fed him bread and water, and locked him in a small room where he was forced to pray on his knees for hours on end."

My stomach turned over at the thought. "That's horrible."

"It is," Callum agreed with a nod. He sat across from me at the table and drank his own coffee. "That's when Marcus felt Tomas for the first time. He intended to intervene but Tomas turned eighteen and moved out of his parents' home. The physical torture stopped, but the damage had been done. He thought that his abilities were witchcraft and that he was going to Hell. Tomas started using drugs, mostly heroin. And his supplier was the vampire I mentioned, the one courting him."

I truly didn't want the coffee now because this story was making me even more sick to my stomach, but I sipped it anyway. My mouth was dry. There was no way this would have a happy ending.

"Finally, the vampire waited until Tomas was out of his mind from the drugs and turned him. Then, he released him in the flophouse where Tomas had been staying. Most vampires develop control within a day or two, but right after they're turned, they're wild and desperate for blood to fuel the change in their bodies. Tomas killed the other eight addicts in the house. Men and women he'd considered friends of a sort. When he came to himself, when he realized what he'd done, he tried to end his life, but his maker stopped him. By the time Marcus made it to Spain, it was far too late. He killed Tomas' maker, but as soon as Tomas was free, he ended his life. That was the last time Marcus connected with someone. He was...broken for a long time after that. I'd hoped that would be the last time. Until you."

I tried to digest everything he said, but I think my brain finally broke after everything that had happened that day.

"I can't do this right now," I said, staring down into my coffee. Coffee that Callum had made exactly the way I liked it after seeing me make my own exactly once. "I can't take on his issues." I glanced up at Callum. "Or yours."

He shrugged. "I have no issues."

I didn't say anything else but we both knew that he wasn't being honest.

"I only wanted you to understand that Marcus isn't sneaky or underhanded." He paused. "Well, in battle he can be, but when it comes to the people he cares about, he's honest to a fault. And he will shoulder the blame. Even though entering your dreams was out of his control, he will blame himself for making you feel as though your privacy has been violated."

"How can he care about me?" I asked. "He doesn't know me."

"If he's seen your dreams for months, would you say that's truly the case?"

He had a point, but I was too numb, emotionally and mentally, to acknowledge it.

"Look, Merry, all I'm asking is that you don't make a hasty decision. Give it a day or two. Because if you leave now, you will never see him again. He'll make sure of it. Even if he keeps dreaming about you, he'll do everything he can to make sure you never know."

"But I will know," I said. "Because he's been in my dreams the last two nights. It's more than dreams *about* him. He sees it all. And I think he's in control of himself during them."

"What are the dreams about?" Callum asked. "Does he do something that frightens you?"

My cheeks heated. "Not exactly."

I expected Callum to tease me about the blush, but he only nodded. "Then, will it really matter if you're here or with Ava and Macgrath?"

"It's a little uncomfortable to see him in person after the dreams," I admitted.

"If you tell him that, and he has control in the dreams as you believe, then is it still a problem?"

"Did you go to law school or something?" I asked. "Because you are way too good at arguing your point."

He smiled. "No. It's a natural talent."

I shook my head.

"Sleep on it."

"I'm not sure I can."

"If you're worried about the dreams, I doubt Marcus will sleep for the rest of the night."

"Do you always speak for Marcus?" I asked, tilting my head to the side.

"He's capable of speaking for himself, but he has a rigid sense of right and wrong. And, despite his advanced age, he's not a dinosaur when in it comes to things like the idea of gender roles. His mother was one of the greatest warriors of our village before she married, so he doesn't have some of the preconceived notions a lot of the males of our generation did. Or still do."

"Do you have those...notions?" I asked.

"Hell, no. If there's anything I've learned in these hundreds of years, it's that women are smarter, more determined, and a damn sight sneakier than most of the men I know. They are definitely not the weaker sex. I also like women a great deal, in general. They're much prettier and smell better, too."

I rolled my eyes. "Couldn't resist the smart-ass remark at the end, huh?"

"Resistance is futile."

"Prepare to be assimilated."

Callum laughed. "Maybe that should be my line." Then, he winced. "Okay, that sounded wrong. Vampires aren't like the Borg. Even the worst of us usually consider turning someone a gift. One that must be earned."

"It doesn't sound like Tomas agreed."

"That sort of behavior is strongly discouraged by Macgrath, Marcus, and me."

"The three of you police the entire vampire population?" I asked.

"Considering all the vampires in existence are our descendants, yes. And they should listen."

I shoved back from the table. "Okay, that's it. That's the last thing my brain can handle. Did you hear that bang? That was my mind blowing up."

Callum's mouth twitched but he didn't smile. "I understand. I know you need to think about everything, um, after your brain recovers, that is. Try to get some rest for the rest of the night and, if you still want to leave, I'll call Ava to pick you up."

I turned to leave the room.

"Merry."

I looked back at Callum.

"You're the first woman that Marcus has seemed interested in for a very long time. If you can't reciprocate, I understand, but if you can..."

"It's not that simple," I argued.

"I know. Nothing ever is. But it could be worth it."

I left the kitchen then. As I shut the guest room door behind me, I realized that the last bit of my conversation with Callum was a little bit like a middle school "Do you like my friend and will you be his girlfriend" sort of interaction and I had to smile.

Though I didn't think I could sleep, I stretched out on the bed. I shouldn't even consider staying.

If Macgrath was one of the first vampires, he'd be just as strong as Marcus and Callum. Ava didn't strike me as a weakling either. I would be just as safe with them as I was with these two.

But I'd also said no more running. At the time, I had been thinking about Rhiannon, but it fit here as well.

I was drawn to Marcus on a level that was deeper than attraction. It was primal. If I ignored common sense, I wanted to stay exactly where I was. I wanted to be close to him. Close enough to touch.

Callum said Marcus hadn't seemed interested in a woman in a long time and I believed him. I was the same. It had been close to two years since I'd had sex. Almost as long since I'd had any kind of interaction with a man I found attractive.

Was I going to let the past and the strength of my reaction to him make the decision for me?

Or was I going to go with my instincts and stay?

CHAPTER ELEVEN

MARCUS

I WATCHED the sunrise from a hill at the back side of the property. Watching the colors of the sky lighten and change calmed me. When the sun was up fully, I rose from the wet grass and walked back to the house. Since she ran The Magic Bean, Ava was an early riser, so I knew she would be awake.

I'd left my cell phone on my nightstand. I would have to go back to the house before I called Ava.

When I walked into the kitchen, I was surprised to find Callum standing at the stove, making eggs, while Merry sat at the kitchen table, drinking coffee.

Shit. I stopped in the doorway and didn't step inside until the screen door hit me in the back. I wasn't sure what to do.

Especially since they were both staring at me as though I had something smeared all over my face.

"Um, good morning." I cleared my throat. "I'll just go call Ava."

"Good idea," Callum said, expertly folding the cooking eggs into an omelet.

My eyes narrowed. When had he learned to make an omelet? He was always bugging me to make breakfast because he "couldn't."

"She could probably set Merry up with a protection amulet for whatever weirdo is stalking her dreams." He smirked. "Well, not you. The other weirdo."

Oh, for fuck's sake.

"But it should help with the awkwardness between the two of you, as well," he continued. "Which should make the living situation more comfortable for everyone."

"Living situation?" I asked. My first instinct was to look at Merry, but I didn't. I kept my eyes on Callum.

Until she spoke.

"I'm staying here," she stated, taking another sip of her coffee as though she'd said something completely mundane instead of blowing my mind.

"What?" I asked, unable to stop myself from looking at her.

"I'm staying here," she repeated. "I thought about it and, if Ava can make an amulet to protect my mind during sleep, then I'd rather stay here."

I had no idea what to say to that.

Callum slid the omelet on a plate, carried it to the table, and set it front of Merry.

"Are you sure?" I asked.

"Yes," she answered. "Callum said a few things that changed my mind."

I turned to Callum. "Tell me you didn't use your mental powers on her. That you didn't impose on her free will."

"Dude, I would never."

"He didn't," Merry insisted. "But he mentioned that you have no control over who you connect with while you're sleeping, which makes sense."

"I—" I stopped speaking, still searching for the words.

"He was telling the truth, right?" she asked, her voice quiet.

"Yes."

"I wasn't in the right headspace to hear and understand that yesterday when I overheard it, but once I calmed down, and Callum explained, it does make more sense for me to stay here with the two of you. And..." she paused to take a deep breath. "I liked talking to you, both of you, before I knew what was happening."

My heart picked up speed and I saw Callum's knowing glance out of the corner of my eye, but I ignored it. She wasn't running away from me.

She actually admitted that she liked talking to me.

And thank God she didn't have the ability to read my mind because then she would know that I was essentially in the midst of an adolescent train of thought.

"Unless you want me to leave," she said.

"No, I don't want you to leave."

"Okay." She picked up her fork and cut a bite from the omelet. She put it in her mouth, chewing for a few seconds before cutting her eyes to Callum. After she swallowed, she asked, "What exactly did you put in this?"

"Onions, cheese, and ham."

"Anything else?"

"A pinch of salt, pepper, and dill. Why?"

"Because it's delicious and you said you couldn't cook."

He grinned. "Compared to Marcus, I don't cook. And I'm kinda lazy, so I prefer for him to do the cooking. I don't mind dropping the dishes in the dishwasher after. It takes less time and effort."

Merry grinned and continued to eat the omelet.

"Want one?" Callum asked.

I shook my head. "Can I speak to you for a moment? Privately?"

With a sigh, he turned off the stovetop and followed me out the back door.

When I faced him, he spoke before I could, "I give you my solemn vow that I didn't subvert Merry's free will."

Callum might joke and make smart-assed remarks but when he gave a vow or a promise, he meant it. And he kept it.

"Okay. Then what in the hell did you tell her to make her decide to stay?"

"I told her what you should have told her."

"She wouldn't have listened to me last night, no matter what I said."

"That's probably true," he agreed. He stared at me for a moment and took a big step back. "I told her about Tomas. And how you can't control the connection when your guard is down."

I understood the step back now. Because I wanted to punch him in the face. Badly enough that I clenched my fists.

"It kept her from leaving," he pointed out.

"Why?"

He groaned and clutched his head in a dramatic fashion. "Are you really that dense?"

"I don't understand."

"Okay, so you are that dense," he said, dropping his hands to his sides. "She likes you, Marcus. She thinks you're hot and, as she said, she likes to talk to you."

"But I violated her privacy."

"She was looking for a reason to stay and I gave her one. Yes, she felt like you didn't have a right to look into her mind, as anyone sane would, but she also understood that it wasn't by choice. You weren't trying to be sneaky or force your way into her dreams, it just happened."

"And that's it? She's just going to let it go? Forget it ever happened?"

"Meh," Callum replied, twisting his hand side-to-side. "Don't forget that we're going to ask Ava to make her an amulet to protect her mind while she sleeps. It should be enough to keep even you out of her head. Now, go call Ava, take a shower, and try not to make things weirder than they already are. I know that's difficult for you, but try your best."

I bit back a growl of frustration. "Try my best? Could you be any more patronizing?"

He pretended to think. "I could, but I didn't think you would appreciate it."

This time I did growl.

"Get some coffee before your shower," he said. "You're grumpy."

I didn't bother to say anything in response. I went back into the house, grabbed Callum's full coffee cup off the counter, and went straight back to my bedroom.

My only alternative was to beat the shit out of him.

MY CALL to Ava took a lot less time than I expected, which shouldn't have been a surprise because I knew how intuitive she was. I drained Callum's coffee cup while the water warmed up in the shower.

Fifteen minutes later, I was clean, dressed, and calm enough that I was confident I wouldn't try to pound Callum into dust.

When I came out of my room, Callum and Merry were nowhere to be found in the kitchen or living room. But Callum had been sure to leave the dishes in the sink for me to wash.

As I opened the dishwasher in preparation to fill it, I heard Merry give an aborted cry. I dropped the pan in my hand with a clatter and sprinted out of the kitchen. The sound had come from Callum's room.

I skidded to a halt just inside the door and found the two of them set up at his L-shaped workstation. Callum was in one corner and Merry was set up on one end with her laptop. They were both crouched over their screens, their fingers flying between the keys and the mice next to their computers.

Considering Merry was human, her speed and accuracy was damn impressive.

"Ah, son of a fucking bitch!" Callum yelled. "How are you doing that? That is so unfair!"

Merry merely laughed, the sound rich and tinged with malevolence. "Still want to take it easy on me, Cal?"

"Fuck that! You're going down!"

There was a few more seconds of intense typing, clicking, and they each leaned closer to their screens.

"Oh, no you don't," Callum hissed. "Don't even think about it, Mer. Don't." He grunted, long and loud, then burst out with, "What are your fingers made of? Fucking magic? Dammit!"

Merry laughed again. "I warned you."

"But you're human! There's no way you can be that fast!"

"The speed of the fingers depends on the speed of the brain, not supernatural abilities," she replied.

It took a few seconds for that comment to sink through Callum's thick skull.

"We're lowering ourselves to insults now?" he asked, affront thick in his tone.

"It's not an insult if it's the truth," Merry said. "And the truth hurts, baby."

"Gaaaaahhhh!" Callum yelled. He leaned back in his chair and linked his fingers together behind his head. "I give up. You are the master."

"That's mistress to you, peasant. If I wore a ring, you would kiss it."

Callum grumbled beneath his breath, but I could tell he was enjoying himself.

"I'm glad to see you're putting Callum in his place," I said.

I expected Merry's triumphant smile to fade when she turned toward me, but it didn't. Instead, she continued to grin.

"Can you believe he actually said he'd go easy on me?" she asked.

This was the woman I'd spent the afternoon with yesterday. The woman who enjoyed a good laugh, even if it was at her own expense.

"I can," I answered, crossing my arms over my chest. "Not too long ago, Ava considered turning him into a pig so his outsides would match his insides."

Merry snickered. "I could see that."

"I don't have to take this abuse," Callum said, getting to his feet. "I'm going for a walk."

From his look, I knew he intended to check the perimeter before Ava and Macgrath arrived.

He moved past me and out of the house with no sound, leaving me alone with Merry.

My palms were damp and my mouth was dry, which made no sense to me. Did my saliva suddenly decide to take a sojourn to my hands and get a different view of the world? It was stupid, wasn't it?

It had been a very, *very* long time since I was a teenager, but I remembered this feeling. This restless energy. The nerves.

I realized that Merry was staring at me, waiting for me to speak.

"Ava and Macgrath will be here shortly."

She got to her feet. "I'd better grab a shower. I have time, right?"

"Of course."

I backed out of the room when she walked toward me. She stopped a few feet away, staring up at me with her head cocked to one side.

"Cal was right, wasn't he? You feel more awkward about this than I do."

I tried to keep my expression blank but must have failed because she laughed, just a little.

Then, her expression grew serious. "Would *you* be more comfortable if I left with Ava and Macgrath?" she asked. "This is your home and you deserve to feel safe and relaxed here."

Once again, she caught me off guard. I was always off-balance around her.

"I'm fine."

She studied me in that way of hers, as if any attempt to shield my thoughts was useless. Merry had no psychic abilities, but somehow she still read my every thought.

"You'll tell me if it's otherwise?" she asked.

"Yes."

"Promise?"

"I promise."

She walked past me and into her room, shutting the door behind her.

I released a long, slow breath. She was right. It would be easier for me if she wasn't staying here.

But it would hurt to let her leave.

That was a worrying thought because at some point, she would leave me behind.

The only question was—would I ever recover from the pain when she left?

CHAPTER TWELVE

MERRY

I WOULD NEVER HAVE BELIEVED it, but I made Marcus nervous. Maybe even as nervous as he made me.

Somehow, that was comforting.

The power dynamic between the two of us should have been skewed toward him. He was a vampire—inhumanly strong, fast, and he drank blood. I was a puny mortal who might be able to use supernatural-strength pepper spray or Taser on him, but that was it. I was food in his world.

But he didn't make me feel that way. Nor did Callum.

Instead, they spoke to me as an equal. There was no condescension, no arrogance, in their attitudes toward me.

Smiling to myself, I closed the bedroom door behind me and went to my bag. After last night's insanity, I'd packed my things. They were still in the bag since I'd spent the last few hours playing games with Callum.

Before I could even open the bag, my phone rang. I fished it out of my sweatshirt pocket and glanced at the caller ID. It was the number of the hotel. Shit. I hoped I hadn't forgotten anything.

I connected the call. "Hello?"

"Merriweather, we need to talk."

The voice was familiar but I couldn't quite place it...

Wait. It was Andre Dumont. I moved to disconnect the call, but his voice rang loud and clear through the speaker and I froze.

"Do not hang up."

I wanted to ignore him. I tried to ignore him but I couldn't move. My hand wouldn't lower the phone from my ear.

"Good. Now, listen carefully and don't speak."

Dammit, now I couldn't even yell for Marcus because I was helpless. Locked in silence by another vampire.

"I hate to do this to you," he said. "But it's necessary. I swear you won't be hurt as long as you cooperate."

The sad thing was that he sounded so very, very sincere. As though he truly did hate putting me through this. A tiny spark of rage flared deep in my chest, white hot.

"Go to the window, unlock it, and climb out," he commanded. "Then, head to your left toward the trees and keeping walking straight ahead. I'll tell you when and where to turn."

The heat of my wrath grew. I'd already been through this before. I knew there was no escaping. I didn't know how he was managing to control me via a phone conversation rather than face-to-face as other vampires did, but he was doing it.

Screams filled my head as my feet carried me toward the window, fighting as hard as I could with each movement. I watched as my fingers manipulated the latches on the window, flicking them open with ease. I had to lift the window with one hand and it was stuck at first. Maybe, just maybe, if he told me to put the phone down, I could break the connection between us.

Unfortunately, my hand pushed the window up another inch and it seemed to release, sliding up smoothly from there.

I pushed the screen out and ducked through the frame.

"Please stop screaming," he said.

I wasn't. I couldn't, even though I wanted to.

"I can hear your mind screaming," he answered. "It's unnecessary and not helpful to either of us."

There was the condescension I expected from Callum and Marcus.

There was the self-righteousness. Right in his voice. He was stronger than I was and he intended to force me to do his bidding, regardless of my willingness. Ire built another notch inside me, heating my core and limbs against the cool air.

A quiet sigh came through the phone. "I swear you will understand once we speak again."

Since he seemed to be able to read my thoughts, I tried to broadcast them louder and clearer.

Seriously? You expect me to fucking believe you when you're FORCING ME TO DO YOUR BIDDING LIKE A MINDLESS MINION?

"Move quickly. Ava and Macgrath are almost there and you need to be out of sight of the house by the time they hit the driveway."

Asshole.

"I may be an asshole, but I'm only doing what's best."

For who?

I sneered even though I wasn't sure if he could see me.

"For all the vampires, witches, and werewolves like your new friends. Like me."

*And you couldn't just **ask** for my help?*

"I knew you would say no and I need you too badly to risk that."

His words were the catalyst to the bomb of rage ticking inside me. That spark detonated inside me and I felt the first crack in the connection between Dumont's mind and mine.

I pushed harder, putting every ounce of my frustration, fear, and pure anger into the blow.

And, finally, *finally*, I screamed, long and out loud. My voice rolled across the open area surrounding the house and birds took flight from the trees nearby.

I could no longer hear Andre Dumont's voice over the blood throbbing in my ears and the sound of my own cry.

He must have released me because my arm fell away and my cell phone hit the ground next to my feet.

I was still screaming, my chest growing tighter and tighter with each beat of my heart.

Suddenly, Marcus appeared in front of me, his eyes glowing with blue fire.

"Merry, what's wrong? What happened?"

He looked around us as he grabbed my shoulders, searching for an enemy that I knew would be long gone.

My scream finally died away and I tried to gulp in air as the band around my chest grew excruciating.

"Marcus..." I choked. "Can't breathe."

He looked down at me and whatever he saw made his eyes flare. He leaned down so our faces were level.

"Breathe, Merry. Just one slow breath in through your nose. You're having a panic attack, but you're safe."

My legs collapsed beneath me but he swept me up as though I were weightless and managed to maneuver us both back through the window and into my room. He laid me on the bed and sat down next to me.

I tried to do what he said, but my body refused to cooperate.

"If you can't slow your breathing, you're going to pass out," he said. "I can help you but I'd have to take control—"

I shook my head, one violent motion, before he could complete his sentence. I didn't want anyone in my head right now, not even him.

His expression flattened. He could have been carved from stone.

"Then, I'll stay with you until you wake up."

I reached out and took his hand before he could move away. I couldn't speak, but I held on tightly.

The room went gray around the edges, then black, and my vision narrowed until the last thing I saw was his eyes, blazing with both anger and fear.

But I could feel his hand grip mine in return as my sight faded completely.

"WE HAVE to stop meeting like this."

Ava's words seemed to be lighthearted but there was no humor in her voice. I opened my eyes to ask her what was wrong and realized I was lying on the bed in the guest room at Callum and Marcus' house.

Ava sat beside me where Marcus had been and her hand hovered over my forehead, a warm golden glow shining in my eyes.

"I agree," I mumbled.

"Good, because we're going to have to do some things you're not going to want to do."

My eyes finally focused and I could see the worry etched on Ava's face.

"Am I dying?" I asked.

Her eyebrows lifted as she shook her head. "No, no, nothing like that. Just, well, given your wariness of any sort of magic, I'm pretty sure you won't like this." She cleared her throat. "Why would you assume you were dying?"

"Because you looked so worried."

She studied me, her gaze sharpening. "I'm going to ask you a few questions and I want you to answer as honestly as possible. Okay?"

I shrugged. "We'll see. There are some questions I prefer not to answer."

"Like what?"

"Like what I weigh."

Her mouth quirked in a small smile. "I won't be asking you those sorts of questions."

"Okay, then we should be fine."

Ava took a slow breath and kept her eyes on mine. I could almost feel the intensity of her focus.

"Can you usually tell when people are upset just by looking at them?"

I shrugged. "Of course. People who are angry or emotional usually have frowns on their faces or their body language announces it for them."

"Have you ever felt the atmosphere in a room change as soon as someone enters it?"

"Yes. Haven't you?"

She smiled again. "Yes, but this is about you. Okay, here's a more

116

complicated one. Have you ever picked up the phone and called a friend because you just *knew* they were upset or in trouble?"

"Yes," I whispered.

She sighed. "Well, I have some good news and some bad news."

"Bad news first."

"You're connected to Andre Dumont. Mentally and magically," she stated.

"Is that how he forced me to do what he told me while we were on the phone?"

She nodded. "It's also how he's been feeding from you."

My heart did a strange twist in my chest. "What?" I asked, aghast. "How?"

"Since you encountered Rhiannon and her minion, you know that not all vampires feed on blood, correct?"

I nodded. "Yes, it felt like he was taking years away from me, sucking the life out of me, when he fed."

"Well, vampires can also feed on other types of energy, depending on their lineage. Some vampires can feed on sexual energy and were often confused with incubi and succubi." She paused. "And others can feed on strong emotions such as fear. When they make a connection with a...victim, they can give them mental nudges. In your case, I'm fairly certain that Andre Dumont has been manipulating your dreams and pushing your nightmares to the forefront when they would naturally subside. It's one of the ways he feeds. And it strengthens his hold over you."

Oh, my God. "How do we break the bond?"

"Well, this is where the good news-slash-thing-you're-not-going-to-like comes in," she answered.

"I guess good news first this time," I sighed.

"The bond can be broken because you've also established a bond with another vampire. A strong bond."

"Marcus," I murmured.

She nodded. "Yes. You and Marcus have created a mental link and, considering he's never fed from you, it's stronger than I would have expected."

"Okay, so this is a good thing how?"

"Your bond with Marcus can be used to break the one with Dumont."

"How do we do that?"

"This is the part you're not going to like," Ava said. I gestured for her to continue. "Okay, part of the good news, bad news, situation is that you're empathic. You're not strong enough to read thoughts or the full scope of emotions, but you have just enough natural talent to read surface emotions. Or draw the attention of vampires."

"Are you saying that I have telepathic abilities?" I asked, incredulous.

Ava smiled and gave a small shake of her head. "Not exactly. You have just enough natural ability to pick up on minute things and to reach out, but you're not quite strong enough to read people's minds or anything like that."

"Marcus said that he didn't connect with me on purpose. Is that how it happened? Did I invite him?"

"Not exactly. He didn't do it on purpose and you didn't ask him," Ava insisted. "Because of your talents, you, for lack of a better word, broadcast. Vampires have very sensitive antennae because it helps them find prey. And you call to them, quite loudly. Marcus can't control his empathic or precognition during his sleep, which is why he locked in on your dreams. It wasn't intentional, I promise."

"Okay, but I'm guessing that Dumont is different?"

"I haven't finished tracing his lineage, but I'm almost certain his maker feeds on a combination of blood and fear. Once he feeds from you the first time, it creates a sort of chain between you. You're bound tighter and tighter each time he feeds on your nightmares."

Shit. I'd been having nightmares since Rhiannon came into my life and even after she left it.

"Yes, you're in deep shit."

I glanced up at her with wide eyes, which made her laugh a little.

"I didn't read your mind. But it is likely that he's deeply bound to you, which means it's going to be very difficult to root him out."

"So what can I do? Marcus mentioned an amulet."

But Ava was already shaking her head. "That won't work. If he wasn't already in your head, it would keep him out, but it won't be fully effective unless he's gone."

"Fully effective?"

She shrugged. "It could work part of the time but not every night."

"How much of the time?"

Ava held her hand up and waggled it from side-to-side. "Maybe thirty percent."

Okay, so that wasn't good enough. Seventy or eighty, I could do, but not thirty.

"What are my other options then?"

"There's really only one."

I waited.

"You solidify your bond with Marcus with a blood exchange. It would break the link between you and Dumont."

"The amulet would be effective against Dumont, but not Marcus, right?"

Ava nodded. "You need to know what you're getting into. Marcus would have the same sort of power over you that Dumont had earlier. He could control your mind anyway, but it will be easier with a blood bond. You'll also be able to speak to each other telepathically. And he'll be able to track you, at least for a while. It takes time for the blood bond to wear off, but it does eventually."

"How long?"

"A couple of..." She hesitated. "Months."

I sighed. "You've known Marcus for a long time, right?"

"Not really. About a year. But Macgrath has known him for over a thousand years and he trusts him with his life. And mine."

"Does Marcus strike you as someone who would take advantage of this sort of...power over another person?"

She shook her head. "Absolutely not." Her response was immediate and vehement. "He is one of the most honorable, honest men I know. His integrity goes down to the bone."

Every person I'd spoken to about Marcus said the same thing. That he was trustworthy. And I wanted to trust him.

This wasn't just staying in the same house. This was giving up my privacy. Inviting a kind of intimacy I'd never had with another person.

But I knew damn sure that I would rather have Marcus in my head than Dumont.

"Have you spoken to Marcus about this?" I asked her.

"Yes."

"And how does he feel about it?"

"I will do whatever it takes to keep you safe," Marcus answered from the doorway. He leaned against the jamb and folded his arms across his chest. "But I'd prefer not to do it against your will." He grimaced a little. "I won't have to give up my privacy as much as you, but I promise that I will do my best not to invade yours."

I nodded.

Coming to Austin. Meeting Marcus. It was all based on my decision to follow my instincts.

Right now, my instincts were telling me to trust not only Ava but the rest of them, too. The thought of having any sort of empathic talent freaked me out. I couldn't even think about it right now. And even if I wanted, Ava was probably right. I wasn't that strong and I doubted I would find it helpful.

I took a deep breath. In for a penny, in for a pound.

"Okay, so what do we have to do first?"

Marcus glanced at Ava. "May I speak to her alone for a moment?"

Ava patted my arm and got to her feet. "I'll be in the living room with Macgrath and Callum if you need me."

She left the bedroom as Marcus came further in and shut the door behind her. He stood at the end of the bed and gripped the footboard. It made the muscles in his forearms stand out and I found my eyes drawn to his hands.

In some of the books I'd read, the hero's hands were often described as capable. I'd always wondered what that meant until now. His fingers were long, the knuckles larger and the skin rough. His hands looked as though he could destroy anything in his path. Or fix something that was broken.

I wondered if I was the broken thing.

"Have you ever been bitten by a vampire?"

I shook my head. Caleb, the vampire with Rhiannon, had fed off my energy from a distance.

Marcus gripped the footboard tighter and I heard the wood groan. He released it as if it burned him.

"Feeding, specifically blood feeding, is intimate. We release chemicals that induce pleasure in our partner."

That strange twisting sensation in my chest returned at his words. He wasn't talking about me as a meal, but as a partner. And the mention of pleasure.

"Are we talking a nice, warm hug or something else?" I asked.

He actually looked sheepish and rubbed the back of his neck with his hand. This conversation was as unsettling for him as it was for me.

"Something else," he answered. A dull flush worked its way into his cheeks. "Typically, if we're in relationships, we only bite our romantic partners, so..."

My own face heated. "So it's sexual?" I asked.

He nodded.

I wondered if my face was a red as his.

"Is there any way to, uh, control it?" I asked.

"A little, but it's an involuntary response, like..." He trailed off as though he were searching for the correct word.

"Breathing?" I asked.

He shook his head. "Not exactly. When you breathe, you can control the tempo, depth, or duration when you think about it. When you don't think, it just happens. This is more like blinking when something gets in your eye or salivating when you smell something delicious. It's almost impossible to control."

I wasn't sure how I felt about that analogy, but I understood what he meant.

"So, it will feel good to me. What about you?"

I hadn't thought it possible, but Marcus' face became a deeper shade of red beneath the olive tint to his skin.

"Uh, well, we find it pleasurable as well because of the, uh...the, um...bond. Our partner's pleasure sort of," he gestured with his hands as he spoke, lifting them and moving them back and forth. "Resonates."

"Long story short, you'll feel what I feel?"

He sighed. "Yes."

I rubbed a hand over my forehead. "Is there any way to...I don't know, stop that part of the cycle?"

"Maybe if you were unconscious," he answered, shrugging.

I had to laugh. "TKO, huh?"

He didn't smile back.

I had three choices here. One, I could continue as I was, letting Andre Dumont feed from me in my sleep and control me anytime he got the urge. Two, I could break the connection with Dumont by cementing the bond with Marcus by blood.

Three, I could run away. It wouldn't really solve anything in the long run, but it was my first instinct.

"We're going to do this," I said, looking Marcus straight in the eye. "I'm sorry if it makes things awkward for you. I don't want that, but I do want to survive. If you can deal with it, I can as well."

"I can handle it."

"Let's just make a pact that we won't let things get weird after this, okay?" I paused. Things were already pretty damn weird. "Not any weirder, anyway."

He nodded. "This is as weird as it gets."

And just as I suspected, the Universe proved that wrong with all possible haste.

CHAPTER THIRTEEN

MARCUS

"WHEN ARE we going to do this?" Merry asked.

She curled up against the headboard on the guest bed, bringing her knees to her chest and wrapping her arms around them. But her gaze was steady as she met mine.

"As soon as we can," I said. "The longer you're vulnerable to Dumont, the longer you're in danger."

"Okay, then let's get it done."

"I'll get Ava from—"

Merry shook her head. "If everything happens the way you say it will, I'd prefer not to have an audience."

That was a relief because I didn't want an audience either. If I somehow lost control, Macgrath and Callum were just in the next room. I didn't point out to her that their hearing was sharp enough to catch every word or whisper from their current position.

"Standing or sitting?" she asked. Before I could tell her it didn't matter, she continued, "Sitting. You're so much taller than me, it would be a bad angle if we were both standing."

"Okay."

She released her legs and straightened as I came around the bed toward her. I moved slowly and tried to appear as non-threatening as possible.

"You know I'm going to take some of your blood, but you're also going to have to take some of mine," I said, sitting on the edge of the bed close to her feet.

She grimaced. "How much is some?"

"A few drops."

"I won't become a..."

I shook my head. "No. There's a process to the change and it does involve a blood exchange, but it's a lot more complex than this."

"That's a relief." Her eyes widened. "I mean, obviously, I don't think there's something wrong with you being a vampire, but I don't want to become one."

"I understood what you meant. No offense taken."

"I'm sorry."

I waved a hand. "Don't be sorry."

She rolled her lips inward and stared at me.

"Merry, I understand that not every human would want to be a vampire. As Callum would say, if I had feelings, it wouldn't hurt them."

"I know you have feelings," she said. "Otherwise, you wouldn't blush."

She smiled when she said it and I couldn't stop myself from smiling in return.

"So which side?" she asked.

"What?"

I had no idea what she was talking about.

"Of the neck?"

My face must have remained blank because it was her turn to blush.

"Which side of the neck do you want to bite me on?" she muttered, speaking so quickly that the words nearly ran together.

"Oh. Um. Well, I thought you would probably prefer the wrist. It's a little less, uh, intimate."

"Oh. Okay. That's...good. I guess. I mean. Definitely." The pink in her cheeks crept to the tips of her ears.

"Ready?" I asked.

She took a deep breath. "As I'll ever be, I guess. This isn't in my realm of every day experience."

"Mine either."

Merry gave me a sidelong glance. "Don't you drink blood every day?" she asked, her tone incredulous.

"No, not anymore. The older we get, the longer we can go between feedings," I explained. "Unless we're mated, we might go days or even a few weeks without feeding if we are healthy and uninjured."

"Really? You don't get," She paused. "I hate to put it this way, but it's the only word I can think of that fits, bloodlust?"

I shook my head. "Usually only the younger vampires or those who are severely injured suffer from bloodlust. I might get a craving for blood, but Ava likens it to when you get a craving for cake or ice cream. It's something I can resist."

Merry laughed. "I'm glad you can because I usually can't resist cake or ice cream when I'm craving them."

Her laughter faded and she inched a little closer. "Okay, I've been stalling, but we should get this done before Dumont tries to reach me again."

I took her hand in mine, cradling her palm face-up. "I'll make it as painless as possible," I stated.

She nodded.

"Since we've already established a connection, I'll be able to control your pain to some extent. Don't panic if you hear a few of my thoughts. At the moment of exchange, my mind will be open to you and yours will be open to me."

Merry inhaled sharply.

"Are you ready?" I asked.

"No, but we're doing this anyway because the alternative is much worse."

I lifted her wrist to my mouth and reached out to her with my thoughts. My fangs elongated and I fastened my lips to her cool skin.

Merry gasped when the tips of my fangs broke through her flesh, but she didn't try to pull away. The taste of her filled my senses, more potent than I expected, and for a moment, my mind went completely blank.

It was only the echo of her pain that pulled me back to reality. I found the light of pain in her mind and drew a veil over it. The light dimmed. Merry's body relaxed again and she sighed.

While I wanted to linger, to enjoy the moment with her, this was about her protection. She wasn't my mate. She didn't think of me as a man but as a monster.

I had to complete the bond. I lifted my mouth briefly from her wrist, just long enough to open a small cut on my index finger. Her eyes met mine as I put my finger to her lips. When my blood touched her tongue, the bond was complete.

For a brief moment, her mind was wide open to me and I knew mine would be open to her. She could see into the heart of me.

But I had to focus on the thin tendrils of her connection to Andre Dumont, deep indigo shot through with silver. Though they were narrow, the threads were strong and twisted deep within her mind. As our bond grew stronger and brighter, the deep blue tendrils dissolved into dust and vanished, leaving only Merry and her shining spirit.

I saw her joys, her regrets. I felt the pleasure that my bite gave her, but struggled to ignore it. Resisted the urge to roll it back to her until it resonated between us like a tolling bell. Images flashed through my head, so quickly that I couldn't keep up with each. Until the last.

It was the two of us, standing in front of the mirror in her hotel room. It was the first dream she'd had after we met and we were both nude.

As that picture flashed, her voice accompanied it, spoken only in her mind.

Don't think about him naked. Don't think about him naked. Shit. Now, we're both naked.

As tantalizing as the image was and as amusing as her thoughts were, I forced myself to withdraw, both from her mind and her wrist. I slid my tongue over the small punctures on her wrist, using my saliva to seal them, and she jumped at the unexpected touch.

She released my finger from her mouth and grabbed my hand to study the tip for a moment. "It's already healed."

I turned her wrist toward her. "So are you."

Her mouth fell open. "How did that happen?"

"My saliva and blood have healing properties," I explained. "I used them to close your wounds."

She ran her fingers over her wrist. "Wow. That's...just wow." Merry looked up at me. "So it's done?"

I nodded.

"I don't feel any different."

"I'm not surprised. Dumont took pains to hide his presence and his influence on you."

There was a light knock on the bedroom door.

Merry looked at me and I shrugged. "It's your room."

"Come in," she called.

The door opened to reveal Ava. "That was quick," she commented, a brow arched.

I cursed silently as my face began to warm and I knew I was blushing. "Merry's safety was the most important thing."

I glanced at Merry and saw she was blushing as well.

"Well, now that that's done," Ava said as she came further into the room. "I have something for you."

She withdrew a slender chain from the pocket of her dress. On the end, a pale bluish-white stone shimmered in a silver setting. "You'll need to wear this. Don't take it off even when you shower," she said.

Ava brushed by me and clasped the necklace around her neck. The stone flared for a moment, emitting a bright light as the enchantment became active.

"This will not only keep Dumont out of your dreams and prevent him from re-establishing the connection and feeding off of you, it will offer you protection from magical attacks from any witches or warlocks you come across."

Merry lifted her hand to the amulet and curled her fingers around it. "You mean that if I met someone like Rhiannon again, this would protect me?"

"Yes."

While Merry's relief was evident in her expression, I could feel it unfurl inside me as it did within her.

I struggled to lift the block between us, to separate her emotions from my own. She understood the link would exist between us, but that didn't mean I should take advantage of it. Merry was entitled to privacy when it came to her thoughts and emotions.

"I know the situation isn't ideal, but if you don't exchange blood again and Marcus doesn't feed from you, the bond will begin to fade with time. I know we discussed it before but I just wanted to make sure you knew it isn't permanent, even if it is intense at the moment."

"I understand."

"Other than that, how do you feel?" Ava asked.

"Well, considering I barely slept last night, I feel pretty good. Energetic."

"That's the vampire blood," Ava said before I could even open my mouth. "It has that effect on humans. If taken in larger amounts, it can aid in healing and slow or reverse aging."

Merry's eyes widened and she looked at me. "You mean vampire blood is the ultimate anti-aging treatment?"

Ava laughed. "Maybe not the ultimate, but pretty darn close."

"Hmmm."

"I'm not sure I like the way you're looking at me," I said. "Like you're figuring out the best way to imprison me so you can harvest my blood."

Merry's laughter joined Ava's. "I'm not, I promise."

Before Ava could speak again, her cell phone rang. She removed it from the other pocket in her dress and looked at the screen.

"Well, well, well, it appears Mr. Dumont would like to speak to me." She tapped the screen with her thumb and lifted the phone to her ear. "Good morning, Andre. Did you sleep well last night?"

I knew Merry couldn't hear what the other vampire was saying, but I could.

"Not as well as I expected to," he drawled.

"That's too bad. I'm sure I could brew up a tincture for you. Or perhaps an amulet." Ava's eyes lit from within.

I had no idea what she was doing, but she was using her magic.

"That's very thoughtful, Ava, but I'm afraid nothing seems to help."

She smiled and I saw Merry inch away from her on the mattress. I couldn't blame her. It was a frightening smile, terrible in its beauty and power. The smile of a Goddess...or her descendant.

"I'm so sorry to hear that. I just prepared an amulet for my friend, Merry. In fact, I think the two of you have met."

Andre was silent for a long moment. "You don't know what you've done, Ava."

"I think you should call me Ms. Amaris, Andre. Because you have no idea what *you* have done. You allowed one of your offspring to terrify a human woman within my territory. You've been feeding from her for months without her consent or knowledge and you had the nerve to try and pull her away from the protection that I have promised her." Ava stopped to take a breath. "I may not play ball with the Council but that doesn't mean that I'm weak or that I will let an insult such as this pass by. Now, you have twelve hours to leave my territory or you will find out exactly what it's like to be hunted by a witch."

"All your power will be useless if she doesn't help me," he said. "You are not a god."

"No, but I am the daughter of a Goddess," Ava snapped. "And the Mother of Vampires, which means that I am the reason you are in this world and I can be the reason you leave it." She took a deep breath. "You have twelve hours. You are no longer welcome in Austin. If I see you again, it will be the last time you see anything."

It had been a while since I'd heard Ava lay the verbal smackdown on someone, but I had heard it before. However, Merry hadn't because she was staring at Ava with huge eyes and I could feel the apprehension brewing inside her.

Ava disconnected the call and tucked her phone back into her pocket. Each movement was smooth and controlled as though she wasn't a hair from losing her shit, but I knew her too well. Her eyes were brilliant amethyst and her hair moved as though it were caught in a slight breeze. Her power swirled around her, so potent that it was nearly visible.

"The Mother of Vampires?" Merry murmured.

Ava turned toward her and Merry winced. The glowing lavender eyes were a bit intimidating if you weren't used to them.

Ava closed her eyes, took a deep breath, and when she opened them again, her eyes were no longer purple coals.

"Yes, Macgrath is the first vampire. He was dying and I used a spell to save him. The magic changed him and he became the first vampire."

Merry nodded, but her eyes were still huge. "Daughter of a goddess?"

Ava sighed. "Yes. I'm the daughter of the Goddess."

"*The Goddess?* As opposed to *a goddess?*"

"Yes."

Merry closed her eyes and shook her head. "I thought nothing could surprise me anymore. But I have to admit that this might be too much for me. I think my mind is finally, literally blown."

Ava smiled and sat down next to Merry's feet on the bed, which meant I had to move back or she would be sitting in my lap. Something I knew Macgrath wouldn't appreciate.

"I'm sorry to spring it all on you, Merry. I work very hard not to let my anger get the better of me, but sometimes I do lose my temper. And say more than I should. Regardless of my lineage or my power, I would very much like to be your friend."

Merry considered her for a moment. "Marcus said something about you turning Callum into a pig."

"I would never do that to my friends."

"I thought Callum was your friend," Merry said.

"He is, but he also acts like a pig on occasion and has to be reminded why that's a bad idea."

A smile spread across Merry's face. "Well, I guess we can be friends if you promise to let me watch the next time you do it."

I couldn't see Ava's face from my position behind her but I knew she was smiling in return because she held out her hand for Merry to shake and said, "Deal."

Goddess help us.

CHAPTER FOURTEEN

MERRY

My body hummed with energy. It was a struggle to sit still.

But I had to.

We were gathered around the kitchen table. By we, I meant Marcus, Callum, Ava, and Macgrath. They were discussing the conversation that Ava had with Dumont.

"He wants something from Merry," Ava said. She glanced at me. "It's likely related to the job he hired you to do. Can you tell us more about it?"

I tapped my fingers on the table top, unable to control the fidgeting. "I didn't have all the details yet. Only what he told me about during my interview with him."

Ava made a gesture for me to continue.

"Essentially, what he outlined was that it would be a security check. He wanted me to attempt to breach one of his systems and find the weaknesses. Once that was done, he wanted me to write a program to shore them up. That's all he gave me. He was supposed to send me more information before I began the job, but..." I didn't finish that sentence because I was too busy remembering the terror of being chased down the street and into Ava's shop.

"He probably intended to impose his will on yours or wipe your memories when you'd finished whatever job he gave you," Ava said.

I saw the look that Macgrath and Marcus exchanged and knew that she was only trying to make me feel better. In all likelihood, I never would have been seen or heard from again if Dumont's man hadn't tried to grab me on the street.

Which brought up another question.

"If he could impose his will on me, why did Marcel come after me? There was no need to kidnap me if he could just make me do what he wanted whenever he wanted," I pointed out.

We all looked at each other.

"Any ideas why he might do that?" Callum asked.

Still all looking at each other.

"That's something we probably need to look into," Ava said.

"Let's go back to the part about how all your power won't save you from what's coming," Macgrath said to Ava.

I couldn't take it any longer. My foot had been bouncing constantly for the last few minutes. I got to my feet. "I need something to drink."

Marcus started to get up. "I can get it."

I shook my head. "I need to move around. I feel like I'm about to bounce off every wall in the house. Please ignore me while y'all talk."

With a nod, Ava answered Macgrath. "He knows something. While we were on the phone, I tried to get through his mental blocks but I couldn't get past the first couple of layers. Since he feeds on emotions, his mental shields are insanely strong. He knows that someone is going to come for him and, eventually, for us. He's frightened. More frightened of whoever is coming after him than he is of either of us."

"Only because he doesn't know what we're capable of," Macgrath growled.

Ava shook her head. "Oh, he knows. Whatever is going on still scares him more."

I grabbed a Cherry Coke from the fridge, popped the tab on the can, and took a sip to moisten my dry mouth. "What could scare a vampire that much? You guys are pretty powerful."

"That may be," Macgrath said. "But we aren't the top of the food chain. There are powerful beings in this realm and in others. Much more powerful than us."

"Things that can kill you?" I asked.

He nodded. "The four of us would be harder than most, but we can die. We aren't truly immortal."

"What about humans? Could one of them kill you?" I asked. When they all focused on me, I lifted my hands as though I were surrendering. "I have no plans to kill anyone. I just wondered."

Macgrath nodded. "Yes. If they used the right firepower and there were enough of them, they could take us down. It would take more than a few bullets, but human weapons can kill us."

"It could either be a powerful being or a group of humans? That doesn't narrow it down much," I said.

"No, it doesn't." Macgrath seemed more grim than usual.

"Think it's too late to ask Dumont?" Callum asked.

Ava's answering laugh was dry. "Yes, I do. I gave him twelve hours to leave the city. And, honestly, his entire approach to this situation makes him a wild card. If we do have a common enemy, I can't say that makes us allies. He's reactive instead of proactive and, in a situation where we are in danger, that's something that could get us all killed. If he'd come to me and been honest and open, I would have helped him. Instead, he played games, tried to use a human woman as a pawn, and then tried to force her to leave our protection. I doubt very much he would answer any questions I had if I called him up and told him that I was willing to help now."

"Then we need to retrace his steps," Macgrath said. "We need to look at where he came from and what he's been doing. Once we know that, we might be able to figure out who may be after him."

"Even if that puts us in their crosshairs as well?" Marcus asked.

I drank more soda because this entire conversation was making all the spit in my mouth dry up.

"I think that we're already on the fringes of their knowledge," Ava said. "Otherwise, why would Dumont come specifically to us?"

I didn't want to interrupt the conversation, but Ava's question had an answer.

"Because he knows what you are," I said.

They all turned to me as though they'd forgotten I was in the room. I guess they'd taken my directive to ignore me literally.

"What do you mean?" Ava asked.

"Let's say that whoever is after him doesn't know about you, but he does. He knows that you're the daughter of the Goddess and the witch who created vampires." I glanced at Macgrath. "And he knows you're the first and probably the most powerful in this world."

They continued to stare so I knew I needed to give them more information.

"When I ran into big trouble as a kid, I always went to my parents. They knew everything and they could fix everything. Maybe this is the vampire version of Dumont running to his parents."

"Well, then he deserves one hell of a spanking and to get his ass grounded for a month," Callum grumbled. "Because this isn't how you ask for help from your parents."

He had a good point. "Okay, so that's accurate. But maybe he doesn't know if you'll care or not. Maybe he isn't sure he can trust you," I said. "What's one way he can find out?"

Ava understood where I was going with this before the men. "You set a trap. Not to kill, but to observe behavior. You want to see what their reaction time is like. Who and what they value."

I nodded. "I was the trap. Dumont wanted to see what you would do if he attacked a human in your territory."

"Maybe, but why wouldn't he come clean to me after that?" Ava asked. "Why would he try to get you out of this house and into his custody before he followed through?"

"The threat of harm," Macgrath said. "She would be a hostage. You've already demonstrated that you care about Merry."

"I think it's more than that. I think he needs my computer skills."

"For what?" Callum asked.

I shrugged. "He didn't divulge any details of the job so I don't know." I looked at Ava. "What do you think he will do now?" I asked.

Macgrath, Marcus, and Callum looked at each other.

"If you can't defeat your enemy," Macgrath said.

"You retreat, regroup, and plan a different angle of attack," Marcus continued.

"Or you hide," Callum finished the thought for all of them.

Ava leaned toward them. "Or you point your enemy in a different direction. You distract and attack their flank."

The men all nodded, approving expressions on their faces.

"But who does Dumont consider his enemy?" I asked. "Us or this unknown entity?"

"That's a good question," Macgrath said. He looked at me with those intense blue eyes so similar to Marcus'.

"Considering he came to us," Ava stated. "I think he would prefer to have us as allies. Since that didn't work, I'm concerned he'll try to use us as his distraction." She sighed. "Should I contact him and rescind my demand that he leave the city?" she asked Macgrath.

To my surprise, he shook his head. "No. Let's see what he does first. We'll watch him and monitor his communications before we do anything."

"Want me to hack his phone?" I asked.

Macgrath grinned. "That's an excellent offer, but I think we'll just clone it."

"Do you have to get close to him to do that?" I asked.

"It shouldn't be too difficult."

Ava rolled her eyes. "Such a show-off."

Macgrath shook his head. "No, I just like to have fun." The mischievous gleam in his eye disappeared. "We're going to watch him and follow him and find out what he knows. Then, we will approach him. He came here and fucked up. He needs to scramble for a little while before we come in and clean up his mess."

"I can help," I said. I wanted to help. I might not have their magic or physical strength, but there were things I could do in this situation that would help.

"Oh, you're going to," Ava said. "I want you to compile every piece of information you can on Andre Dumont. Everything. Banking information, property he owns, vehicle registration, emails, texts, anything you can find or think of. See if he has any aliases or shell companies.

Go crazy. Make a file on him that any government agency would want on one of their adversaries. Or allies."

I put my soda down and rubbed my hands together. "I can do that."

Ava got to her feet and Macgrath followed suit. "We're going back to the shop. All my tools and herbs are either there or at home. I believe I'm going to put a tracking spell on our friend, Andre. It'll make it easier for Macgrath and Callum to find him and clone his phone and place an actual tracker on it."

"If you can track him with magic, why do you need the technology?" I asked.

"In case one fails or he blocks one of them," she answered.

That made sense.

"I'll get to work," I said.

"I can help."

I glanced at him. "I don't know. Your fingers are fast, but your brain is slow. Remember the game?"

He laughed without humor then made a face at me. "It's bad sportsmanship to gloat," he said.

"It's not healthy to remain in denial."

He made another face at me.

"Children, don't worry, you can all help," Ava said.

I grinned at her. "But I was having so much fun."

"Tease him later when he's still fumbling around to find things that you've already dug up."

"Hey!" Callum said, looking at her. "No ganging up on me."

"Try to take this seriously, Callum." Macgrath put an arm around Ava's waist. "I know it's difficult."

"But she—" He stopped and stuttered. "She started it."

"And you're a lot older," Ava answered, folding her hands at her waist. "You should know better."

Callum kept sputtering as Ava and Macgrath headed out of the kitchen toward the front door.

"We'll touch base tonight and compare notes," Ava stated. She turned and gave me a pointed look. "Be sure to take breaks to eat and stretch. I don't want you passing out on me."

"Yes, Mother."

Ava shook her head. "You're rubbing off on her already, Callum."

After they left, I glanced up at Marcus. The entire day so far seemed surreal. "What's your job going to be?" I asked.

"Watching your back."

I liked the sound of that.

CHAPTER FIFTEEN

MARCUS

Callum emerged from his room, stretching and yawning. It was late, nearly two in the morning, and he and Merry had been working for hours. I'd made them take a couple of breaks to eat and stretch their legs, but they were on a mission.

"Hey, do we have any snacks?" he asked, going to the fridge and opening it. He put one hand on his hip and stared inside as if it held the secrets of the universe.

"Yes. There's dip and veggies."

He scoffed and pulled a pitcher of cold brew coffee out of the fridge. We made it by the gallon because he loved it so much. "Veggies. Real snacks are full of preservatives and carbs. Or fat. Or sugar. Or all of the above."

"You mean the stuff that will clog your arteries and give anyone human a heart attack?"

"Well, yeah."

I groaned. "Look in the pantry."

"Sweet."

"Where's Merry? Do you think she's hungry?"

"Nah," he answered, gathering a bunch of junk food in one arm while holding the cold brew in the other hand. "She's asleep."

"I didn't hear her go to bed."

"Oh, no. She's facedown on her laptop."

"You just left her like that?" I asked, anger rising.

"No, I'm telling you so you can do something about it."

"Jeez. Why bother doing something yourself when you can have someone else do it?"

He set everything on the counter with a plunk and turned toward me. "Oh, so you'd be fine with me picking her up, holding her in my arms, and then gently tucking her into her bed? Then, that's what I'll do."

I snarled at him, sounding more like a shifter than a vampire, and he laughed.

"That's what I thought. Now, go put her to bed before she wakes up with a crick in her neck."

I left him in the kitchen and found Merry exactly as he described her. Her arms were folded under her head and the hood of her sweatshirt was pulled over her head.

I walked over to her and leaned down, sliding one arm under her legs and another around her shoulder.

She stirred, went rigid, and the next thing I knew, lights were exploding behind my eyelids.

My body locked up and I couldn't stop myself from dropping her as I fell back. The back of my head hit the floor with a thunk and white-hot pain seared every nerve ending. A dull roar filled my mind, blocking out any other sound.

The pain released me from its grip and my muscles finally relaxed. The bones of my legs must have dissolved under the intense shock because they refused to obey me and resembled jelly.

"Oh, my God, Marcus." Merry's face appeared above me, her eyes wide and her cheeks pale. "I'm so sorry. You startled me and, well, I zapped you."

"S'okay." My cheek was wet and I wondered if it was because my eyes were tearing or because I was likely drooling.

"What?"

"S'okay," I repeated. I tried to enunciate clearly but my tongue had gone the way of my legs and was refusing to cooperate.

"What in the hell?" Callum asked from the doorway.

"Callum!" Merry cried. The sound was so loud that I winced. My ears were ringing louder now. "I accidentally tased Marcus and I can't tell if he's seriously hurt or not."

"You're joking."

"No. I ramped up a police-issue Taser I bought so that it would be effective on vampires and I was sleeping when he picked me up so I—"

Callum interrupted, repeating what she'd said earlier. "Zapped him?"

"Yes. Can you please come and make sure he's okay? He hit the floor pretty hard."

"Well, I'd say your Taser is definitely effective against vampires," Callum drawled as he sauntered over to me and crouched down. "Wouldn't you, Marcus?"

I glared at him since my tongue still wasn't working right. Which, of course, made him laugh.

"Think you'll live?" he asked me.

I nodded, short and jerky.

"See? He's fine," Callum told Merry.

She smacked his arm. "I could have really hurt him, Callum! Stop joking around."

She leaned over me and put her hands beneath my head. Her fingers were gentle as she lifted my skull and touched the small knot that was rapidly disappearing. It was tender where she pressed on it, but she gasped as the swelling vanished within a few seconds.

My limbs were still tingling like crazy, but my tongue no longer felt as if it had been superglued to the roof of my mouth.

"I'm a'right," I slurred to her. "Just nee' a min't ta...ta..."

"He needs a minute for his brain to unscramble," Callum finished for me. "He's not seriously injured, but electrical pulses can mess with our brains just like a human's. Good job figuring that out, by the way. If he'd been Dumont, he'd have been in for one hell of a shock. Literally." He chuckled to himself.

I was able to roll my eyes and saw that Merry did the same.

"Ah, after a couple thousand years, you can be punny. How cute," she said.

Callum pressed a hand to his chest. "Me?"

Merry had rapidly adjusted to his ridiculous ways and ignored him. "Think you can sit up?" she asked me.

My answer was to do exactly that. The room spun in a single, slow circle before it settled right side up.

"I'm okay," I said, glad my mouth was no longer numb. "But now I understand how the dice feel when Ava makes me play Yahtzee."

Merry smiled at me. "I'm so sorry."

I shook my head and immediately regretted it because the room tried to spin again.

"Don't be sorry. You did exactly what you should have done if someone grabbed you while you were sleeping. You reacted without thinking and took me down. If I'd been an enemy instead of a friend, it would have given you time to call for help or run away."

Merry's fingers were still tangled in my hair, her palms resting against the back of my neck. "Does your head hurt? The lump on the back of it was pretty big a few minutes ago."

"Already faded," I assured her.

"If you were human, you'd probably have a concussion," she argued. "Surely a vampire can't heal from one of those so quickly."

Callum and I glanced at each other, just for a split second, but she caught it.

"But you two aren't just any vampires, are you? Besides Macgrath, you're the oldest."

Callum nodded. "Macgrath isn't much older than us. Maybe by a year or two. We heal almost instantaneously now. And as the years pass, we get faster and stronger. It may take a century or two, but after twenty of them, we're almost impossible to kill."

Merry must have realized she was still touching me because she lowered her hands from my head to her lap and clenched them together. I wished she hadn't.

Callum rose to his feet. "Well, I hate to kick y'all out of here, but

I'm ready to hit the hay." Merry opened her mouth, but he pointed a finger at her. "If my eyes are blurry, yours must be too. Take a break. Sleep a few hours. We'll pick this up in the morning. We've already given Ava her update for tonight and worked an extra six hours. You'll miss something important if you don't rest."

Merry shut her mouth with a snap and glared at Callum, who seemed completely unperturbed by her sour attitude.

I leaned to one side and started to push myself to my feet. The dizziness from the shock was almost completely gone, but I was still just a bit shaky. Merry realized what I was doing and abandoned her stare-down with Callum to help me up. Her arm wrapped around my waist and she tried to prop me up with her weight.

I laid my arm over her shoulder and let her help me because I didn't want to sit there while she bickered with Callum all night. I knew all too well that he would do exactly that just for fun.

"Night, you two," Callum called as he shut the door behind us.

Merry sighed and turned toward my room. I tried to shift out of her grip, but she held firm.

"I'm helping you to bed," she stated. Then, her cheeks turned fiery red and she blinked rapidly. "I mean, I'm helping you to your room."

"I really am—"

"Fine. I know. I'm still helping you."

I sighed because even from the strange angle, I could see the hard, stubborn set of her jaw. I couldn't see her eyes, but I was certain they were glinting with pure obstinacy. There was no use arguing with her because there was no winning the argument. I'd learned a long, long time ago to never go into battle if I was certain of defeat.

I'd left my door open and she guided me through and to the bed.

"Sit down," she ordered.

I sighed again and did as she commanded.

"And stop sighing as if this is the end of the world. I'll be gone in a few minutes."

"I'm not sighing as if it's the end of the world," I argued. "But you're overreacting."

She mulled that over for a second as she crouched down by my feet and started to unlace my boots. I tried to pull away but once again she held fast. This time, she tilted her head back to stare at me.

"If I am, then you'll just have to deal with it. I could have hurt you tonight."

"Did you miss the part where Callum said that we're nearly impossible to kill?"

Merry shot me a gimlet eye and went back to untying my boots. "Doesn't matter. There's a first time for everything and it would be just my luck that I would kill one of the few people who have helped me in the last year."

I realized her hands were trembling so badly that she couldn't unknot the ties. In fact, her entire body was shaking so hard that I had no idea how she was staying upright in her squat.

"Hey," I said, reaching down to take her hands in mine. They were cold and tense beneath my fingers. I pulled her up and onto the bed next to me. Without thinking, I put an arm around her. Fine tremors rocked her shoulders as I hugged her to my side. "I should have woken you up instead of just trying to carry you to bed. After everything you've been through, it's not unexpected that you'd react like that to being startled."

She tucked her face against my neck and tears wet my skin.

Unable to stand it, I put my other arm around her and hugged her close. "I'm unharmed and grateful that you're at least able to protect yourself from a vampire or shifter if you need to. Please don't cry."

After a year of reaching deep for strength, Merry broke. Her sobs were silent but they wracked her body in huge waves. Tears soaked the collar of my shirt and her hands clutched my waist before wrapping tight around my middle.

She held me as though I were her anchor in the center of a tempest.

I kept my arms wrapped around her and rocked with her as she cried. I had no idea what to say, so I settled on soothing, wordless murmurs as I stroked her heaving back.

Finally, after long moments, the storm of her weeping subsided and her forehead rested against my neck. Small hiccups occasionally ran through her, but she seemed content to lean against me, so I didn't release her and move away. I couldn't have, even if I wanted to, because her hands were still fisted in the back of my t-shirt.

"If I had met you before," she whispered. "I wouldn't be so fucked up now. So afraid even though I'm beginning to realize you would never hurt me. Things could be..."

She trailed off and sighed against my throat.

"Be what?" I asked.

Her pause was long. "Be different."

I stroked a hand over her hair. "If Rhiannon hadn't found you, I probably never would have known you existed. Nor would you have known I existed. Our paths were destined to cross because of her. I hate the pain that you've been through, but I'm not sorry that you're here now."

She didn't move, but her next breath was shaky. It was a huge temptation to reach through our new bond and see what she was thinking and feeling, but I squashed the urge like a bug. I would not do that to her.

Merry lifted her head and her deep brown eyes were still damp from her tears as she looked at me.

Then, she did the last thing I expected.

She kissed me.

CHAPTER SIXTEEN

MERRY

I kissed Marcus.

There was nothing else I could do. Or wanted to do anyway.

For a man who didn't say much, he used the right words when he did speak.

The craziest thing of all is that he was kissing me back. He didn't pull away or gently explain to me that I misunderstood his feelings.

No, his arms pulled me closer until I was draped across his lap. I sank into the kiss, letting go of everything else. The stress of the day, the fear that had dogged me for months, and the wariness I'd used to keep distance between us.

When his mouth moved to my throat, I let my head fall back. He hadn't been lying when he said that a vampire's bite only hurt when they wanted it to. Earlier, I'd been frightened by the way my body responded to his mouth on my wrist.

Not because it hurt or was uncomfortable, but because it wasn't. It was pleasure. Bliss.

His lips touched the base of my throat, where my pulse throbbed, and a ragged sigh escaped my lips.

Somehow, that tiny sound seemed to wake Marcus up because he lifted his head and looked down at me.

His blue eyes glowed with unearthly light, brilliant and hot. I could see the edges of his fangs as he spoke.

"This is a horrible idea," he said.

Okay, scratch the thought I had before about him saying the right things when he spoke.

I sat up and stared at him in disbelief. "Really? Kissing me is a horrible idea?"

I started to get to my feet, but his hand touched my arm and I found myself settling back down next to him.

"That's...it's just that...I mean...that's not what I meant," he finally said.

Any other time in my life, I would have backed down from this. I wouldn't have confronted him. I wouldn't have done anything to make either of us uncomfortable.

But not this time.

I wanted to know why.

"Then what did you mean?" I asked.

He turned toward me, lifting one leg on the bed, effectively putting more space between us. Oh, poor vampire, he must have been afraid I'd throw myself at him again.

"Only that I don't want you to regret this and I think you would. Bonding is a strong experience, whether it's between a vampire and human or two vampires. It can create...a desire to be closer. To repeat the experience on a regular basis, which only strengthens the bond with each one. I don't want you to wake up tomorrow and realize that you made this decision when you weren't quite yourself."

Okay, so that was a decent explanation, but also a load of bullshit because I was fully aware of my own thoughts and feelings. Not in some fog of lust because he'd bitten me once and now I was dying for more. While he was feeding from me and when he'd given me the small amount of his blood, I'd felt the bond snap into place. I couldn't hear his thoughts, but I knew that he felt the same attraction I did. I could feel it, like the tolling of a bell.

"You think this is a byproduct of the bond and has nothing to do with my real emotions or thoughts?" I asked.

He shook his head. "I don't know and that's what worries me. I'm blocking the bond right now so neither of us is feeling its full effects."

"Well, I hate to burst your bubble," I said. "But I have had my thoughts controlled before and that's not what's happening here. I kissed you because I wanted to. Because, in spite of everything that's happened to me, I like you." This time, when I got to my feet, he let me go. "But I'm not going to force the issue. I don't want you to have regrets in the morning."

Maybe it was petty of me to throw those words back at him, but he'd essentially implied that I wasn't capable enough to decide my own emotions or thoughts right now and that stung like a pissed-off wasp.

Marcus gaped at me as I walked to his door, through it, and closed it behind me.

I went into my own room, shut the door behind me, and tried not to groan. Even with all the doors and walls between us, Marcus would hear me and I wouldn't give him the satisfaction.

Irritation buzzed inside me. I was finally emerging from the cocoon I'd wrapped myself in over the past year, only to be swatted down by the first man I found attractive in a long, long time.

I paced from one side of the room to the other, trying to think past the annoyance. Rejection sucked, even if it was dished out with kind words and sincere eyes.

The crux was that I hadn't thought Marcus would reject me. We were drawn to each other, like two magnets that came into close contact. I saw into his heart when he bound me to him. His emotions ran deep and he felt something for me. Something I'd never experienced before. It was more than appreciation or affection.

I had no frame of reference or ability to describe it because it wasn't a feeling I'd experienced before. He hadn't lied when he said he would do whatever it took to protect me. I'd sensed that grim determination through the brief connection.

Based on all of that, I never expected him to push me away when I reached for him.

I rubbed my sternum and realized that the irritation, the annoyance, was only a mask for my true emotions.

It hurt.

My throat tightened and I knew tears weren't too far behind, so I took a deep breath and let it out slowly. I would not cry over this. He had just as much right to say no to me as I did to him.

I had to give him the same respect I would expect in return if our roles were reversed.

I reached up and ran a finger over the amulet Ava had given me and felt the metal warm beneath my touch, as though it were responding to my heightened emotions.

Maybe it was.

And at the very least, tonight I probably wouldn't have nightmares.

"That's one win for today," I murmured to myself as I got ready for bed.

By the time I stretched out beneath the sheet and blanket, exhaustion was mugging at me once again.

I'd sleep a few hours and then get back to work.

And I would not act weird around Marcus tomorrow. At this point, it was a matter of pride.

I SHOULD HAVE EXPECTED the dream. Ava warned me it was likely.

The water in the pool was hot, steam rising from the surface in thin tendrils. The interior of the cavernous room was dim. There were torches and candles lit along with walls and on stone ledges, but the flickering lights didn't reach the ceiling or the end of the room.

Water swirled and sloshed in the far corner of the pool. I shifted on the shelf and peered into the darkness.

"Who's there?" I asked. My voice travelled in a hushed echo.

Marcus appeared out of the darkness, his eyes shadowed.

I laughed quietly before I sighed. "No escaping each other, is there?"

He moved to the opposite side of the pool and settled on the same underwater shelf I sat on. A good five or six feet separated us.

He lifted his arms as he settled into the corner, resting his elbows on the stone edge of the pool. His chest and arms were bare and the water came up to the top of his ribs.

I wondered if he was naked beneath the water. Because I was. The water was deep enough and dark enough to keep me covered, but the heated liquid lapped at my skin like a kiss.

I couldn't read his expression, but he was watching me. Everywhere his eyes touched, my skin tingled. His silence shouldn't have been disconcerting because I knew that he wasn't talkative by any means, but the air between us felt ripe, heavy with unspoken thoughts.

My mouth wanted to move and I wanted to ramble and fill that empty space, but I held back. If he wanted to sit here and stare at each other all night, I would freaking oblige him.

Okay, so maybe I was still hurt from his earlier rejection.

Marcus must have realized that I wasn't going to speak, because he asked, "Why did you kiss me?"

His voice was low and his question soft, as though he didn't want to ask but he couldn't stop himself either.

I turned to put my back against one side of the pool and pulled my legs up to my chest, wrapping my arms around them. "Because I wanted to."

He didn't respond in any way, not even a nod. He just sat there and stared at me with hidden eyes.

"Why did you think I kissed you?" I asked, arching a brow at him.

"Because I wanted you to."

My heart gave a single, hard thud against my breastbone and I inhaled a shaky breath. Wow. Okay, that wasn't quite what I expected him to say. I thought maybe he would admit he found me attractive but say it wasn't the right time. Or that I was human and it could never work. Anything but that.

"Why would that be a problem?" I asked.

He waited a few seconds before he answered and my hands clenched my arms where they wrapped around my legs as I waited. Jeez, it was like pulling teeth getting him to answer my questions.

"The connection between us is stronger now that we shared blood," he finally said. "And even though I work very hard at blocking my emotions from you, I couldn't be sure that I wasn't projecting my thoughts. Not completely."

"I don't feel anything from you," I said, my arms relaxing. He opened his mouth as though he meant to argue and I shook my head. "It was there during the blood exchange, but then it was like...you slammed a door in my face. You're right next to me and I still have no idea what you're thinking or feeling. Do you sense anything from me?" I asked.

"Not really. I'm blocking you as well as I can. I can sense your presence or if your emotions were extremely heightened, such as in terror, but nothing else."

"Okay, then you know that you had nothing to do with that kiss."

His expression finally changed and I saw the tiniest hint of a smile on his mouth. "That's not entirely true."

I had to laugh, just a little, because he had kissed me back. At least at first. And it had been amazing.

Without thinking, I lifted my hand from the water and touched the tips of my fingers to my bottom lip. Though his eyes were still shadowed, I knew he watched me.

I lowered my hand because my skin suddenly felt hotter than the water surrounding me.

"What do we do about this?" I asked.

He shrugged and I couldn't tear my eyes away from the play of muscles in his shoulders and chest. "I don't know. I haven't courted a human since I was one."

"Courted?" I asked, laughing.

He scowled at me. "What would you call it?"

"Dated? Hung out with? Spent time with? Had a relationship with?"

"Okay, all of those," he growled.

My heart rate spiked before I spoke again. "I guess the most important question is if you would want to spend time with a human."

"I'm spending time with you now."

I rolled my eyes to the ceiling and, if I hadn't been naked, I would have gotten out of the pool and stomped away.

But I was trapped in the water unless I wanted to flash my naked ass at him.

When I lowered my gaze, I gasped and shrank back against the pool wall.

Marcus was right in front of me, his face fully in the light since the dream began. His eyes weren't glowing, but his gaze was intense.

"I like spending time with you," he whispered.

"Okay."

"But I'm not human, Merry, and your experience with vampires hasn't been the best. I'm worried that you would regret getting involved with me."

I relaxed against the wall. My foot brushed his leg as I leaned back. He didn't pull away. "I know what you are, Marcus. What's more important is *who* you are." I swallowed around the sudden lump in my throat. "Would you regret getting involved in a human? You said you hadn't dated a human since you were one yourself."

His hand came out of the water and brushed my cheek. "I wouldn't regret getting involved with you."

I leaned into the caress. "Then, we don't have any obstacles, do we?"

That hint of a smile returned. "I think we have plenty of obstacles."

"Outside obstacles," I argued. "And even humans have those."

He seemed closer as he lowered his hand to rest on the ledge next to my ankles. His chest made contact with my shins and I realized he had moved, just a bit.

"Merry, I don't think you realize what having a vampire lover means," he stated.

"What are you talking about?"

"We bite our lovers. It's intimate and it strengthens our connection."

"Oh my God, you want to bite me?" I gasped dramatically. He scowled at me, but I ignored him. "I understand that part, Marcus. I'm not naive."

"But—"

I put my fingers over his lips, stopping the words before he spoke them. "You're different. You treat me differently as well. I trust you. Probably more than I would a human man."

He blinked several times before he reached up and removed my fingers from his face. "I want to take you at your word, but I'm afraid to."

"Why?"

"Because it will hurt if you don't mean that. Or if you change your mind."

"You could hurt me, too," I pointed out. "A lot more than I could hurt you."

He fell silent and we stared at each other from inches away.

"You'll have to trust me," I said. "Just like you want me to trust you."

"You have a point," he agreed.

When he didn't say anything else, I nodded my head. "And?"

"Just that. You have a point. What else can I say?"

"Nothing, I guess."

He smiled at me, not a small one this time, but one that reached his eyes and lit his entire face.

"Are you angry with me?" he asked.

"Annoyed," I answered.

"Why?"

"Because you've seen into my mind even more than I've seen into yours. I know how you feel about me. You have to know how I feel about you."

"I do," he replied.

"Should I back off? Is that what you want?"

"No."

I lifted a hand and touched the tips of my fingers to his neck. "Then, what do you want me to do?"

His eyes dropped to my mouth and his irises began to glow faintly.

"Just...tell me if I scare you."

This time, I knew what the light behind his eyes meant. He was hungry, but not for blood.

Our lips had barely touched when the edges of the dream shredded.

"Don't go," I whispered.

It was too late. I opened my eyes and stared at the ceiling of the guest room. I glanced around, wondering what had woken me.

The screen of my phone was lit up. I had an email. The vibration of the notification must have been enough to wake me up.

I picked it up and clicked on the banner. I sat up and read the words on the screen carefully.

They are all in danger. You're the only one who can help them. They are being watched and plans are in motion. Contact me if you want to save his life.

A. Dumont

As I stared at the screen, there was a knock on my door.

I don't know why I did it, but I tucked the phone under the blanket. "Come in."

I had an inkling of who it was anyway.

Marcus opened the door and came inside, shutting it behind him. "You okay?"

"Yeah. Just woke up for some reason."

Like the dream, I couldn't see his face due to the shadows in the room.

"Are you okay?" I asked him.

"Yes."

"Are we going to have to go through the entire dream conversation again or can we move on from there?"

He came to the end of the bed and grabbed the footboard. "Does being awake change your mind about anything we discussed?"

I shook my head. "You?"

"No."

"Then, will you hold my hand until I go back to sleep?"

He hesitated.

"If you're worried about your virtue, you can lay on top of the blanket and I'll stay underneath."

I saw a flash of his teeth when he smiled. But he didn't say anything. He just came to the opposite side of the bed and lay down next to me, holding out his hand. I took it and tucked it beneath my chin.

"Thank you," I whispered.

"For what?"

"Keeping the nightmares away."

"Go to sleep, Merry," he murmured. "I'll be here as long as you need me."

I closed my eyes and held his hand a bit closer to my chest. "Good night."

CHAPTER SEVENTEEN

MARCUS

I HATED to get up before Merry woke, but I couldn't sleep anymore and my stomach was growling.

I carefully extricated my hand from hers and slipped off the bed. The door opened on silent hinges. I closed it behind me without a sound. Callum's door was still shut but I could hear his snores coming through the wall. We really needed to invest in some soundproofing for his room because the man sounded like a comatose grizzly.

As I went into the kitchen to make a cup of coffee and grab some breakfast, my thoughts went back to last night.

Merry was coming out of her shell around me. She was no longer as hesitant or wary. It was both beautiful and dangerous, as most women were.

I loved seeing the true Merry, the one I knew from her dreams.

But it was dangerous because I wanted her. All of her.

Merry talked about dating, about spending time together, but she didn't understand that I was past that.

If we went down this path, I would want her, body and soul. She would be my mate. I couldn't accept anything less.

I needed everything she was, or I would have nothing.

I'd tried to talk to her about it in the dream last night, but the way she looked at me, the way the water lapped at her bare skin, had clouded my mind. The heat of the pool had intensified the scent of her skin until she was the center of the world—all I could see, hear, or smell.

I'd wanted so badly to touch her and she wanted to be touched. I could feel her yearning as intensely as I felt my own.

I had to resist.

If she wanted to be courted, I would do it.

But we would have to talk, and soon. Because I wouldn't be able to hold back for long.

She needed to understand what she was in for with me, and if she rejected me, I would have to accept it, no matter how much it hurt.

I had to set it aside for right now and focus on the most important thing—protecting the woman I was beginning to love.

After I ate and drank a cup of coffee, I changed into a pair of workout pants and grabbed my sword and staff.

First, I had to check the perimeter and make sure that no one lurked in the woods around the house. Ava had set wards different distances from the house, the first to warn us of someone's approach was a half-mile away. The second would stop anything non-human a quarter-mile from the house. It was keyed to allow in people we trusted, such as Arien, Harrison, Savannah, Rhys, and Caleb, but any other creatures would be stopped. They could eventually break through, but it would give us ample time to fortify or run if necessary.

The final ward started at the tree-line and it would take a sorceress or wizard of Ava's power to break through.

Since I seriously doubted that there was another witch of her caliber in this world, I felt that we would be safe in the house.

But I never wanted to take it for granted.

I used the perimeter check as my warm-up, running the border of the ward nearest to the house before I moved out to the second ward. There was nothing. As I circled the furthest ward, the sun peeked over the horizon.

When I finished, I found no sign that anyone had been on the

157

edges of the property and I ran back to the house. My muscles were loose and ready for a more intense workout.

I went through a series of push-ups, sit-ups, and pull-ups on the bar that Callum and I installed in the backyard. Sweat soaked my shirt as heat began to rise of my body. I stripped it off and tossed it aside before I grabbed the staff.

I went through a slow series of strikes and blocks, focusing on technique rather than speed, and turned when I heard the back door open.

Callum stood on the back porch, a cup of coffee in his hand and his hair sticking up in several different directions.

He took a sip from his cup before he said, "You're up early. Couldn't sleep?"

I shook my head and picked up speed with the staff. "Considering what time you went to bed, you're up early yourself."

"Yeah. I heard all the heavy breathing out here and thought you'd finally made a move on Merry."

I lost my grip on the staff mid-twirl and it swung around to smack me in the back of the head before it fell on the ground.

Callum laughed so hard that he spilled some of his coffee. "You should see the look on your face."

I picked up the staff and placed one end on the ground. "Watch your step."

He drained the cup and set it on the patio table. "Or what?"

"I'll teach you how to keep your mouth shut."

His eyes sparked with humor and devilry as he came down the steps onto the grass a few feet from me. "Haven't you figured out after nearly two thousand years that it's a losing battle?"

"There's always a chance that this time will finally be the one that breaks through your thick skull," I answered.

"Planning to use that stick to do it?" he asked, holding his hands out to his sides.

I tossed the staff onto the ground and barely had time to step back as he rushed me. I turned, letting him go past me, and smacked my elbow in the back of his neck. It was a light hit, just enough to get his attention.

Quick as a snake, Callum twisted with the blow and swept my legs from beneath me. I fell on my back but managed to kick him away before he could land on top of me. Callum grinned and danced lightly on the balls of his feet as I rolled to mine.

"You're slow this morning," he drawled.

He'd barely finished speaking when my fist landed on his chin. We exchanged jabs, low kicks, and a few knees and elbows, looking for openings and not providing any to each other.

I heard the back door open and I realized that Merry must be up. That moment of inattention cost me because Callum took me down hard and landed on top of me. Grappling was his strength.

He tried to shift his grip and I knew he was going to try for an arm bar. If he got me, I would never be able to get out. He was too damn slippery. I lifted my knee to knock him forward and then lowered my leg to bridge my hips and threw him to the side, rolling with him so that I was on my knees.

Callum clamped his legs around my ribs and lifted his hips to shove me back before I could land a punch. Then, he jerked me forward and managed to avoid my strike before he locked me down into a chokehold.

I aimed a blow at his ribs but he just grunted and tightened his grip on me.

"Want me to make you look good?" he murmured as he tried to cut off the blood flow to my head.

"Fuck. That," I growled.

Instead of trying to pull out of the hold, I shifted more of my weight onto him and ground both of my elbows against the inside of his thighs. It loosened the hold of his legs just enough for me to put space between us.

Before I could break his hold, ice-cold water splashed over us.

I yelped and tried to scramble away as the stream hit the back of my head. Callum released me and a high, piercing scream at the same time.

159

We rolled apart and stared up at Merry in shock.

She released the lever on the spray attachment connected to the garden hose and nodded once.

"Now, y'all play nice," she said.

I was suddenly very aware of how cool the morning air was against my now soaked skin and pants.

"What the hell, Mer?" Callum asked, getting to his feet to follow her as she rolled the hose up and then turned off the water at the faucet.

She faced him, pressed the lever again to release the water still in the line, and he jumped back. "You were being an ass. I could tell just by the way you winked at me when I came outside. I figured you needed something to cool you down."

"You're right," he said. Then, he held out his arms wide. "How about a hug to make up for it?"

He lunged forward as though he intended to grab her. Merry dropped the hose, shrieking, and darted around him. "Don't you dare!" she yelled, running toward the back door.

Callum laughed as she dashed into the house and slammed the screen door behind her. There was a small click and I knew she'd locked the screen door. Not that it would stop Callum if he really wanted inside.

"What? You don't love me anymore?" he asked, standing at the screen door with his arms still out to his sides.

"I never loved you," she replied, but I could see her struggle against the smile that threatened to break out on her face.

Callum clutched his chest dramatically. "You wound me so, my beautiful Merriweather."

She scowled at him and this time she meant it. "I told you not to call me that."

Without waiting for his response, she closed the solid wood door between them and locked it for good measure.

Callum was still grinning when he turned back to me. "It's really a shame you saw her first, brother, because I like the feisty ones."

Possessive instincts rose inside me, sharp and hot, and I bared my fangs at him. "Careful, or we're going to fight again and she won't be here to save you."

He opened his mouth, likely to needle me again, until he saw my expression. "Shit. Your instincts are kicking in, aren't they?"

I swallowed hard and nodded. I didn't say anything else as I went over to grab my shirt off the lawn and shrug it on. My skin was still damp but I was getting cold.

"I'm sorry. I'll mind my words in the future."

"It won't matter," I said. "She's going to leave eventually."

The expression on his face said that he didn't want to have this conversation again, so I lifted a hand to silence him.

"Even if she stays, even if she falls in love with me, do you think she'll ever want me to turn her? I'll have to fight the urge to push her into it every single day we're together."

"You're putting words into her mouth again," Callum pointed out. "But you do have a point. She knows nothing but bad things about vampires, with the exception of us. Fucking Dumont only made it worse, so, yeah, I understand your concern. But you still need to give her a chance."

"I can't wait forever. The longer she takes to make up her mind, the harder it will be for me to let her go."

"I won't let you keep her against her will," Callum said.

He was trying to reassure me, but the thought of being that far gone scared the hell out of me.

"I know."

"Can we go inside and get some more coffee?" he asked, abruptly changing the subject. "I'm getting cold."

"I don't know if she'll let us in," I said.

"You don't have your key?"

I shook my head.

"Shit. I guess I'll go start groveling."

I laughed and followed him to the back door.

He knocked and called out in a thin, trembling voice, "May I trouble you for a crust of bread? We're so cold and hungry, you see."

"It's open, you asshole!" Merry called back.

I laughed again when he winced and actually tried the knob. It turned in his hand. Neither of us had heard her unlock it.

"Damn lucky you saw her first," he murmured.

I jabbed an elbow into his kidney as we walked inside. He didn't even grunt. Probably because he was afraid that Merry would yell at us again.

Since our bond snapped into place, she seemed less and less afraid of us both. She slid seamlessly into our lives as though she belonged here and always had.

That was a dangerous thought.

"Give me a few minutes to shower and I'll make breakfast," I said.

Merry shook her head. "Don't worry about it. I already had a couple of Pop-Tarts and some coffee. I need to get back to work."

I wanted to argue, but knew better. Not because I knew her, but because I understood what drove her. She wanted to know everything about Dumont she could because it made him less of a threat. Less scary.

"Then, I'll take a shower and figure out what we're having for lunch."

I ignored the image that flashed in my mind of me, naked under a stream of hot water. It was her thought and I knew she would be embarrassed if I reacted in any way. I was careful not to look directly at her as I left the kitchen.

But I smiled when I knew neither of them could see me.

Merry no longer regarded me as a monster, but as a man.

And it wasn't because of the bond. I would have felt it otherwise.

After so many years of loneliness and failure, she was my chance at redemption.

When I came out of the bedroom, I found Callum and Merry in his room, working in silence on their computers. Both of their coffee mugs were empty, so I made them each another cup.

I couldn't help with the computer work, but I could make sure they were fed and caffeinated.

I despised feeling useless and found myself back outside, checking the perimeter wards again.

The feeling of being watched took hold of me. It was like an itch between my shoulder blades or a burn on the back of my neck. I could feel the eyes on me, but there was no one there. Dumont nor his men had breached the wards. Not even a human had stumbled upon us out here due to the nature of Ava's spells.

Yet I couldn't shake the sensation.

Somewhere out there, we were being watched, but I couldn't be sure if it was by vampires or any other supernatural creature.

Whoever they were, their magic was well-hidden.

Still, even if I couldn't see or hear them, I knew they were there. My instincts screamed it.

I headed back to the house to check the interior fortifications and maybe set a few traps of my own.

When they came, we would be expecting them.

But they wouldn't be expecting us.

CHAPTER EIGHTEEN

MERRY

IT WAS OFFICIAL.

My brain was utterly and completely fried. If I tried to dig out one more piece of data on Dumont, I would know more about him than God himself.

I stood up and stretched my back, twisting and bending to loosen the tight muscles. I would give someone a thousand dollars for a decent massage. If I had a thousand dollars.

Callum groaned and got to his feet as well. "I think we found everything there was to find," he said. "I even know what size briefs Dumont wears now."

I grimaced. Andre Dumont was a handsome man, but his attitude and actions ruined those good looks, so imagining him in his under-pants wasn't exactly pleasant.

"We have everything we possibly can," Callum continued, reaching toward the ceiling. I heard his back pop. "It's time for you to sit back and let the rest of us do our work."

I wasn't going to argue with that. I didn't want to face Dumont or another of his vampires any time soon. My Taser worked and my vampire-strength pepper spray probably would, too.

But I'd rather not test it out for the first time in a real-life situation.

"About that," I said. "You know you can clone his phone without being in the same room, right?"

Callum's eyes sparkled with humor and mischief. "Yes, I know, but Macgrath wants to plant some bugs, eyes and ears. He wants to see and hear everything happening."

"But how will that work if he's on the move? Won't the cameras be useless?"

He grinned. "Nope. We have our ways."

Okay, I didn't think I wanted to know.

"You and Marcus will stay here while I go to the planning session with Ava and Macgrath."

"If Marcus is going with all of you, shouldn't he be there, too?"

"Nope. We're not leaving you here alone," he said.

"What about the wards? Didn't you say they would keep out anyone but the most powerful magic user?"

"Doesn't matter. I can promise you right now that Marcus won't agree to leave you here alone."

"Doesn't he need to be involved in the planning?"

Instead of answering my question, he asked, "Are you trying to get rid of both of us for a few hours or something?"

"No, I just want to make sure he doesn't get hurt."

Callum's smile faded a bit. "You care about him too, don't you?"

"I care about both of you."

"We've been doing this sort of thing for a very, very long time. We'll be fine, even if Marcus can't present us with his usual grumpy face during the meeting."

"What grumpy face?" Marcus asked from the door.

I jumped and whirled around to face him. "Don't sneak up on me like that!" I yelped, clutching my chest.

Marcus stood in the open doorway, his arms crossed over his chest, and wearing the exact grumpy expression that Callum mentioned.

When I laughed, he looked at Callum for clarification, but all he did was shrug. "What's so funny?" he asked me.

I waved a hand at him. "You. You're funny."

He frowned harder and his biceps flexed, which only made me laugh harder. "I don't understand."

"You're wearing the grumpy face right now," I said, giggling like an idiot. But there was no stopping it.

Marcus seemed to realize what he was doing because his face cleared and he dropped his arms to his sides.

Since I was still snickering, Callum changed the subject. "Merry was worried about you missing out on the planning session and getting hurt when we go on our mission. I was just trying to reassure her that even if your grumpy self wasn't present, you've done missions like these for longer than the United States has existed and you would be fine."

I picked up a pen and flicked it in Callum's direction. "You don't have to repeat everything that I say," I griped.

He caught the pen in mid-air. "I didn't."

I rolled my eyes and looked back at Marcus. "I just thought it would be best if you were in on all the details," I said to him.

"I understand. Thank you for your concern, but Callum is right. We've been a team for a long time and we work well together."

"Okay," I sighed.

Callum clapped his hands, which made me jump. "I have an idea! Why don't you two have a nice dinner and a quiet night in while I'm in town?" He looked at Marcus. "Merry could use some relaxation. And probably a massage. My back is killing me so I'm sure hers hurts as well. She doesn't heal as fast as I do."

Oh, he was so damn lucky I'd already thrown the only pen on the desk at him. Otherwise, I would have done it at that moment.

"Is your back okay?" Marcus asked.

"It'll be fine after a little stretching and a glass of wine," I answered. I shot Callum an angry look, which seemed to slide right off him.

"I'll see the two of you in the morning," Callum said as he gathered up his things. "I probably won't be back until after you both are all tucked up in bed."

The innuendo was heavy in his voice and if I'd had the ability to kill with my eyes, his carcass would be smoking on the carpet.

"I'm going to go start dinner," Marcus said. "Is there anything you'd like?" he asked me.

"Anything is fine," I answered.

As soon as he left the room, I lunged at Callum and pinched his side. He didn't have a lot of extra flesh around his abdomen, but I got a good grip.

"Ouch! Hey!"

"Why are you such a pervert?" I hissed. "Or were you just born that way?"

He rubbed his side. "Pretty sure it's genetic as my father had a way with the ladies—"

I reached toward him again and he ran backwards, lifting his hands in surrender. "Okay, okay. I'll stop."

"Stop meddling," I said. "We'll muddle through this on our own."

"Muddling is about right," he muttered.

"Oh, and your love life is better?" I asked, arching my eyebrows at him.

"Ouch." He grimaced. "Okay, good point."

Shit. He laughed and joked so much that I forgot he had feelings underneath the amiable facade.

"I'm sorry. That was rude." I cleared my throat. "I appreciate what you're trying to do, but Marcus and I are awkward enough as it is and it only feels worse when you start in with the innuendo. I...like Marcus. A lot. And I think he likes me, too."

"You know he likes you," Callum said. "But I understand and I'll back off."

"Thank you. Now, be careful tonight."

"Yes, ma'am."

I left his room and went into mine. I didn't really need another shower, but the hot water would probably help loosen up my back.

I would have loved a massage, but I wasn't going to ask Marcus for one. If he put his hands on me, I'd want more. And I wasn't sure I was ready for that. Not after everything he'd said in the dream.

C.C. WOOD

Marcus was intense and driven. If he said he would want more than my body, then he would work extremely hard to get it. Loneliness had been my constant companion for so long that I questioned my own judgment. I had strong feelings for Marcus, but I wasn't sure if I was ready for anything permanent. With anyone.

∼

WHEN I EMERGED from my room, Callum was gone and I could smell something delicious coming from the kitchen. I shook out my hands and blew out a breath. Damn Callum and his little comments. Now, I was nervous when I hadn't been earlier.

Once I felt a little calmer, I headed into the kitchen. Marcus turned from the stove and smiled at me.

"Feel better?" he asked, looking completely at ease.

"Yes. Thanks." If he could act naturally, so could I. "That smells great. What are we having?"

"Shepherd's pie." He paused. "Technically, I think it would be considered cottage pie since I'm using ground beef instead of lamb, but it's what I had."

I smiled back at him. "Sounds great. I'll, uh, set the table while you work."

"No rush. Once the sauce and potatoes are ready, I'll still need to bake it for a little while."

I grabbed plates, cutlery, and glasses out of the cabinets and took them to the table. I hesitated, wondering if I should put his setting directly across from me or at the head of the table to my left.

Before I could decide, Marcus said, "Put mine at the end of the table please."

As I did it, I asked, "Why?"

"So I can see both doors and have my back to the wall."

Hmmm. That made a strange sort of sense. I noticed both Callum and he disliked sitting with their backs to a door or window. Which now made me nervous. Shit.

"It's habit," he said. "Nothing more. We'll be safe here."

168

I glanced over my shoulder at him. "Are you reading my mind now?"

He shrugged. "Not exactly. I'm just beginning to understand you a little better."

I finished setting the table and saw an open bottle of red wine sitting on the counter next to the sink. "Want a glass of wine?"

"One wouldn't hurt. All we have are juice glasses, though."

"A glass is a glass when it comes to wine," I commented.

He pointed to the cabinet that held the glasses and I grabbed two. They were small, maybe four or five ounces, which was perfect. I didn't need to drink half a bottle of wine and end up throwing myself into Marcus' lap before the night was over.

I poured us each a glass and put his on the counter to the right of the stove.

"Thanks."

I carried my glass to the other counter. I boosted myself up on top of it and watched as he stirred the sauce to thicken it.

"Thanks for making dinner," I said. "And lunch."

"You're welcome. I can't do what you and Callum do, but I can help in other ways."

"Does it bother you?"

"No. In times of war, everyone pitches in however they have to."

"Do you think we're at war?"

He hesitated. "It was a figure of speech. We're not necessarily at war, but we are on high alert."

"I don't know. Over the last year, it's felt a lot like war to me."

He poured the sauce in the bottom of an oval casserole dish before he topped the mixture with the mashed potatoes in another pot. After he slid the entire thing in the oven and set a timer, he faced me.

"Why does it feel like war?" he asked.

He sipped his wine while I tried to think of the best way to express my thoughts.

Finally, I said, "Every day is another battle to get a piece of myself back. Pieces that may be lost forever. Rhiannon and Caleb took so much from me. It was only a week, but it's also every day. Every night.

Sometimes I'll see something out of the corner of my eye and turn around, expecting one of them to be there, just waiting to pounce on me." My mouth was dry so I drank a bit of my own wine. "I don't have days where I feel like just Merry anymore. It's like I've been shattered and glued back together, but there are slivers missing. Not just one or two, but hundreds. Some days, I feel like I've found one of them and it slides into place. Other days, I wonder if this isn't all a dream and I'm still trapped in that house with them."

I hadn't meant to say all of that. Marcus didn't need to know the fucked-up state of my mind. Sure, he probably had a pretty good idea of how messed up I was since he'd been in my nightmares, but somehow this felt different.

I had a choice to tell him all of these things.

In my dreams, that choice was taken away from me.

Marcus put his wine aside and walked over to me, stopping only a few inches away. His eyes were calm and kind as his gaze locked on mine. His blue eyes were no longer brilliant jewels, but darker, like the ocean at night.

"I can promise you that this isn't a dream. You're free from Rhiannon. She is gone and she is never coming back. I know what it's like to find yourself in a totally new world, feeling as though you've been broken beyond repair. I've seen into your heart and your mind, Merry. You are stronger than anyone I've ever met, including me. You will continue to get better. You might never be the same as you were, but this is forging you into the person you were meant to be. And brought you to the people you were meant to meet."

His fingers touched my hand and I stifled a gasp. The simple contact brought my entire body to attention. As I looked into his eyes, I realized that the difference was his intention.

Right now, Marcus was looking down at me with pure emotion in his eyes. He wasn't hiding what he felt behind the stoic mask he seemed to wear most of the time. He wanted me to know what he was thinking. What he was feeling.

And, boy, did I feel it.

He'd said something to this effect earlier and part of me had dismissed it, but I couldn't any longer.

I was meant to be here, right here, with Marcus.

I'd never believed in fate. Until this moment.

He squeezed my hand and took a step back. "I need to finish dinner."

I wanted to reach out and stop him, but I held myself back.

I remembered the kiss in our dream last night. I wanted to experience that in reality, but Marcus seemed determined to give me time. I knew he worried that I would change my mind.

But I couldn't shake the feeling that time was running out.

CHAPTER NINETEEN

MARCUS

IT WAS TIME.

For the first time in my long life, I didn't want to do what needed to be done. I wanted to stay with Merry.

Two days had passed since the night we had dinner together. After dinner, we watched a few more episodes of One Punch Man. She laughed at my inability to understand certain aspects of the show and teased me relentlessly.

No trace of the scared woman I'd met only days ago remained.

I couldn't bring myself to touch her that night, to ask her if she wanted what I wanted.

I knew she wanted to touch me and be touched in return, but I could still sense a certain hesitancy. The warning I'd given her had sunk in. She understood that for me it wouldn't just be sex. It would be a great deal more.

Still, she kissed me before going to her room, just a light brush of lips against mine.

Tonight, we were going to the house that Dumont was using as a base. As Ava suspected, he left Austin, but he didn't go far. He rented a house between Austin and Houston and he'd remained there rather than returning to Louisiana.

None of us were certain if he was waiting for orders from someone or planning something, but we agreed it would be best not to wait and find out.

"Be careful," Merry said.

I focused on her and saw that her mouth was tight. "We all will. It will be fine. I promise."

She didn't say anything else but I could see that worry still gnawed at her.

"We'll be back by dawn," I continued, hoping that it would reassure her.

"I know. Will you call me when you're done and on your way home?" she asked.

It was the first time anyone other than Callum or Macgrath had asked me to check in after a mission.

"It will be late. I don't want to wake you."

She laughed, a short, harsh sound. "I don't think I'll be sleeping so feel free to call and text."

"Okay. I'll call you."

"Promise me," she said, her gaze piercing.

"I promise."

"Good."

Without warning, she stepped into me, put her arms around my neck, and pulled me down so her lips closed over mine.

The kiss stole my ability to think. I wrapped my arms around her, pulling her onto her toes and into my body. She tasted of the coffee she'd been drinking and the Andes mints Callum had brought home after his planning session with Ava and Macgrath.

A shrill whistle interrupted the kiss and Merry pulled her mouth from mine. She didn't back away, but I wanted her mouth back. I wanted to forget everything and lose myself in her.

"Celebrate when we come back," Callum yelled. "We have a mission."

Merry's eyes opened and she sighed. "I don't suppose you could just forget him and leave him behind when you're done, could you?"

"I'm definitely considering it," I murmured.

She smiled, her dark eyes sparkling. The anxiety had faded from her face. "Just come back to me in one piece. I have plans for later."

"Oh, God. I don't need to hear this," Callum griped. "Marcus, meet me in the car in two minutes or I'm leaving without you."

I heard him stomp through the living room to the front door before it slammed behind him.

"I have to go."

"I know," she replied. But she still held on.

"I'll come back."

"I'll find you if you don't."

Her arms loosened and I released her. We stared at each other as I stepped back.

"Are you still here?" Arien asked, appearing in the kitchen out of thin air.

Merry jumped and I bit back a sigh.

"Yes, Arien. I'm leaving now." I looked at the shapeshifting witch that would be staying with Merry while we were gone. I knew she was powerful, but she'd sacrificed a great deal for the Goddess who sent her to watch over Ava. She walked with one foot in our world and another in the realm of magic. She could protect Merry, but I worried she wouldn't sense a threat or act upon it until it was too late.

Ava, however, insisted that Arien would be suitable to stay with Merry and that we would need Rhys and Harrison for this mission.

I'd given in, but with reservations.

"Stay in the house," I said, looking at them both.

"I'll keep her safe, vampire," Arien stated, folding her hands in front of her. "You have my word."

Power flared and I knew that the witch had put her magic into that vow. She would protect Merry or die trying.

I doubted it would come to that, but a shadow nagged me, lurking in the back of my mind.

It wasn't a vision or even another person who needed my help. Just the sense that this night would somehow spiral out of control.

"I'll be back soon."

Merry wrapped her arms around her waist. "Be safe."

Arien only waved at me as I left the kitchen.

When I climbed into the car with Callum, he looked at me and said, "It seems things are progressing extremely well between you and Merry. Do I need to give you *the talk* again? I mean, it has been a few centuries."

"Shut up and drive. The sooner we leave, the sooner we'll be back."

I ignored his laugh as he started the car and roared down the driveway.

~

Ava, Macgrath, Harrison, and Rhys were all ready to go when we arrived at Ava's house. Savannah was there. She promised Rhys that she would stay at Ava's until we returned. Something about the wards being stronger.

When we came inside, Harrison looked to me and I nodded. "She made it safely."

Sooner or later, his ability to keep his distance from Arien would end. But I doubted it would be his doing. More than likely, Arien would force the issue and things would either fizzle out or explode.

I was betting on the latter.

"Let's go over the plan one more time," Macgrath said.

Callum groaned but the rest of us ignored him. He might bitch and moan about preparation, but he always showed up and he always paid attention. The rest was just for show.

Macgrath kept the plan simple. Instead of tracing to the house, we would drive. Tracing was similar to the science fiction idea of teleportation. We could get from one place to another in the blink of an eye. But, much like the sci-fi version, it was safer and more accurate if we'd actually been to the location. It wasn't quite the same as GPS coordinates, but close enough. Also, if Dumont had a witch or warlock among his people, the magical signature would announce our presence immediately.

We would rely on stealth rather than force to enter the grounds, plant the bugs, and get out. From a distance, Ava would handle any wards or spells that might arise. Harrison and Rhys would be our back up, and Macgrath, Callum, and I would get into the house, planting bugs in several of the rooms. The phone would be taken care of remotely because Merry was right, we didn't need physical proximity to clone it or hack into his microphone to listen to his conversations. Which was a frightening thought.

If we could do this to him, who could do this to us? I rarely carried my cell phone but Callum, Ava, and Macgrath were addicted to theirs. Even Harrison had his phone with him most of the time.

As we slipped on our weapons, Rhys turned to me. It had been a while since we'd spoken as he preferred to avoid public places whenever possible. Crowds of people made him...itchy.

"Caleb is returning from Dallas," he said.

Shit. "When?"

"In four days."

I nodded, my thoughts racing ahead to how I would have to tell Merry that the vampire she feared the most was actually a friend. To all of us.

"I have no idea how to tell her," I murmured.

"Should we keep him away from her?"

I shook my head. "That won't work."

Rhys frowned at me, his question written on his face.

"If things work out the way that I want them to, she'll be here permanently. We can't hide him from her. I just have to think of the best way to explain what he is and that the pain he caused her wasn't his choosing."

"Good luck with that," Rhys said, his tone dry.

My answering laugh was without humor. The dread that had nagged at me all evening increased.

I would have to think about this for a day. Honesty was a necessity. Merry was finally beginning to trust me and I didn't want to break that trust.

I feared this information would smash it beyond repair.

"Thank you for letting me know," I said to him.

Rhys nodded and finished placing his knives in their sheaths. He had one on each hip, his right thigh, and his left ankle. A short sword would go into the sheath down his back when we arrived at the house. Riding in a car for an hour and a half with a sword against your spine wasn't comfortable.

He moved away toward Savannah and pulled her into an embrace.

I thought of the kiss that Merry had given me before I left and heat filled my gut. As I promised her, I hadn't used our bond to read her thoughts or emotions, but even without magic, I knew that she was on the brink.

She wanted my body and she enjoyed my mind.

All that was left was for her to accept my heart.

"Ready?" Callum asked me.

I nodded.

"Good. Let's get this done so we can go home."

We loaded up into our car. Rhys rode with us because Harrison couldn't tolerate Callum and his teasing for that long. Ava, Macgrath, and Harrison took Macgrath's SUV.

With each mile, the urge to turn around and go back to the house grew. I did my best to ignore it, knowing that the bond between Merry and I was likely the culprit. The temptation to reach out through the magic that connected us and check on her was strong, but I resisted.

I doubted she would thank me.

We drove for over an hour, pulling over several miles from the house. Though I doubted Dumont had a magic user with him, Ava still checked for wards and spells.

"Nothing," she said. "Not even a basic protection spell on the house." She sounded confused and a little worried.

"That's good, right?" Callum asked.

"Yes," she said, her eyes distracted as she stared at the house in the distance.

Only two windows had lights shining through them. The rest were dark. There were blinds over each of them and no shadows moved inside. There were cars in the drive, but the house had an aura of emptiness.

The sensation of wrongness nagged at me again.

"You feel it, too?" I asked Ava.

She didn't look at me but nodded. "Something's off."

"Think they set some booby traps?" Harrison asked.

Ava continued to study the small home. "No. I don't think they're there at all." She glanced at Macgrath. "Do you sense anyone?"

He shook his head.

"There's not even a speck of magic either," she said.

"I'll go take a quick peek," Callum volunteered just before he disappeared from view.

Ava sighed. "Well, I sure hope I'm right about the wards and lack of magic, otherwise he might come back looking like he's been through a food processor."

A few moments later, Callum reappeared, an expression of consternation on his face.

"The house is empty. All the cars are cold." He paused. "And there was a note."

He held it up for us to see.

Thank you for the visit. Please call ahead first next time. It's good manners.
~Andre

Macgrath's face became thunderous and Ava only frowned.

Before anyone could say anything else, panic blossomed in my mind. A short, sharp stab of fear hit me dead center in the chest.

"Merry," I whispered.

The feeling vanished and the terror I felt then was purely my own.

"He went after Merry," I said. I closed my eyes, pulling my power to me. A trace of this distance would be difficult, but I'd managed it easily before.

As soon as I pushed out my power, aiming to propel myself back toward my house in Austin, lines in the shapes of runes flashed on all of the trees, killing my magic.

Oh, that goddamn son of a bitch. I would kill him. I would rip his entrails from him while he screamed for mercy.

He had the woman I loved and I was trapped here with no way to return to her.

I forged my power into a hammer and smashed it against the spell

178

surrounding us. The shock reverberated through the circle like a giant chime and everyone cringed, holding their hands over their ears. I drew back to do it again, but Macgrath tackled me.

"Stop!" he yelled. "You're hurting Ava."

I looked over and saw a small trickle of blood trail from one of her ears. The mindless fury vanished. I quashed it without mercy. In its place was ice-cold anger. My thoughts cleared and I knew the only way we would escape this trap was with Ava's help. If I kept hammering at the spell with brute force, I would only end up hurting my only chance to get to Merry in time.

"I'm okay," I said to Macgrath.

"I don't believe you."

"Fine. I'm not okay, but I am in control."

"That I believe," he said, climbing off me and holding out a hand to help me up.

I went to Ava. "I'm sorry."

She waved me away. "I understand. Are you calmer now?"

I shook my head. "Not exactly, but I can help."

"Good, because I think it will take both of us to get out of here."

"And me," Harrison said, coming up behind us.

I reached down the bond connecting me to Merry.

I'll be there soon.

Silence was the only response.

CHAPTER TWENTY

MERRY

I SAT at the kitchen table with Arien, trying to teach her how to play Go Fish. Originally, we started with Gin Rummy and quickly realized that neither of us had any interest in learning all the rules. So we went with something simple.

After this, maybe we could play War or Slapjack.

"Do you have any fours?" Arien asked.

"Go fish."

As she drew the card, she glanced at me and said, "You don't seem to fear me."

"Should I?"

"No, I don't think so."

Okay, that gave me pause.

"You don't *think* so?" I asked cautiously.

She blinked several times. "That didn't come out correctly, did it?"

"I'm not sure because I don't know exactly what you meant."

"Only that you have nothing to fear from me unless you mean to harm the people I care about," she explained.

"Then, that's probably why I'm not afraid of you." Or at least, I hadn't been. "Do you have any sixes?" I asked.

Her light blue eyes focused on me, piercing in their intensity. "Are you cheating?"

I shook my head as she handed over a six. I paired it up with the other six I had and laid them next to my growing row.

I took a sip of my soda, waiting for her to ask me for a four. I'd pointed out to her that it wouldn't be right to ask for the same card over and over if I told her to "go fish" since the objective was to pair up all of your cards before the other player, but she ignored me and continued to ask for a four.

"Have you had sexual intercourse with Marcus yet?" she asked as she studied the cards in her hand.

I choked on my Coke and had to run to the sink to spit it out before I spewed it all over the table. I leaned over the sink and coughed for several minutes, trying to get my breath back. Once I was done, I rinsed my chin with cool water and took the paper towel that Arien held out to me.

"I am sorry," she apologized. "The others are used to my questions, even the ones that aren't considered socially appropriate. I didn't think it would distress you so."

I cleared my throat as I dried my dripping face. "It didn't upset me. I just wasn't expecting it."

She took the paper towel from me and tossed it into the trashcan under the sink. "You don't mind that I asked?"

I hesitated. I liked what I knew of Arien so far but she had an indescribable quality about her. Almost as if she wasn't wholly human. The way she walked and moved her head was oddly feline.

"I don't mind that you asked," I finally said. "But I usually don't talk about my sex life with people I don't know very well. Most people don't."

"Ah, I see," she said with a nod. "The vampires and shifters are usually so open. I forget that humans are different."

Yep, definitely not completely human because she obviously didn't lump herself into the same category as me.

"To answer your question, no, Marcus and I are not involved in a...sexual relationship."

181

"Why not?"

Thank God I wasn't drinking soda this time.

"Arien, may I say something without offending you?"

She smiled, a small curve of her lips. "Would you like me to stop asking questions like that?"

I sighed and nodded.

"Okay. I can do that. Again, my apologies if I've made you uncomfortable."

"You didn't. Though I am wondering why you asked."

"I wanted to talk to another woman about sex."

Now, I was really confused. "Um, can I ask why?"

"Because I want to have it and the male I am most attracted to won't speak to me. So, I will probably need to find another male to copulate with, likely a human. I thought that another woman, especially a human, would be able to tell me how to go about doing that."

Oh, this was so above my pay grade, which was zero since I wasn't getting paid for this endeavor.

"Ummm..."

Before I could formulate a response, the air in the center of the kitchen shimmered and then undulated like the surface of a lake when a drop of water fell onto it.

"What is that?" I asked.

"Get behind me," Arien commanded, her somewhat childish demeanor vanishing. A cold mask took over her features, turning her from a slender, pretty woman into a warrior. The sense of *otherness* grew stronger and the air seemed to thicken and heat. It wasn't steam I was feeling. It was magic.

Holy shit. Arien was a badass. I never would have suspected, but it did explain why Ava was okay with leaving me here alone with her.

Arien murmured a few words in a language I couldn't understand and made a sideways slashing motion with her right hand. A bright blue-white circle appeared in the center of the kitchen around the disturbance. It flared until it was almost blinding before it faded to a dull glow.

Out of the rippling air, a man appeared. A familiar man with black hair and eyes and a handsome face. Andre Dumont.

"Seriously?" I asked.

The shimmering air around him vanished and he remained in the center of the circle. Arien muttered a chant beneath her breath and punched her fisted right hand into her left palm. The circle around him shrank a few inches. He glanced down and his eyes widened.

"Wait!" he called, holding out his hands, palm first. "I mean no harm. I came only to talk."

Arien ignored him and continued to chant. She punched her left palm again and the circle shrank once more. I had the mental image of it eventually closing on him and squishing him in the center like a tube of toothpaste. It wasn't a pleasant thought.

Dumont seemed to realize that he'd better start talking faster because he spoke so quickly his words nearly ran together. "The humans know about us. And about you. They're watching every move you make and you can't protect yourself from it because you don't even know it's happening. I'm not sure what they're planning, but they have soldiers immune to vampire mind control and others who are immune to magic. We are all in grave danger. They are not only watching, but they are planning to come for us."

Arien's chant halted and she stared at Dumont for a prolonged moment. "And how do you know this?"

"Because I'm spying on them as well." He hesitated. "Please. I don't have the skill to get into their system and figure out exactly what they know or what they plan, but you do," he said, looking straight at me. "You can help me."

Suddenly, things made a little more sense.

"Was this the job you offered me?" I asked.

He nodded.

"You had to know I wouldn't break the law for you."

"I had all the credentials in place. You would have thought it was a government contract. What I couldn't lie to you about, I would wipe from your mind."

"Then why send Marcel after me?"

183

He sighed. "He was only supposed to keep an eye on you, keep you safe. But when he saw you heading toward Ava Amaris' store, he thought you weren't what you seemed. I swear to you that he wasn't going to harm you, only bring you to me. I would have told him that was a stupid idea because I knew you weren't a threat."

That reminded me.

"Yes, because you invaded my mind and fed off my fear, asshole!" I yelled.

He winced. "I'm sorry about that as well. I prefer not to create a mental bond that way, but I needed a way to control you if you realized what was happening and tried to run away."

Without thinking, I scooped up my glass of soda and threw it at the circle. It bounced off and sent liquid flying everywhere. Dammit.

"Considering how much you've fucked this up, why should I help you now?" I asked him.

Before he answered, Marcus' voice filled my mind.

I'll be there soon.

He'd used our bond to reach out to me. Any other time, it would have pissed me off, but at this moment, I was glad to know that he was on his way.

"Well?" I prompted him.

"Because they won't just take me and mine, they'll come for Marcus and Callum. And Ava and Macgrath. Harrison. Rhys. Savannah." His gaze fixed on Arien. "And you. You'll be worse than prisoners. You'll be test subjects. They'll tear us apart to see how we can put ourselves back together. They'll use our blood to create atrocities and unspeakable human hybrids in the name of protection of the country. And no one will save us because no one knows we exist or that we've even been discovered."

I could see exactly what he was talking about, oh so clearly. Marcus strapped down to a table as a doctor performed a live autopsy on him, recording how his body healed injuries and trauma. The vials and vials of blood they would draw to use in experiments on animals and people. Their smug agreement that it was in the best interests of national security if they made their soldiers stronger, better. Invincible.

"You know I'm right," he said to me, his dark eyes glowing with power. "You know what they'll do to us. We won't be considered human, even if we started out that way. Any pain or suffering we experience will be in the name of a safer future for humans, even as it puts them in grave danger from the very people sworn to protect them."

I remembered Ava's words about my slight empathic ability. The instincts that I'd been following since I met Marcus were related to that talent. I knew it somehow.

Right now, all those instincts said that he was finally being honest with me.

"Let him go," I said to Arien, my voice faint.

"What?" she asked, gaping at me.

"Release him from the circle. He's telling the truth."

"I know he's telling the truth," she agreed. "But I can't release him. He could still grab you and trace away."

I stared at Dumont. I could see both the determination and desperation on his face.

"No, he won't. Let him out."

Arien hesitated for a long moment before she spoke a few words and swept her hands outward, about waist high.

The dull circle of pale blue light vanished.

"If you try anything, vampire, I will crush you like a fly beneath my boot," Arien said.

Dumont nodded and I could see the small beads of sweat around his hairline. "May I have a glass of water?"

Arien didn't move so I went to the fridge and got him a chilled bottle of water. I carried it to the table and sat it on the opposite end of where Arien and I had been playing cards.

"Here. Let's all sit down and you can tell me everything you know from the beginning," I said.

Dumont moved slowly to the end of the table, keeping his hands up. I kept the table between us and sat in my seat. I knew he could move quickly enough to grab me at this distance, but I didn't think he intended to do that. Especially with the way Arien watched him.

Before, she seemed feline to me, but now her stare was distant and cold, like that of a raptor searching for prey.

He sat down with a slow, careful motion, as though he was exhausted or his entire body was sore. Dumont picked up the water bottle, cracked it open, and drank nearly half the bottle.

When he lowered it, his eyes met mine. "From the beginning, then?"

I nodded.

"It started with you," he said.

I blinked several times. "Uh, what?"

"You were under government surveillance for some of your activities when Rhiannon kidnapped you."

"But I haven't done anything illegal..." He shot me a look that said he knew that was a lie. "In years. I was in college the last time I did things I wasn't supposed to and I almost got caught."

"They didn't want to arrest you. They wanted to hire you. For something big. Something classified. We were never able to find out because it was buried so deeply."

Okay, I guess that made sense. "Fine, what did my kidnapping have to do with it?"

"Rhiannon and her creation were caught on camera and by their agents doing some very strange things. They were getting ready to intervene when Rhiannon left town and you fell off the grid."

"How do you know all this?" I asked.

"One of my men was involved before he was turned." When he saw Arien's angry expression, he shook his head. "Willingly turned. He was mortally wounded by Rhiannon when we found him. I offered to save him and he accepted. Once he realized that we weren't all possessed by demons or even evil, he shared information with us."

"How did all of that lead them to Austin?" Arien asked.

"They figured out how to track Rhiannon and followed her here," he said. "Now, they have satellite imagery and long-distance listening devices, among other things, set up to watch every move that they make."

"How do you know that?" I asked.

"Because we piggy-backed off of them. We hear what they hear. We see what they see."

"And you know what they know?" I crossed my arms over my chest.

He nodded. "That's the reason I came to Austin. They're getting ready to do something, but I can't get into their system to see. The audio and video feeds were difficult enough, even with Evan's help. Their internal system is beyond my reach."

"I'm not sure it's in my reach either."

"But would that change if Evan was able to give you information?"

I considered it. "Probably."

"We have to try," he said, leaning forward. "They'll come for your friends first. Then, me. Then, the rest of us. The shifters. The witches. There are so many supernatural creatures that they could capture and experiment on. It would be genocide and no one would save us."

After what he'd put me through, I didn't really give a crap about Andre Dumont, but I cared about Marcus and Callum. And all the rest of them.

Dumont read my mind. "I know you couldn't care less about me, but think about the others."

"I am."

He opened his mouth.

"Zzzt." I held up a hand. "No more talking while I'm thinking."

I mulled it over.

"I'll help you. But you'd better give me every single shred of evidence, knowledge, text, phone numbers, codes, and anything or everything that could help me with this...this project of yours. If I find out you're hiding anything from me, I will feed you to the sharks and worry only about everyone else."

"I understand."

"Yes, but do you accept?" Arien prompted him.

"I accept."

C.C. WOOD

"Swear it," she said. Her light blue eyes glowed and her long dark hair lifted in an invisible wind. "Bound by magic."

"I vow to you that I will not hide anything from you if you help me," Dumont said, his eyes locked on her.

"The promise is made," Arien said. Her voice was deeper and vibrated with magic. "You realize what will happen if you break it?"

He nodded. His head turned toward the front of the house. "I believe we'll have company soon."

Dumont rose to his feet and put his back to the wall.

Marcus and the others were on their way or already here. I got up as well and went to the front door.

"What are you doing?" Arien asked.

"Telling them everything's fine. You and I both know they're probably lurking out there, planning how to infiltrate the house without alerting the intruders."

I jerked open the front door and yelled, "Everything's fine! He comes in peace!"

Marcus appeared in front of me before the last word even faded and grabbed me, pulling me out of the house and halfway down the drive in a near blur.

As soon as he stopped, I put my hands on his shoulders, shoving, and said, "Oh, my God. I think I'm going to puke."

"I'm sorry. Sorry," Marcus murmured. "You'll be safe now."

I smacked his shoulder as I leaned over and tried to take slow deep breaths so I wouldn't yak all over his shoes. After a second, I was able to say, "I was safe before, which you would have known if you'd listened to what I just said."

"I thought you may have said it under duress."

"The only one under duress was Dumont." I straightened. "Did you know that Arien is a freaking badass?"

"What do you mean?"

"I thought she was going to squish him like a bug in a neon blue circle."

"What?" he asked.

"She did this chant thing and a ring of bright blue formed around

188

him. Every time he even blinked, she'd shrink the circle. I imagined it would have ended like she was popping a giant zit."

"Ew," he said, frowning.

"I know. Really gross, but now I have this morbid curiosity."

He shook his head. "You'll have to ask her yourself."

"Well, then we should get back to the house so I can do that. And before your buddies rip Dumont to shreds."

"I don't really see an issue with that."

I sighed. "Just...come listen to what he has to say."

"Fine."

He reached for me and I held up my hands. "Let's go a little slower this time."

"Yes, ma'am."

CHAPTER TWENTY-ONE

MARCUS

THE URGE TO rip Dumont's head from his shoulders was strong. The only thing that stopped me was Merry holding my hand.

And not clutching it in fear.

Just holding onto me because she seemed to want to. Our fingers were interlaced and she held onto me but her fingers weren't gripping hard.

This small human woman had the strength to distract me with a mere touch of her fingers against mine.

Merry nudged me with her elbow. "Are you listening to anything he's saying?" she murmured.

"Not really."

She rolled her eyes but kept her hand in mine. "Okay, I want everyone in the living room. I'll make a pot of coffee and we'll talk."

Macgrath crossed his arms over his chest and stared at Dumont. "I'm not sure he deserves coffee. More like a punch to the throat."

Merry released my hand then so she could mirror Macgrath's pose. "I'm telling you that you need to listen to what he has to say."

Macgrath ignored her until Ava turned toward him and smacked his arm. "Ewan," she growled.

"Ewan?" Merry asked.

Macgrath stared at her, a brow arching, and said, "Merriweather?"

"Ugh. Fine. Be a butthead," Merry said, throwing her hands in the air.

Ava gave Macgrath's leg a light kick. He groaned and relaxed his position. "Fine. Coffee for the vampire who trespassed on our territory and got through Ava's wards."

He left the kitchen.

Ava studied Dumont. "He does have a valid point. How did you get past my wards?" she asked.

"Magic," Dumont answered.

I growled and both Callum and I took a step toward him. He raised his hands in surrender.

"Sorry. I couldn't resist," he said. "I've always wanted to say that."

"Stop trying to be funny and go into the living room so you can explain things to them," Merry said as she moved over to the coffee maker. It was the type that did single cups or pots, depending on the settings you used. When Dumont didn't move, she glared at him. "Now."

To my shock, he picked up the water bottle sitting on the table in front of him and left. Apparently, he wasn't immune to Merry's glare either. Callum followed him into the living room. Ava gave me a pointed look that I had no idea how to decipher and went with them.

Merry set about making coffee. "Do you have a tray or anything to carry the cups and pot on?" she asked as she started the pot brewing.

I thought about it for a second and remembered that Ava had brought one over months ago. It was on the top shelf of the pantry, leaning against the wall.

"I'll get it."

I scrounged around, got the tray out, and carried it to the sink to wash the dust off. After I dried it, I put it on the counter next to Merry. Together, we got out the cups needed.

I watched her movements and realized that I could have lost her tonight. My hands wanted to shake, but I couldn't allow it. Not now.

Later, after everyone was gone and I was alone in my room, I would face it, deal with it, and put it away.

Once all the cups, sugar, creamer, spoons, and coffee pot were arranged on the tray, I carried it into the living room, much to Merry's amusement.

"I can do it," she insisted, grinning.

"I can do it just as well."

"My hero."

"It's not chivalry, it's good manners."

She laughed behind me as we headed into the living room.

Dumont was sandwiched between Macgrath and Callum on the couch, but he seemed unperturbed. Ava and Arien sat on the coffee table, but got to their feet so I could set the tray on the table.

"I'll get some chairs from the kitchen," Merry stated.

"No, I'll get them."

She sighed. "Do I need to ask permission to pour the coffee or do you want to do that too?"

She sounded annoyed.

"Um, of course not," I answered.

Merry didn't say anything. She just set about pouring coffee.

I grabbed three chairs from the kitchen and brought them into the living room. I would stand while we talked.

Once everyone had a cup of coffee, even Dumont, Merry said, "You need to tell them everything from the beginning."

I really didn't want to listen to anything he had to say, but I forced myself to focus.

After Dumont had been speaking for a few minutes, I no longer had the urge to roll my eyes. As he explained how the humans had discovered our existence and followed Rhiannon to Austin, my stomach clenched. Dear God in Heaven, we were being spied upon. They were listening to us right now.

"Now they know that we know," Macgrath said. "We've lost the element of surprise."

"Not exactly," Dumont said. "I'm wearing a device that jams their audio abilities. They can still see the house, but they can't hear anything we're saying."

"And you don't think they'll find this suspicious?" Macgrath asked.

"Doubtful. They have outages from time to time. Since I traced in, they have no idea I'm here. And they don't know anything about me at all," Dumont pointed out.

Merry waved her hands. "Before y'all get into it, I'm just letting you know that I intend to help him."

Forget ripping his head off. I was going to start with his legs, then move to his arms. I was going to save his screaming-in-agony head for last.

The room erupted.

~

AN HOUR LATER, and against my better judgment, Dumont traced out of the living room. None of us were happy.

He wanted a promise of aid and we didn't want to let him leave, period. None of us got what we wanted. But Ava promised him that she would call him the next day and they could discuss it further. When he pointed out that the government was watching, she told him not to worry about it. That technology wasn't infallible.

Merry wasn't happy either. I could see it in every line of her body.

As soon as everyone left, I had no doubt I would hear all about it.

Sure enough, when Macgrath, Ava, and Arien left, Callum took one look at Merry and said, "I'm going to go patrol the perimeter."

He vanished before I could tell him that I would do it. The coward.

Merry turned to me, her expression thunderous. "We have to help him get into their computers."

"We don't have to do anything," I replied. "Or have you forgotten that he sent his minion after you?

"I'm not happy about that, but this is bigger than my irritation."

"Well, I'm not sure it's bigger than mine."

"You didn't even know me then!" she yelled, waving her hands.

"Yes, I did!" I yelled back, immediately wishing I hadn't. I didn't want her to fear me again.

I shouldn't have worried because her anger increased and I could see the blood rush to her cheeks. Her eyes sparked with brown fire.

"You know what, that's not the point," she said. "The point is that even if you aren't going to help him, I will. Because they aren't going after him. They're coming after you. And Callum. And Ava and Macgrath. And everyone else here."

"You won't."

She took two steps, closing the distance between us to less than a foot. "Do not presume you can tell me what to do. I'm staying with you because I knew I'd be safer. But you aren't my keeper or my jailor. If I want to help him, I will." She wasn't yelling any longer, but her voice vibrated with intensity.

Any control I had snapped. I reached for her, pulling her to me. "Do not put yourself in danger for me. I wouldn't be able to stand it if anything...happened to you."

"Then, help me," she pleaded, putting her hands on my cheeks. "Because I don't want anything to happen to you either."

My internal brakes were gone. I lifted her up on her toes and kissed her.

Merry threw her arms around my neck, pressing her body closer to me.

Desire ignited inside me, exploding from a single spark into an inferno. Her tongue was in my mouth and her hands fisted in my hair. I never wanted her to stop, but I had to know.

I ripped my mouth from hers and asked, "Are you sure you want to do this?"

Her eyes were heavy-lidded as she stared up at me. "Oh, hell yes."

Before I could ask again or decide what I was going to do next, Merry kissed me again. She jumped up and locked her legs around my waist. Instinctively, my hands went to her ass, hoisting her higher.

Her lips moved to my ear, then my neck, and my legs nearly went out from under me. "Bed. Now," she demanded.

"Uh. Ah."

"Before Callum comes back."

That got my legs moving. I carried her through the house, trying not to drop her or bump into walls as her mouth explored my throat.

"Merry, you need to stop for a second."

"No," she said, her voice nearly a purr.

"I don't want to ram you into anything."

She laughed in my ear. "You mean you want to be the one to ram me."

I had to laugh too as I stumbled into my room. I kicked the door shut behind us, stopping for just a second to lock it. Callum wouldn't interrupt us if he came back while we were in here, but I wouldn't put it past him to sneak in here after we were asleep and prank us.

I lowered Merry down onto the bed and took her mouth with mine. Her legs stayed wrapped around me and her hips cradled me. She moaned against my lips, her body undulating beneath me.

I was so hard that it nearly hurt.

Merry's hands tugged at the bottom edge of my shirt, pushing it up my abdomen. Her fingers trailed over my chest and stomach, painting thin lines of heat on my skin. Then, she shoved it up until it caught on my chin. I had to release her and yank the damn thing completely off.

Her eyes were dark and hot as she studied my body. She pressed her palms to my pectorals.

"You're beautiful," she whispered. Her hands moved over my body, touching, learning.

"So are you."

She started to say something, but I covered her mouth with mine. Her fingers clutched my shoulders, her short nails digging into my skin.

I slipped my hand beneath her shirt at her waist. The skin of her stomach was soft and warm. I moved slowly, giving her a chance to tell me to stop or to pull away, until I cupped her breast. Her body arched, pressing her breast deeper into my palm.

"Don't stop," she murmured against my lips.

She reached down between us and tugged her shirt up, over her head, and dropped it on the floor. Her bra followed. She took my breath away. Merry took my hand and put it to her breast.

"Touch me."

As if she had to ask.

195

I rubbed my thumbs over her nipples, enjoying the way she gasped at the caress. Her hands moved to my belt, tugging it loose.

I lowered my head and took one of her nipples in my mouth. Her hands clenched in my hair and she moaned again.

I wanted to hear that sound again. Over and over.

I licked and sucked, tasting her breasts. Then, her hand slid beneath the waistband of my underwear. Merry curled her fingers around my cock, stroking me.

Dear God, it had been too long. If she continued, I would embarrass myself like a teenage boy with his first woman.

"Wait," I said, lifting my head.

Merry lifted her upper body and put her mouth on my chest. "I can't. It's been too long. I need you."

Ah, shit. I could take my time the next round. Because I needed her, too.

I stood next to the bed and shucked my pants and underwear. I nearly fell when they caught on my boots. Dammit. I bent over and ripped at the laces of my boots, jerking them and my socks off. My pants followed.

When I straightened, the sight of a naked Merry greeted me.

She knelt on the bed next to me, waiting.

Merry reached for me, pulling me in for another kiss. My skin felt scorched where her body touched mine. Her hands moved from my shoulders, down my back, to my ass. She tried to pull me closer, but there was no space between us.

Her fingers kneaded my ass. "I need you inside me."

I tasted her neck and shoulder. I wanted to move my mouth over every inch of her skin.

"Right now, Marcus," she murmured.

"In a second."

Once again, Merry shocked me. She moved back and shoved me down onto the bed before she threw her leg over my hips.

"Now," she repeated.

I had to smile. Her reticence was completely gone.

Merry leaned down and kissed me again. Her hips moved against me, her wet heat tight against my cock.

"Help me," she murmured, reaching between us and running her fingers over me.

I helped her line up my cock with her entrance and groaned as she sank down on me. She lowered a few inches, lifted up, and then lowered again.

Merry bit her lip as she finally engulfed me completely. Her nipples were tight and I reached up to tug them. Her head fell back and she moaned.

Then, she moved, riding me slowly. I slid one hand down and rolled my thumb over her clit. She tightened around me, her movements growing quicker.

Suddenly, I was on the edge of orgasm. I gritted my teeth as Merry grew tighter around me. Desperate, I circled her clit, putting more pressure into the caress.

She gasped and her pussy clamped down on me hard. "I'm going to come," she whispered.

Thank God because I wouldn't be able to hold out much longer.

Merry's hips crashed into mine and she threw her head back and cried out as she came. My fangs descended and I had to stop myself from pulling her down in order to sink them into her neck. It was too late anyway.

I locked my hands on her hips, holding her against me, and came.

In that moment, time froze and I knew I would never be able to let her go.

CHAPTER TWENTY-TWO

MERRY

I STRETCHED and ran a hand along Marcus's torso. His skin was hot. I'd never had a lover with a lot of chest hair, but I liked it on Marcus.

He turned toward me and threw his arm over my waist.

"That was—" I had no words.

"I agree."

I smiled at him. "You don't know what I was going to say."

He settled deeper into to the mattress. His bed was a double and the two of us almost didn't fit on it. "Was it horrible?" he asked.

"No, it wasn't horrible."

"Mediocre?"

I laughed. "No."

He pulled me closer. "Then, maybe we should try again so you can figure out the words."

"It was mind-blowing," I said. "And I need a little time."

Marcus smiled. He seemed relaxed. I hadn't seen him like this before. Then again, I hadn't seen him naked before either. Maybe nudity chilled him out.

Yeah, probably not. If the sex had been half as amazing for him as it had for me, then he was definitely relaxed from the orgasm.

"Merry," he murmured, his fingers trailing over my cheek to my shoulder. "I have some bad news."

My heartbeat stuttered at the look in his eyes. Doubt pricked me for a moment.

"I'm not sure I can let you go," he said.

The trickle of fear vanished. "Who said I'm leaving?"

His hand stilled on my shoulder.

"And if I do, I may kidnap you so I can have a sex slave."

His smile returned. "Is it considered kidnapping if I'm willing though?"

I pretended to think about it. "Probably not."

"Are you saying you'll stay with me?" he asked.

"For now, yes. We'll have to talk again in a few weeks."

"Do you think I'm going to change my mind?" he asked.

I knew he wasn't reading my thoughts because I could feel the wall between us. It had vanished for a split second when he came and I got a flash of his thoughts. But it was back now.

"You might," I said. "I'm not exactly easy to live with."

"You haven't been difficult so far," he said.

"Oh, really? Is that why you were so upset in the kitchen earlier?"

He laughed. "No. I was upset because I don't want anything to happen to you and you seem determined to plunge yourself into danger."

I ran my hand over his chest again. "Not exactly. Just trying to protect the people who have protected me."

"I'm not going to change my mind," he said. "Callum would tell me to shut my mouth, but I'm going to be honest with you. It's been decades since I met a woman I wanted to make love to, much less live with."

Oh, my God. Decades? He was gorgeous, kind, gentle, funny, and strong. He should have been swatting women off with a stick.

"I don't need to read your thoughts to know you're surprised," he said. "Why?"

"Well, you're hot and nice and you can cook. Women should be bumping each other off for a chance to be with you."

"You forgot something very important," he said.

"What's that?"

"I'm excellent in bed."

I laughed. "That too. But, seriously, decades?"

He gazed at me for a long moment. "Time moves differently when you've been alive for thousands of years," he said, his voice soft. "Decades seem like nothing after such a long time. You start to look for something different. Someone different and you begin to recognize a special person when you see them."

Ah, shit. This was it. I was in love with Marcus Vane. He was literally the man of my dreams.

"You can't say things like this to me," I said, my voice breaking.

"Why?"

"Because then you'll never get rid of me."

"You're assuming that I'll want to."

In my head, I was already planning our future...until it hit me that I would eventually grow old and die while he stayed the same.

"But I'm going to get old," I said.

He studied me. "Not necessarily."

I waited but Marcus didn't say anything else. "You have to explain that," I said.

"I will, I'm just trying to figure out how to explain it in a way that won't freak you out."

"Forget freaking me out and just tell me."

"Well, if we continue to exchange blood on a regular basis, you'll stay the same age you are now. Physically."

"Regular basis?"

"Several times a week. You would only have to take a few drops each time. But there's another option. You could become a vampire."

I looked into his eyes and considered it. "That's a big commitment."

"I don't expect you to decide tonight. Or even tomorrow. But it is an option that you should consider if you decide to stay with me."

"Okay. Yeah, I think I need a while to mull it over. Especially the whole drinking blood thing."

"If I turned you, we would only drink from each other."

"Good to know."

He smiled again, something he seemed to be doing with more regularity.

"You should do that more often," I said.

"Do what?"

"Smile."

He kissed me, long and slow, and rolled over so that he was on top of me. I spread my legs to make room for his hips. His lips left mine for a moment.

"We went too fast earlier."

"You said that before," I said as his mouth trailed down my neck. His lips were scorching against my skin and there was a faint scrape of sharp fangs. "Is that why you didn't bite me?"

He hesitated and lifted his head, his eyes glowing faintly as he looked down at me. "Each time I bite you, it cements the bond between us further. I thought you didn't want that."

When he first told me that, I hadn't. But now, I wanted all of him.

"I—" Shit, I didn't know how to say what I was thinking, so I reached down the link between us, tapping against the mental wall he'd erected.

"Merry?"

"I can't explain how I'm feeling," I said. Okay, in all honesty, I was too much of a coward to voice my thoughts.

Marcus removed the wall between us and suddenly we were linked. I gasped as his thoughts and feelings flooded my mind. I knew he was feeling the same sensation.

God, it was so intense, almost too much. Information inundated me. But one piece of information caught my attention.

He loved me. He never wanted me to leave.

The surge of emotion leveled off to the point that I could think again.

Until his mouth crushed mine.

Marcus kissed me like I'd never been kissed before.

I wrapped my arms and legs around him, pulling him into me. His mouth moved over my throat to my breasts. He sucked my left nipple deep into his mouth, the edges of his fangs digging into my skin.

I inhaled sharply and my back arched. Heat flooded my body. My clit pulsed. His mouth grew more insistent as he moved to my right nipple and my arousal peaked to nearly unbearable.

"Marcus!" I cried.

He reached between us, sliding a finger deep inside me, and I nearly came. I realized that his desire resonated inside me. We were sharing everything. Every touch. Every kiss.

I whimpered when his finger vanished. I needed him inside me. Before I could voice the demand, his shaft thrust deep. I cried out again, my hands clutching at his ribs as he rode me hard.

The pleasure crested uncontrollably and just as it peaked, his fangs sank into my neck.

The orgasm shot through me so hot and bright that I was surprised I didn't burst into flames. Wave after wave crashed over me until it rode the sharp edge of pain. I was caught between Marcus' climax and my own, the echoes vibrating within my body until my vision darkened.

His mouth left my neck after one last, slow lick and the tremors that shook me began to calm.

Marcus slowed his thrusts, his movements losing their desperation.

Finally, he stopped, still buried deep inside me.

"Wow," I panted. "I think my soul left my body for a second."

Marcus released a short bark of laughter. "That didn't go quite the way I expected."

"Any better and I'd probably be unconscious."

He laughed again and my hips lifted as another spasm shook me. A hiss left his lips as I clamped around him.

"I wanted to take my time," he said.

"Next time?" I suggested.

"I guess we'll have to keep trying until we succeed," he said.

"Sounds like a plan."

~

I TALKED Marcus into coming into my room to sleep. His mattress was great but too small for both of us to fit on it comfortably. I also slipped into a tank top and a pair of shorts. Like Marcus, I knew Callum wouldn't be above pranking us while we slept. He wouldn't be able to help himself.

In the meantime, I got to fulfill my fantasy of Marcus in my bed. He lounged against my sheets as I tossed my dirty clothes in the hamper and finished getting ready for bed. When I put my pajamas on, he'd slipped on a pair of briefs.

I couldn't complain though because he looked like an advertisement for designer underwear. Especially with his arm raised above his head and his left leg cocked to the side.

"Stop looking at me like that or neither of us will get any sleep," he said, his eyes flaring with blue light.

As great as that sounded, I was a little sore. After nearly two years of no sex and suddenly having a lot of it, my vagina was letting me know I'd overdone it.

I climbed into bed next to him, drawing the sheet and blanket over us. My head rested on his shoulder and I draped one thigh over his. Marcus reached out and turned off the lamp on the nightstand.

I snuggled closer to him. "You're warm."

"So are you," he said, his hand gliding up and down my arm.

"I hate to bring this up now, but we still need to help Dumont."

Marcus sighed. "I know."

I lifted my head and looked at him in the dim light of the bedroom. "You know?"

"Yes. But I don't have to like it."

"If you know, why did you yell at me?" I asked, my voice rising.

"Because I couldn't bear it if you got hurt."

Shit. My irritation faded.

"And I feel like things turned out well, considering," he continued.

I had to agree with him. I settled my head back on his shoulder.

"Then, we'll call Dumont tomorrow and let him know that we'll help him."

He growled beneath his breath but didn't say anything.

"Good night," I murmured.

I closed my eyes and let myself drift.

I felt like I'd just fallen asleep when a faint noise woke me. The bed next to me was empty and the house was eerily quiet.

I glanced around the room. The corners were deeply shadowed. The exterior house lights were out. Their glow usually peeked around the corners of the curtains, giving the room just enough light for me to see when I got up at night.

I realized that the house was quiet because there was no power. There was no ambient noise.

Another quiet sound caught my attention and my head swiveled. I peered into the darkness but couldn't see anything.

"Marcus?"

The shadows shifted, coalescing into the shape of a man. A large man. His torso looked like a square block set on thick legs. His head was misshapen.

I backed up against the headboard and sucked in the air to scream.

Before I could let loose the sound, electricity shot through me and locked me in place.

I lost my breath. Then, I lost consciousness.

CHAPTER TWENTY-THREE

MARCUS

My head was splitting in half. That was the only explanation for the amount of pain I was in.

I bit back a groan, trying to come up with a clear memory of what happened. With my healing abilities, I hadn't been in this much pain in a long, long time.

It came rushing back. The exterior ward had gone off, waking Callum and me. We'd met in the living room, armed ourselves, and exited the house.

That was the last thing I remembered.

My muscles tensed and I cracked my eyelids open. Light filtered through woven black cloth. They'd put a bag over my head. I had to smile. It might make things a little more difficult, but not impossible. I closed my eyes again and focused on my other senses.

The air was cool against my skin and the light had been artificial. I was inside a building somewhere. I let my focus shift to what I could hear. There were three humans in the immediate vicinity. I could hear their heartbeats, their breaths, and the minute sounds of their clothing as they shifted their weight.

Wait, there was a fourth heartbeat. It was slower. I inhaled deeply. Even with the bag over my head, I could smell Callum.

But I couldn't smell Merry.

She wasn't with us.

Fuck.

I reached for her with our bond. She was there, but she wasn't conscious. She seemed okay, just out of it.

I heard a door clang and footsteps approaching. Three more people. One woman and two men.

"It's time we had a chat," a man said.

The bag was ripped off my head.

I blinked against the lights and looked around. I was in a huge white room. More like a warehouse. I was chained to a chair and the chair was screwed to the floor. Callum was next to me, his head drooping and also covered with a black bag.

"Good morning," the man said.

I looked up and narrowed my eyes.

The man standing before me was a human in his mid-forties. He looked like a former soldier—his hair was cut short, almost a buzz cut, he was clean-shaven, and he wore a suit over a body that had been hardened by years of training.

"Let's chat," he said, taking a seat in the chair across from me.

The other man and the woman ranged themselves behind him, both wearing dark grey suits with guns beneath their jackets. They assumed identical positions with their arms in front of them, one wrist clasped by the other hand.

I stared at the man, waiting. Callum was still unconscious and I couldn't fight them all and carry him out at the same time.

Finally, he spoke. "Aren't you going to ask me what I want?"

Again, my only response was a glare.

He seemed nonplussed by my unwillingness to speak. He shifted his weight on the chair, leaning forward.

"My name is Edward Channing. And we are going to work closely together for the foreseeable future."

Callum laughed. One of the guards behind us stepped forward to whip the black bag off. He straightened and glared at the human man in front of me.

"I'm so glad you could join us," Edward drawled.

Callum and I glanced at each other. One look and he knew what I intended to do.

"Why exactly did you invite us here?" Callum asked. "I mean, kidnap us and drag us here in chains."

"Because I have an offer for you," the human answered, crossing one leg over the other. He felt in control of the conversation now. His body language screamed arrogance.

I took in the man and woman standing behind him. The man kept his eyes straight ahead, looking at the far wall. The woman, however, was looking at me. I felt the first tentative touch of her mind and shoved it away. Her eyes widened slightly but she withdrew.

My gaze went back to Edward Channing. "If you want to chat, keep your pet telepath to yourself." I glanced pointedly at the woman.

Edward turned toward her. "Interesting. You and I should talk after this."

The woman's facial expression didn't change but her heart rate increased. He hadn't known about her abilities. That was interesting as Channing put it. She gave him a single nod but I could sense the tiny undercurrent of panic that ran beneath her stoic facade.

The man turned back to me and I saw the male behind him glance at the woman. His eyes were burning with hatred. For some reason, he loathed her. Whether it was because he'd just found out about her abilities or another cause, I couldn't know without reading his thoughts and I didn't have time. I needed to focus on Channing.

This was our opportunity for intel on what the humans knew about us. Before Callum or I acted, we needed information.

"Now, let's get down to business," Edward Channing said. "We've seen your abilities and would like to offer you an opportunity to help your country."

I shot Callum a look. Did he seriously just say that?

Callum smirked and offered a shrug. Yep. He did just say that.

"And this required you kidnapping us?" I asked.

Channing lifted his hands as if he had nothing to do with it. "We only wanted to talk and weren't sure what our reception would be."

"I can tell you it would have been a lot friendlier if you'd approached me with a phone call or in-person visit."

"Let's just say I didn't want you to dismiss the opportunity out of hand. I wanted to make sure I had your full attention."

What he meant was that he wanted to make sure we knew he could get to us if he wanted to. He obviously didn't realize that we could get to him as well.

"How long have you been watching us?" I asked.

Channing shrugged. "A while."

"Callum?" I asked.

"I can't do it," he muttered in answer.

Shit, these must have been the men and women who were immune to vampire power. But what they didn't realize was that the older we got, the more powerful we became. And that I wasn't an ordinary vampire.

My power snapped out of me and latched onto the man and woman standing behind Channing. "You should take a nap," I suggested, nudging them with my power.

The man fought my hold for a moment, just one or two seconds, before he laid down, closing his eyes and going to sleep. The woman resisted.

I used a telepathic link to reach out to her. *I don't want to hurt you.*

I don't believe you. She bared her teeth at me, which I had to respect. She was a fighter.

I would have to show her. I traced free of the chains that were draped around me, appearing right behind her. She gasped and whirled to face me.

I could have killed you as soon as I woke up. I don't want to hurt you. Either stop resisting or leave.

She stared at me for a split second and then the block on her mind dissipated and she sank to the floor, curling up like a child. I didn't know how long the order to sleep would work. Her psyche was strong.

I turned on Edward Channing and found him standing in front of his chair, pointing a handgun at me. Callum was gone, having traced outside to take care of the guards.

"Don't move or I'll—"

"*Put the gun down,*" I ordered, using my abilities against him. It seemed he wasn't immune as his lackeys had been.

His hand trembled for a blink then slowly lowered. His face was filled with terror as his hand released the gun and it dropped to the floor.

It was finally beginning to dawn on him that he didn't have the upper hand. His fear perfumed the air.

"Have a seat," I said.

He collapsed into his chair as I walked around to the one I'd been sitting in. The chains were a pile on the floor, wrapped around the legs. I kicked them out of the way and sat down facing him, crossing my legs.

"Now, why don't you tell me exactly what you intended to accomplish tonight?"

"I wanted to gain your cooperation."

"Again, you could have just asked," I said. "What are you really after?" I pushed with my power, breaking the small bit of resistance he put up.

"We want to use you to help us in military missions and research your condition so we can replicate it."

"You're military?" I asked.

He shook his head. "No, we're a defense contractor. We weren't going to approach them about this until we had everything in place and your cooperation."

"And how did you intend to ensure that cooperation?"

"By whatever means necessary. Such as the woman who was in your house."

My body stiffened. "Have you harmed her?"

He shook his head. "No, she's sedated for now. But if you refused to help us, we would."

I leaned forward and clenched my hands into fists. "Would you really?"

Channing nodded even though his eyes were wide and terrified. "But only if you gave us no other choice."

"How many other people here know what you're up to?" I asked, relaxing back against the chair. I needed to know in the event I needed to kill someone.

"Only the people in this room."

"How did you get past our defenses?"

"What defenses?" he asked.

"The wards. The lights. Everything."

He shrugged. "I have no idea what you mean by wards. The lights and power we cut from the road in the event you had a sensor in the driveway or an alarm on the house. We knew you'd be stronger than the average human based on our surveillance, so we built a Taser that will send out enough power to knock out a rhino."

For fuck's sake. All the wards that Ava set were meant to keep out everything but humans because we didn't want to hurt someone who came on our property to make a delivery or check the water meter or anything like that. We never thought the humans would be watching us or planning to harm us in any way. They didn't even know we existed. Or so we thought.

"I'll need a list of names of everyone involved in this project," I said to Channing. "Written with their contact information. If your boss knows what's going on, you'll need to put his information on here as well."

Channing nodded. His fingers shook as he withdrew a pen and notepad from the inner pocket of his suit. As he made the list, I looked up as Callum returned. My first instinct was to kill Channing, but I also didn't want to raise questions that might bring more attention to us.

"You came back just in time. He's going to share everything he knows with us."

THIRTY MINUTES LATER, Callum and I were on our way to an adjacent building to grab Merry and get the hell out of here. She was locked in a cell with a single human guard. Before we knocked Channing out, he'd called over and told him that two men were coming to get the prisoner.

"You should have let me kill him," Callum complained.

"Too many questions."

"Like they won't have questions when they wake up in the warehouse with two chairs and chains lying on the floor in front of them."

"Did you shut off the cameras and erase the video memory?"

"Yes, Father." His answer was dry. "I am serious, though. You should have let me kill him. This is going to come back and bite us on the ass."

"If it does, we'll deal with it, but we can't go around killing humans without drawing attention to ourselves. Especially humans who've managed to find us once before."

Callum made a face but stopped arguing, which meant he was either done talking or he was planning to circle back around and kill Channing anyway. Either way, it was out of my hands.

We entered the building and walked down the hallway. It looked like any other generic office building, even though it was fairly small.

We turned the corner and saw the guard standing at the end of the hall in front of the door. I'd been checking my bond with Merry periodically and she was still out, which worried me. She should have been conscious by now.

Since Callum and I had both been in our underwear, we'd stripped two of the male guards in the warehouse. The suit I'd taken off Channing's bodyguard was a bit tight in the shoulders and thighs, but Callum was a little bigger than I was and had to take the fatigue pants and tee off the other guard. The shoes hadn't worked out so well though. We'd had to take combat boots from both the guards.

The human didn't say anything as we approached, but he did adjust his stance, straightening a little.

"We're here for the prisoner," Callum said.

The guard nodded, glanced at my shoes, and tensed.

Before he had a chance to do something stupid, I grasped his mind. "Sleep."

C.C. WOOD

Unlike the others, he sat down immediately, leaning against the wall, and passed out.

Callum tried the door and the knob turned easily in his hand. "Dumbasses. Did they think that Merry would just stay in the room when she woke up?"

As soon as we saw her, he swore. "I guess they did."

They'd laid Merry on a metal twin bed but secured one of her wrists to the metal frame with a pair of handcuffs. The bed was screwed to the ground as the chairs had been. She could sit up but she couldn't go far.

I walked over and knelt beside the bed. "See if you can find the key to the cuffs in his pocket," I said to Callum.

He didn't argue for a change, just did as I said.

I leaned over Merry and stroked her hair. "Can you wake up for me, Merry?"

She remained so still.

"Merry, you have to wake up," I said, a little more forcefully. "I need to know you're okay."

"I'm fine," she slurred. "Jus' tired."

I bent closer until my nose was nearly against her skin and inhaled. Shit. They'd drugged her. That's why she was still out of it.

Callum dropped to the floor next to me and handed me the hand-cuff key.

"Is she okay?" he asked.

"They drugged her," I growled, unlocking the cuffs.

Her hand was so limp in mine.

"If you're not going to let me kill that Channing asshole, let's get the hell out of here," he said.

I stood and picked Merry up off the bed. Her body felt boneless and the urge to slaughter every human here gripped me. I reined in the impulse. She was more important than they were. We'd shut down the cameras, erased the video footage, and Callum had installed a virus on one of the computers, promising that it would destroy every computer in the network.

We'd also adjusted everyone's memories. They thought they'd discovered supernatural creatures but been proven wrong.

Even if they found a small piece of evidence to the contrary, they wouldn't believe it.

"Let's go," I said.

Magic swirled around us as we traced out of the building, back to our home.

CHAPTER TWENTY-FOUR

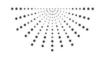

MERRY

I WOKE up alone in my bed. It was like déjà vu.

Only the sun was out this time. And my head was splitting open.

I sat up slowly, groaning as the pain in my skull increased and the room swayed.

Holy crap. What a weird dream. I wondered if it was because Marcus bit me the last time we had sex. Had he accidentally taken too much blood?

Before I could figure out if my legs would hold my weight, the door opened on silent hinges and Marcus entered the room. He looked relieved to see me sitting up as he came over to the bed and sat on the edge.

"How are you feeling?" he asked, his voice little more than a whisper.

I appreciated his efforts to be quiet. "Horrible. Like I'm hungover. And I had the weirdest dream. I'm not sure I want you to bite me again if I'm going to wake up feeling like this. And it's strange because I didn't feel this way the last time you bit me."

Marcus winced. "This isn't because of my bite. Did your weird dream include people in black breaking into the house and zapping you with a Taser?"

"How did you know?" I asked. "Ugh. I need some water."

Marcus reached over to the nightstand and cracked a bottle open for me. "That wasn't a dream."

I nearly choked on the water I was sipping. My stomach clenched and threatened to revolt. "What do you mean, it wasn't a dream?"

"Humans broke into the house last night and kidnapped us all."

"What?" I asked. "How? I thought that Ava set wards to prevent stuff like that from happening."

Marcus frowned. "She did, but they were set to allow humans in because we didn't want to risk harming the people that deliver packages or end up here accidentally. But that's going to change today. Macgrath has already called and arranged to have a security gate installed at the end of the drive. Anyone who has a delivery will deposit it into a box attached to the fence. And Ava's working on the wards right now."

"Why did they come here and take us?" I asked.

"That's a long story," he said.

I lifted my pillow so it rested vertically on the headboard and leaned back against it. "I've got time," I said before I took another sip of water.

Ugh. The inside of my mouth tasted bitter.

"When she kidnapped you, Rhiannon managed to catch the attention of a man who works for a defense contractor. They'd been hired to approach you about a job, but instead he followed her here and found us. We've been under surveillance for months and never knew. They'd already planned to snatch us last night when Dumont showed up. If I hadn't spoken with the man in charge of the project and surveillance myself, I would blame Dumont for this entire mess."

"You think he snitched on us?"

Marcus shook his head. "No, I know he didn't. He was being honest with us."

"How do you know that?" I asked.

"The man in charge told me."

I sipped more water.

"Okay, what now?"

215

"Well, Callum is insisting we install counter surveillance equipment and that we monitor this contractor. He said we'll need your help for that."

"Of course."

Marcus studied me for a prolonged moment. "Are you okay?"

"Physically or mentally?" I asked.

"Both."

"Physically, I don't feel great, but a little food and a huge cup of coffee will probably go a long way to fixing that. Mentally, I'm freaking out that I was kidnapped and missed the entire thing. I went to sleep here and woke up here. Those guys in black seem like a bad dream rather than a traumatic experience."

Marcus nodded. "Why don't you stay in bed and I'll bring you a cup of coffee before I make you lunch."

I winced at the thought of actual food. "Can I just have some toast or a banana for right now? My stomach is still upset."

"Whatever you want," he said. He leaned forward and touched his lips to my forehead.

He got to his feet and left the room. I stayed where I was for a moment, thinking about everything he said. My head throbbed in unison with my heart. I was going to need something other than coffee and food. While I would love some prescription-strength painkillers, an ibuprofen would have to do.

I moved slowly to the edge of the bed and turned so my legs draped over the side. I gripped the headboard as I pushed myself to my feet, my legs trembling from the effort it took to hold my weight. When I was sure that I wasn't going to go splat, I took a few shuffling steps to the end of the bed. I held on to the footboard as I rounded the mattress and made my way to the bathroom.

Now that I was on my feet, I was desperate to use the toilet. My legs were slowly regaining their strength and I was able to move faster.

I shut the bathroom door behind me and hurried over to the toilet.

Five minutes later, I was back in bed, bladder relieved, hands and face washed, and teeth brushed. I tossed two ibuprofen tablets into my mouth and washed them down with water.

My head still hurt but my mouth no longer tasted like something disgusting.

Marcus came into the room with a huge mug of coffee and a plate of toast. "You got up?"

"Yeah. Nature called and I had to brush my teeth. Whatever they gave me made my mouth taste like a sewer."

He put the toast on my lap and handed me the mug.

"Thank you," I said.

"You're welcome. I know you said that you were freaking out about missing the kidnapping thing, but I'm glad you weren't sitting there, terrified, for hours while I wasn't there to protect you."

"You won't be able to protect me from everything, Marcus," I said.

"Maybe not, but this was something I should have been able to protect you from."

"You can't predict what people will do," I argued.

"Maybe not, but I should be prepared for anything."

"Why? Because you've been alive for nearly two thousand years?"

He stared at me as though I were speaking another language.

"What?" I laughed. "Being ancient doesn't mean you're omniscient. You can't be everywhere at once."

"Ancient?" he asked.

I drank some coffee and batted my eyelashes at him.

He sighed. "You do have a point. Except about me being old."

I made a show of looking at his hair. "I do see a few silver threads in there."

"Stop," he said.

I laughed again and took another gulp of coffee. It was delicious, exactly the way I liked it. Further proof that Marcus paid attention. He knew how I liked my coffee and he knew how my brain worked.

"Whatever happened, I'm safe for now. What I'm curious about is this defense contractor. What's the name of the company? And the guy in charge that y'all were talking to?"

Marcus shook his head. "Eat your toast and drink your coffee. Once that ibuprofen kicks in and you feel better, we'll talk more."

I made a face at him, but picked up a piece of toast and took a bite. My stomach tried to slide sideways as I chewed but settled as I swallowed. I ate the rest of the toast slowly and washed it down with more coffee.

By the time I finished the toast and the coffee, the meds were working and my headache had faded into a dull throb rather than a piercing stab.

"Okay, all done," I said. "Tell me more about this company and the guy."

"Let me get Callum. He was the one in their computer system and he knows more than I do."

He got up and stuck his head out the door. "Callum!"

When he turned around, I was standing next to the bed. "I want another cup of coffee. I'll come into the kitchen and make another cup while he talks."

Marcus opened his mouth like he wanted to argue, but he shut it quickly after getting a good look at my expression.

"Fine, but if you start to hurt again, you need to come back in here and lay down."

"I'm smart enough not to argue with that."

He sighed and opened the bedroom door for me.

Callum emerged from his room at the end of the hall. "I'm glad you finally woke up. Marcus was worried."

Judging by the expression on his face, he had been worried, too.

"I can't believe I missed the entire thing," I said.

"I'm glad. It was underwhelming and not worth any anxiety it would cause you."

I rolled my eyes. Only Callum would consider being kidnapped underwhelming.

The guys followed me to the kitchen where I found Arien and Harrison sitting at the table, staring at each other. I didn't want to interrupt out of worry that their eyes would cut me to the bone if they looked at me.

"Will you two cut it out?" Callum said. "It's creepy when you sit there and stare at each other in complete silence."

Arien blinked and looked over at us. Then, she smiled at me. "Merry, I'm so happy that you're okay. I wanted to help heal you, but Marcus said you weren't injured, just drugged. Are you still suffering from ill effects?"

I held up a hand and made a seesaw motion with my outstretched fingers. "Sort of. The coffee, toast, and ibuprofen helped."

She nodded and got to her feet. "Please call me if you need anything. I'm going to go help Ava with the wards now that you're awake."

"Thank you, Arien," I said, walking over to her and giving her a hug.

She stiffened for a second before she relaxed and put her arms around me. "You're welcome, Merry."

Arien released me with a smile and left the house.

Harrison had watched this exchange in silence. As soon as Arien was gone, he said, "I'm also happy that you're well, Merry. I'm sorry we weren't able to prevent this."

"It's not your fault. You couldn't have known that this would happen."

"Maybe not, but we should have been prepared."

"You sound like Marcus," I commented.

Harrison shrugged. "There are worse things."

I sat at the table and smiled at Marcus when he brought me another cup of coffee. "Thanks."

Then, I fixed my gaze on Callum. "It's your turn to talk. I need to know all about this company and the guy who grabbed us."

He sat down across from Harrison in the seat that Arien had vacated. The wolf didn't growl, but I could see his lip trembled as he fought a snarl.

"The company is the Fallon Group. Edward Channing isn't the top guy, but he does head several projects. According to what Marcus got out of him and his computer, he was keeping the information about us on the down low. He wanted proof we existed before he brought us to the attention of his boss. Apparently, he was worried that someone he worked with would get the jump on the information and nab us first."

Oh, my God. This was incredible. Unbelievable.

Callum cleared his throat and continued, "This is the only thing that prevented me from killing him. Marcus and I erased us from the memory of everyone there, got rid of audio and video recordings, wiped Channing's computer, and loaded a virus that will spread to any computer networked with his. They might have a stray piece of information here or there, but they shouldn't know what to make of it when they see it."

"So all of you will be safe?" I asked.

Callum's affable expression vanished. "Oh, yes. We will be safe. Now that we know about them, we'll keep an eye on them."

His tone was ominous. I almost felt sorry for Edward Channing and his employer. They were now on the radar of predators and they would not rest until they were certain they were safe.

"How are you going to keep an eye on them?" I asked.

Callum grinned, his fangs sharp and longer than usual. It was a scary smile, one I'd never seen on his face before.

"I planted a few devices while we were there. And as soon as they get their computers up and running again, I'll install some spy software. Now that I know the layout of their business, it won't be too difficult to get back inside."

It was clear he hadn't told Marcus about any of this because Marcus glared at him. "You're not going back in there."

"I am."

"Okay, then you're not going back in there alone."

"I am. There's no discussion here, Marcus. This is what's best for all of us and I'll do it, whether you agree or not."

"No, you won't because you could put us in more danger."

Harrison and I looked at each other then back at Callum and Marcus. They were both on their feet, facing off as though they were ready to resort to physical violence.

"Neither of you is doing anything without input from Macgrath or me," Ava said from the doorway.

The vampires turned as one to look at her. Her eyes glowed lavender and a few strands of her hair moved in a phantom wind. Her power filled the room. Even I could feel it and I shouldn't have been able to as a human without power.

Huh. How did I know that? Probably from the mind-meld thing that Marcus and I had done the last time we had sex. That could be handy in the future. Maybe I could learn to fight by osmosis or whatever they called it.

"You know I need to do this," Callum argued.

"No one said the opposite," Ava replied. "But you do need a well-thought-out plan and you know that. If you go off half-cocked, you'll bring them right back on us again."

Callum didn't argue with that. Probably because she was right.

"And you're not going alone," Macgrath said.

Callum opened his mouth this time, but Macgrath just shook his head and he shut it again.

"You're absolutely right to keep an eye on them," he continued. "But we won't make rash decisions that put everyone in danger."

The stiffness went out of Callum's posture. He was finally accepting what they were saying.

"I won't," he said.

Ava nodded and the light faded from her eyes. Her hair settled around her shoulders and she turned to the table.

"Merry, you're up. How are you feeling?"

"A little hungover," I admitted. "But better now that I've had some coffee and toast."

"Good." She cocked her head to the side as she studied me. "You look more relaxed than the last time I saw you."

My face heated. Shit. Could they tell that Marcus and I had sex?

Marcus glanced at me and I realized he'd heard that stray thought. Mostly because he gave a short, almost invisible nod. Holy crap. Everyone knew.

I hid behind my coffee cup and tried to pretend that I wasn't now aware of this knowledge.

"Since I need permission, I'd like to talk to you about observing the Fallon Group and their activities," Callum said to Macgrath.

Macgrath and Marcus both scowled at him.

"Let's go outside," Macgrath said.

Harrison got up from the table and followed the three vampires outside.

Ava went to the fridge and took a bottle of water out before she came to sit at the table facing me. "They're probably going to spar to let off some steam," she commented, cracking the seal on the bottle. "If we give them five or ten minutes, they'll probably strip off their shirts."

I laughed. "So, are we going to ogle the men?"

"Why not?"

"Good point." I fell silent. "Do you really think all of you will be safe?" I asked.

She nodded. "I do. At least for now. And if we're not safe in the future, we'll know better than to assume we're safe just because we're not dealing with supernatural creatures." She paused. "So...you and Marcus?"

I groaned. "Is it that obvious?"

Ava shook her head. "Not to most people, but we're not humans." She paused. "You look happy, even though you're still half sick from the drugs they gave you."

"I am."

"You can tell me to mind my business, but are you planning to stay?"

"I won't tell you to mind your business. You've been the closest thing I've had to a female friend in years." I sipped my coffee. "And I am staying. At least for now."

"You're planning to leave eventually?" she asked.

I shrugged. "Not exactly."

Her mouth twitched as though she wanted to smile. "Then, what are you planning?"

"Um, on staying until Marcus kicks me out?"

She did smile then. "You realize that won't ever happen, right?

When vampires mate, they take it very seriously. Especially when they're mating for love."

"Vampires don't mate for love?" I asked.

"They do, but they also mate for power, money, or other reasons, just like humans do."

I nodded. I understood that.

"So, if you're going to wait for Marcus to kick you out, it won't happen. He's crazy about you. Anyone can see that." Ava's eyes were alert as they scanned my face. "But you already know because of the bond, don't you?"

"I'm having trouble believing it," I admitted. "We barely know each other."

"He's seen your heart and you've seen his. Do you really think you don't know each other?"

I sighed. "No. Yes. I don't know. This isn't exactly something I've dealt with before."

She nodded. "I understand. Just...try to keep an open mind."

"I will."

Ava glanced out the back window. "Ha! I was right. They're sparring and they're shirtless."

Without thinking, I got to my feet and walked to the window over the sink. "Oh, my."

Ava laughed. "I know. I love Ewan with all my heart but I'm not blind. They're all built."

I had to laugh with her. "That they are."

She put an arm around my shoulders. "I'm glad you're here, Merry. And I think that you'll be here for a long time to come if you don't let doubts cloud your head."

I glanced at her and she gave me a squeeze before she released me.

"Just promise me you'll talk to me if you decide to leave," she murmured.

"I will, I promise."

Even as I vowed, I realized that I didn't want to leave. And I probably never would.

CHAPTER TWENTY-FIVE

MARCUS

THE AIR WAS CHILLY. Austin was far enough south that we rarely had cold weather, but every now and then, a cold snap would come through. Today was one of those days.

I watched as Callum and Macgrath clashed together, punching and grappling. I knew that Macgrath had dragged Callum out here to provide our brother an outlet. Since the kidnapping, Callum was wound tighter than I'd seen him in centuries. Not since Macgrath helped Lisandra vanish.

Callum had loved Lisandra to a distraction over a century ago. She managed to convince him she was helpless. Delicate. She'd looked the part. Her body was slender and fine-boned and her face formed in clean, fragile lines. Even as a human, there was something compelling about her brown eyes. They were almost black when she gazed at you and it seemed she could see right through you. Her dark brown hair was always styled in a loose topknot and a few curls inevitably floated freely.

She'd played her role to perfection. Until she met Rhiannon.

Rhiannon had immediately seen through the facade to the duplicitous creature beneath. And she liked what she saw. Especially when she realized that Lisandra had power. It was small, but Lisandra's personality was malleable and she was willing to do things she shouldn't.

Macgrath had seen what was happening and feared that Rhiannon would use Lisandra against Callum. So, he'd given Lisandra money, more money that she could spend in a lifetime, and taken her far away. Callum's woman had been more than willing, particularly after Macgrath named the amount he was willing to pay. She had even haggled for more money to leave the man she loved.

Callum hadn't believed it at first. Not until we ran into Lisandra thirty years later. She was still young and beautiful, but there was a coldness to her that hadn't been there before. She was remote, her eyes flat and empty, even as she preened and flirted with Callum.

And he saw it then. When he asked her about the past, she admitted that Macgrath had given her money to leave. That she'd gone willingly.

It had irrevocably changed something within the vampire I considered my brother. Even after two thousand years, there had still been a part of him that had remained naive. And that innocence had been destroyed and he'd become stoic for a long while. It eventually gave way to his usual affability, but it had taken a while.

Callum had that same grimness today and he needed a way to release it.

Macgrath, in his usual astuteness, sensed this and provided the outlet.

After two hours of sparring, we were all shirtless and sweaty despite the crisp fall air. Steam rose off Callum's body as he attacked ferociously.

Harrison came up next to me with my shirt in his hand.

"Thanks," I said as I took it from him and slipped it over my head.

"Is Callum going to be okay?" he asked quietly.

"Yeah. He's just...shaken."

Harrison gave me a sidelong look and I shrugged.

"It may be more than that," I said. "But he hasn't spoken to me about it."

As Harrison and I watched. Macgrath threw Callum, who grabbed him on the way to the ground and brought him down, too. They were grappling, moving so quickly that the human eye probably couldn't see each movement, and grunting.

A slight sound caught my attention and I watched as Arien appeared out of the trees at the rear of the property and walked toward us. Her hair was loose and tangled, wild as though she hadn't brushed it. Her shirt was buttoned incorrectly and her eyes were a little wild as well.

She'd gone for a run in animal form. Unlike Harrison, who was a wolf shifter, Arien was a shapeshifting witch. She used magic to change forms. For several years, she'd taken the form of a cat and lived with Savannah so she could keep an eye on Ava, who lived nearby. She had revealed herself last year when Macgrath and Ava found each other again.

Though she usually stayed in human form, she did occasionally like to change and run through the woods as a cat or fox or even a wolf. Much to Harrison's irritation.

Harrison growled low in his throat and I bit back a sigh.

"Stop antagonizing her," I muttered.

"She antagonizes me with her existence."

Abruptly, I'd had enough. "Just stop," I said, turning toward him. "I know you have strong feelings about Arien and that they're mixed, but we no longer have the luxury of being at odds with each other."

"I'm not at odds with her," he argued. "She...disturbs me."

"I know, but you can't keep treating her the way you have."

"I have to," he murmured, watching Arien as she walked closer to us.

"Why?" I asked, completely exasperated.

"Because the distance keeps us both safe."

I had no idea what he meant by that, but I couldn't ask him because Arien was now within earshot. She approached on my left and nodded to Harrison before turning to me.

"Is Merry still inside?"

I glanced at the kitchen window, where I'd noticed Merry and Ava watching us earlier, and saw that they were no longer there.

"She was in the kitchen with Ava earlier."

Arien nodded. "Thank you." She glanced at Harrison, her light blue eyes as cool as the air. But an alien intelligence looked out of them. I wondered how much of the animal remained with Arien after she shifted because nothing human was looking at us now.

She glided past Macgrath and Callum, who were locked together on the ground. Macgrath had Callum in an armlock and he wasn't letting up. Callum was refusing to tap out.

Arien flicked her fingers at them and two small streams of water hit them both in the face simultaneously.

I laughed as they both stopped fighting and blinked as they looked up at her.

"If you're done putting on a show for everyone, it's nearly lunch time." Arien swept up the back stairs and into the house without waiting for a response.

Even Harrison cracked a smile as the two vampires on the ground swore and broke apart before rolling to their feet. They grabbed their shirts from the back porch and pulled them over their heads.

We trooped into the house and found the women seated around the kitchen table. Arien ran a brush through her hair as she chatted with Merry.

Ava faced us. "Great. You're done with your..." she trailed off. "Planning session. I'm starving," she said to Macgrath. "We should head back into town and have lunch."

He grunted in what I assumed was assent and went to the sink to wash his hands.

Ava came over to me and patted my arm. "I'm going to get everyone out of here so you can talk Merry into resting. I'm certain her head still aches. Especially after our discussion earlier."

"Discussion?" I asked.

"About her plans now that she's no longer in danger. Where she plans to go next and what she plans to do."

Her words managed to do what the chilly air outside had not—they froze my blood.

"She's leaving?" I asked.

227

But Ava was already walking away. Within minutes, the house was empty. Callum decided to go with them for lunch, despite the fact that he was still sweaty from his bout with Macgrath.

Merry came back from the living room with a smile on her face. She'd walked them all out while I remained in the kitchen.

"Are you okay?" she asked, coming closer. When I didn't answer, she put a hand on my chest. "Marcus?"

"Are you leaving?" I asked.

Her mouth fell open but she didn't say anything. She only blinked a few times before she pulled back. "Uh, do you want me to leave?" she asked, answering my question with a question.

"No, I don't."

"Okay, then I suppose I'm staying."

"Merry, are you thinking about leaving? Making plans?"

She frowned at me. "No, but I'm wondering if I should be. What's going on?"

"I..." Shit. I had no idea what to say.

"You, what?" she asked.

"I don't," I had to stop and clear my throat. "I don't want you to leave."

Merry smiled up at me, her hazel eyes warm and sparkling. "That's good, because I don't want to leave."

Her hand was still on my chest. I held it gently in mine. "You don't understand. I don't want you to leave at all."

Her smile faded. "Maybe not now, but what if you change your mind? If I stay here for months, I'll essentially be starting from scratch. I'll have to pick up the pieces and move on and I'm not sure I can do that."

"I've waited hundreds of lifetimes for you," I said, lifting her hand to my mouth so I could press a kiss to her palm. "I won't change my mind. I'm not going anywhere and I don't want you to either. The question is how do you feel about me?"

She didn't speak for so long that I was afraid I'd pushed too hard, too fast. My thoughts raced as she stared at me with wide eyes.

Finally, she opened her mouth and said, "I'm all in. I want to stay here and sleep with you every night and have coffee with you in the morning. I want to know what makes you angry and what makes you smile." Her fingers flexed in mine and traced the edge of my lips. "I want to make you laugh. You smile and laugh so rarely and you should do it more often. I...I'm falling for you and it's nothing I've ever experienced before."

I pulled her closer and she leaned into me.

"It sounds ridiculous when I say it out loud," she said. "But this, everything I'm feeling, is scary as hell."

"It scares me, too," I admitted.

She tilted her head back and one corner of her mouth lifted in a crooked half-smile. "Really?"

"Really. Other than Macgrath and Callum, I haven't depended on anyone in a very long time. But I'm depending on you."

Her arms stole around my waist and squeezed. "Would it make me a horrible person if I said that I was relieved?"

I had to laugh. "No."

"So no expiration date on...us?" she asked.

"No."

"One day at a time?"

"One day at a time."

She sighed and leaned forward to rest her head on my chest. "I can do that."

I stroked a hand over her hair. "That's all I can ask."

After a moment, she lifted her head and pressed her lips to mine. "Do you realize that we have the whole house to ourselves for the foreseeable future?"

"I do now."

The smile that spread across her face was very nearly wicked. "Want to take a shower with me?"

She squealed when I swept her off her feet and carried her down the hallway to her bedroom.

～

A FEW HOURS LATER, Merry was asleep again. Her head rested on my shoulder and her arm was draped over my waist. I listened to her quiet breathing and wondered how long it would take me to convince her to marry me.

After we made love in the shower, I made lunch and we sat on the couch and watched a movie together.

Until Merry came into my life, I hadn't realized I was lonely. I lived with Callum but we each went our own way most of the time. It never occurred to me that I was lonely.

I had been sleepwalking through my life and she woke me up.

Merry brought color and vibrancy to each day. Seeing the world through her eyes made me see what I'd been missing.

I didn't want to miss anything else.

I heard the front door open and realized that Callum was back. He must have traced from Ava and Macgrath's home.

Gently, I slid Merry's head off my shoulder before I slipped out of the bed. I grabbed my pants off the floor and pulled them up before I left the bedroom. The door shut silently behind me.

I could hear Callum moving around in his room, opening drawers and rummaging in the closet. He looked up when I entered his room.

"Hey. How's Merry?" he asked as he stuffed a couple of t-shirts into a duffel bag.

"She's sleeping." I gestured to the bag on his bed. "What are you doing?"

"Macgrath and I talked after lunch and we decided to keep an eye on our friend, Edward Channing, and the Fallon Group. Harrison, Rhys, Macgrath, and I are going to take turns on surveillance. I took the first shift so you and Merry could have some privacy." He disappeared into his closet again and reappeared with a pair of boots. "I figure they'll have their network up and running in a few days and I want to sneak back in there to plant a few little devices."

He jammed the boots into one end of the duffel and turned to the dresser.

"Hang on. Wait," I said, coming further into the room. Callum

230

ignored me until I stepped in front of him and said, "Stop and talk to me."

Callum tossed the socks in his hand on the bed and put his hands on his hips. "There's nothing to talk about."

"Why wasn't I invited to this meeting that you had with Macgrath and the others?" I asked.

"Because I didn't want to interrupt your banging," he retorted.

My hands fisted and I resisted the urge to take a swing at him. I'd forgotten how he could push my buttons when he wanted to. Callum rarely acted like an asshole, so when he did, he made up for it in spades.

"Fuck you, Callum. Don't say shit like that."

He sighed and the aggression went out of his stance. "I'm sorry. That was an asshole comment."

"Apology accepted. Now, tell me the truth."

"The truth is that you need to stay here with Merry. For her and for yourself. You need each other and you need time together. Alone. We also need to keep an eye on Channing and his employers. As much as I would like to believe that the steps we took the other night will be enough to keep them off our backs, you and I both know better. Humans are a crafty lot and I don't want to be caught by surprise again."

"I'm grateful that you and Macgrath took my attachment to Merry into consideration, but that doesn't mean I can't take a turn on the stakeout."

Callum arched his brows. "How effective do you think you'll be when you're worried about Merry every second? The mating urge has you in its grip. You won't be able to stay away from her. You'll want to hear her voice, see her, touch her."

"I'm not a young vampire. I can control my instincts."

"Fine," he said, waving his arms. "After Macgrath, Harrison, Rhys, Caleb, and I each take a week of surveillance, it will be your turn. That's five weeks. We'll discuss it then."

"Fine."

He went to the bed, gathered up the scattered socks, folded them and tucked them into the bag. He went into the bathroom and came out with a toiletry kit that went on top and zipped up the bag.

He came over to me and held out a hand. I grasped his forearm and pulled him in for a hug.

"Be careful," I said.

"I will."

"And check in every day."

"Yes, Mother Dearest," he drawled, pulling away.

I scowled at him. "It's not mothering, it's safety. I need to know if you're still in place or if we need to come rescue your ass."

"Ha! I've never needed rescuing."

"Should I list all the times I've had to save your ass?"

Callum went to the bed and shouldered the bag. "Go ahead and write it down. I'll read it and point out all the mistakes when I get back."

There was his usual sarcasm.

"I'll call you tomorrow," he said. Then, he was gone.

Unsettled, I went back into Merry's room, dropped my pants on the floor, and crawled in next to her. Still asleep, she turned toward me and threw her leg over my hip as she nuzzled her nose into my chest.

I held her close and tried not to worry about Callum.

A shadow loomed in the future, but I had no idea when it would swallow us.

CHAPTER TWENTY-SIX

MERRY

THREE DAYS LATER, I talked Marcus into taking me into Austin for lunch. And for a stop at The Magic Bean for coffee and pastry.

At first, he didn't want to go anywhere, but I'd talked him into it. I pointed out that we were no longer being watched by the humans and Ava and Macgrath were on good terms with Dumont, so there was no reason we couldn't go out.

When he still resisted, I might have mentioned that he'd never even taken me out on a date.

So, we went into town, had lunch at a cafe near SoCo, and then went to Ava's shop for a caffeinated beverage and dessert. Marcus had difficulty relaxing at first, but by the time our food arrived at our table, he wasn't swiveling his head to watch every person in the cafe.

The last bit of tension drained out of him when we entered The Magic Bean. Harrison and Savannah were there, but the store itself was empty for now. Savannah looked pretty and fresh in a light green dress and her hair in a thick braid down her back.

"Hey!" Savannah said. "Long time no see."

"Hey. How are you?" I asked, walking to the counter.

"I'm good. How are you doing? Ava told me about what happened a few days ago. I can't believe it."

I shrugged. "It's scary when I think about it but I missed the entire thing because they zapped me with a stun gun and then drugged me."

Savannah's eyes shifted to Marcus. I could feel him next to me, doing his best imitation of a thundercloud. "Uh, well, I'm glad you're okay."

I nudged Marcus with my elbow. "Quit staring at her like that."

"Like what?" he asked, crossing his arms over his chest.

"Like you're ready to rip her head off."

Savannah giggled when Marcus frowned at me. "I wouldn't categorize it as that. More like he's annoyed with me."

"What?" Marcus asked again, this time sounding more bewildered than irritated.

I imitated his stance and put a scowl on my face, scrunching up my lips and lowering my eyebrows into an exaggerated approximation of his facial expression.

Savannah laughed outright and tried to cover it up with a cough. "Uh, sorry. I, uh, choked on my own spit." She continued to cough so much that I was genuinely worried about her.

Harrison sighed and went to the fridge. He took out a pitcher of water, grabbed a cup, poured out some water, and brought it over to Savannah.

"Here," he murmured. "Have some water."

"Thanks," she said, her voice hoarse. "I actually did choke after I said that."

He rolled his eyes and went back to the fridge to put the pitcher of water away.

Marcus was no longer scowling, but staring at both of us with astonishment.

"I don't look like that," he said.

Savannah and I both smirked at him and he grunted.

"Maybe just a little," I said, holding my index finger and thumb close together.

"Sorry I laughed," Savannah said, her cough finally under control. "You don't look exactly like that, but you do frown a lot."

Marcus dropped his arms as I laughed. "I do not. I just don't smile very often."

"That's true, too," I said. "But you still frown a lot."

"I do not."

I pointed to the reflective surface of the bakery case. "You're doing it right now.

Marcus looked down, saw his expression, and stopped frowning. "Dammit."

Savannah and I both laughed and I gave him a kiss on the cheek. "That's okay. You have a sexy frown."

His brows lowered further and I smiled sweetly at him.

"Maybe some dessert will sweeten your mood," I said.

"We have your favorite today, Marcus," Savannah said. "Apple galette."

"Sounds good."

Savannah turned to me. "We also have lemon mousse cake."

"Oh, that sounds good, too. Can we get both of those and two cappuccinos?"

Savannah smiled. "Of course."

Marcus insisted on paying for the food, but I pulled a few bucks out of my pocket and dropped them in the tip jar.

"You didn't have to do that," Savannah said as she got our desserts.

"Yes, I did," I said.

She smiled and shook her head, sensing that it would be useless to argue with me.

I turned to Marcus to say something, but he was looking out the front window. The door to the shop opened and Ava came in first, followed by Macgrath and two other men. One was dark, with black hair and bright blue eyes. The sun blinded me momentarily as the other man came inside. I blinked until my eyes focused and my heart stopped for a moment.

Dear God. It was Caleb. Rhiannon's pet vampire. He was here.

My legs lost their strength and I leaned against the counter.

I had to run. I had to get away. But my body refused to work.

"Merry? What's wrong?" Marcus asked.

235

I couldn't think, much less speak. Panic clouded my mind.

Heavy bands wrapped around my ribs. I couldn't breathe.

"Rhys! Caleb!" Savannah called, coming around the counter to give them both a hug.

Why was she hugging him? Didn't she know that he was dangerous?

I tried to cry out, to tell her to stop, but my mouth wouldn't work.

Marcus leaned down and his face filled my vision. "Merry. Talk to me."

I couldn't say anything. I was staring in horror as Caleb hugged Savannah back, smiling down at her. He looked normal. Nothing like the monster I knew he was. Ava, Macgrath, and Rhys seemed to know him well. None of them were concerned.

"It's him," I finally said.

Marcus sighed. "I know. It's okay. He's not a threat to you anymore."

Those words captured my attention and I looked from Caleb to him. "What did you say?"

Marcus seemed to pale. "When Rhiannon came here last year, Caleb was with her. She created him and thus had a magical hold over him. She controlled him and used him, much as she used you. He didn't want to do the things that he did any more than you."

Betrayal spiked through my abdomen, straight into my heart.

"You know him?" I asked.

Marcus didn't answer, so I asked again. "You know him?" This time my voice was louder and it attracted the attention of everyone standing by the door.

Marcus reached for my hand but I jerked away. "Do not touch me," I snapped. "I poured my heart out to you. I told you about my past and my...my time with Rhiannon. I told you what he did to me!" I was yelling now, my voice cracking with anxiety and anger. "And this entire time, he's been here. You know him and he's your *friend*. And you never said anything to me about it!"

"Merry," Marcus began. "Please, just listen to—"

"No! You had a chance to tell me about this for the last week and you didn't say a word. You kept him a secret from me."

I tore myself away from the counter, putting space between us. "You lied to me."

Ava appeared next to Marcus. "Merry, what's wrong?"

"Did you know?" I asked her.

I had to give it to Ava, she didn't try to pretend that she had no clue what was going on.

"Yes, but I thought Marcus would have told you about Caleb by now." She shot Marcus a sidelong glance.

I shook my head, backing away from them all. "You all lied to me."

Savannah approached me. "Merry, what are you talking about?" She came up beside me, ignoring the way I tried to sidestep her. I had nowhere to go because Marcus was standing right there. "Here, let's go back to Ava's office. You can tell me what's going on."

I realized that she didn't know. I wanted to leave. To escape. But I knew I couldn't run. My legs wouldn't support me, even if I wanted them to. My body was trembling and my breath came in pants.

"Come with me," she said, her voice gentle. Savannah put a hand on my forearm. "Please. Let's go sit down and you can talk to me."

She didn't wait for my reply, merely slid her hand down to mine and led me through the swinging door that led to the back of the store.

I let her guide me to Ava's office.

Once we were inside, she urged me toward the couch and went to the small fridge behind Ava's desk. I sat down, rested my elbows on my knees, and dropped my forehead in my hands.

"Here," Savannah said, holding the water bottle in front of my downturned face.

"Thanks," I said, taking the bottle from her.

Savannah sat on the coffee table, her knees in my line of sight. "Take a sip and tell me what's going on."

I leaned back on the couch and took the lid off the water bottle. After a small sip, I set it to the side and folded my hands in front of me.

"I've met Caleb before. When he was with Rhiannon."

Savannah nodded. "Okay."

I stared at her but she didn't seem to understand, so I explained, "She sicced him on me like a damn attack dog, Savannah. Any time I displeased her, which was nearly every day, she would let him feed from me. Just enough to terrify me and enough for him to fight against her when she held him back." Tears welled in my eyes. "I thought that she would let him kill me eventually."

Savannah leaned forward and took both my hands in hers. "I'm so sorry, Merry. I didn't realize."

"I know."

"And this is the first time you've seen him since then?" she asked.

I nodded.

She squeezed my fingers. "No wonder you freaked out." She paused. "You do realize that she controlled him the way she controlled you, right? He's not evil."

I huffed out a laugh. "He definitely seemed evil to me," I argued.

Savannah nodded. "I'm sure he did and I know he feels horrible about it."

"How do you know that?" I asked.

"Because I've known him since he came here with Rhiannon and he's told me about the things she made him do."

"You're friends with him?" I asked.

She nodded. "Yes, because he's like my fiancé, Rhys. He was created with magic and used for someone else's benefit, just like Caleb. They're called *animavore* and there are only two in the world. Rhys and Caleb."

I leaned away from her, wanting to put some space between us. She released my hands.

"What are *animavore*?" I asked.

"They feed on the life force of others. Humans, vampires, shifters, just about any living thing," she answered. "But like vampires, they don't need to kill to feed. And as they gain control and get older, they don't need to feed as often."

There was a knock at the door and Ava stuck her head in. "Are you feeling any better?" she asked me.

"If you mean 'are you done panicking?', then yes," I replied. "If you're asking if I'm still angry about being lied to, then yes also."

She came inside and shut the door behind her. "I'm so sorry about that." She sat on the table next to Savannah. "I encouraged Marcus to tell you about Caleb when he returned from Dallas, but I didn't realize that he hadn't taken my advice."

"You knew all this time, too?"

Ava nodded. "If I'd realized..." she trailed off. "I should have told you."

"Savannah was just trying to convince me that Caleb isn't evil," I said, crossing my arms over my chest.

"Having trouble believing it?" she asked.

My only answer was to arch an eyebrow at her.

There was another knock on the door and it opened to reveal Rhys and Caleb.

I inhaled sharply when Caleb's gaze met mine. I was frozen again, unable to move.

"I know that I hurt you," he said, ignoring everyone else in the room. "And I'm very, very sorry. I was not in control of my actions, but that's no excuse. I hope that someday you'll be able to forgive me."

I had no idea what to say. My mouth opened, but no words came out.

"If I was able, I would give back what I took from you," he continued. "I know I can't, therefore I'm in your debt. If you ever need anything, anything at all, you have only to ask."

Caleb turned and walked away, leaving me with Ava, Savannah, and Rhys.

Savannah's fiancé looked at me. "You have every right to be upset and angry with him. I hope that when you have time to calm down and think about it, you'll eventually be able to forgive him. I realize you've only dealt with him when he was under Rhiannon's influence, but he's a good man and he deeply regrets hurting people, even though he didn't have a choice."

As I sat there, blinking at him, Rhys shut the door.

Ava patted my hand. "I'll go get you some cake and a cappuccino. You can sit back here and relax for a little while. I'll keep the others out."

"Thank you," I said faintly, lost in thought.

Ava left the office and Savannah leaned forward, snagging my attention.

"Do you want a little time alone?" she asked.

"I'd appreciate it."

She smiled and patted my arm. "I'll go help Harrison out front and tell the rest of them to give you some time."

"Thanks."

"I'm glad you're here, Merry," she said. "I hope that you stay."

Savannah left the office as well, leaving me completely alone.

I had a lot to think about.

CHAPTER TWENTY-SEVEN

MARCUS

IT WAS a struggle not to shove my way through the door at the rear of The Magic Bean and back into the office. I wanted to tell Merry that I hadn't meant to lie to her. That I fully intended to tell her about Caleb and that I'd been distracted by Dumont and the humans.

But Macgrath and Harrison planted themselves in front of that door. Savannah and Ava had come back out from the office and made it clear that Merry wanted some time alone.

Ava had taken a cup of cappuccino and a thick slice of lemon mousse cake and returned already.

I paced around the storefront until Savannah shoved a cappuccino into my hand and an apple galette in the other.

"Go sit down. Eat your dessert and drink your coffee," she commanded. "You're making me anxious."

I sighed and did as she said. I forced myself to eat and drink. The galette was delicious, sweet and spiced. It tasted like autumn, but it didn't make me feel any better.

By the time I was finished eating and drinking, I was no longer worried. I was depressed. Merry had every right to be angry with me. I only hoped I could convince her not to leave.

An hour later, Merry reappeared with an empty cup and plate in her hand. She put them behind the counter.

"Thanks for the dessert and coffee," she said to Ava.

Then, she turned around and looked everywhere but at me.

Caleb and Rhys had left right after she vanished into the office and Savannah was in the reading room with a client. Only Ava, Harrison, Macgrath, and I remained in the shop. A couple sat at a table near the front windows, but there were no other customers at the moment.

Finally, after a few long minutes, Merry came over to me. "Can we go home?" she asked.

That was not what I expected.

"Um, of course," I answered, getting to my feet.

We said our goodbyes and walked out to the car. As I pulled out onto the street, I glanced at her out of the corner of my eye.

"Are you sure you want to go back to the house?" I asked. I should have bitten my tongue instead of speaking, but I couldn't control the urge.

"I'm sure," she murmured. "But we do need to talk."

"I know."

The half-hour drive was silent.

When I pulled in front of the house and parked, Merry turned to me. "Let's take a walk."

Fall temperatures in Austin would be considered warm compared to other areas. The afternoon was sunny and in the low eighties.

We got out of the car and I followed Merry around the house. There was a large open area between the house and the trees. Callum and I kept the grass cut short since we liked to exercise outside.

I trailed behind her as she walked toward the wooded area.

Merry glanced over her shoulder. "Are you going to lurk behind me or come up here so I can bitch at you?"

She didn't sound angry anymore. Just tired.

"I'm sorry."

Merry stopped walking and turned toward me. "What was that?"

"I'm sorry, Merry," I repeated, a little louder this time. "I didn't tell you about Caleb when you first came to stay with us because I was afraid you'd run away. You were so anxious and your nightmares..." I paused. "I was selfish. I wanted more time with you. So I didn't say anything."

She nodded. "Okay. What happened after that? Why didn't you mention it?"

"The honest answer is going to piss you off," I said.

"More than I already am?"

"Good point." I cleared my throat. "I forgot about it. I was more concerned with Dumont and then being kidnapped by humans. Ava brought it up when Caleb returned from Dallas and advised me to tell you about him, but so much happened."

Merry crossed her arms over her chest. "Your excuses are that you were selfish and you forgot?"

I winced at the stern tone in her voice. "Well, when you say it like that, it sounds really bad."

Her lips tightened as she glared at me. "Seriously?"

"I really am sorry. I screwed up. I should have said something."

"Yeah, you did screw up." She studied me for a long moment. "But I suppose I can understand considering we were dealing with a rogue vampire, spying humans, and then being kidnapped."

Wait, what?

"Yes, I'm letting you off the hook," she said. "I figure at some point in our relationship, I'm going to screw up and I'll want you to be sympathetic and understanding rather than bitchy and whiny." She inhaled and let it out with a sigh. "So, I'm trying to give you what I would want from you when that happens."

I took a step forward and put my hands on her waist. "I'm not going to ask you if you're sure because I don't want to give you a chance to change your mind."

She shook her head and leaned her forehead against my shoulder. "I'm not going to change my mind. Against my better judgment, I love you, you big lughead."

I kissed the top of her head, unable to think of what to say.

"Anything to say to me?" she mumbled against my shoulder.

"Um..."

She pinched my side and I yelped. "Okay, okay. I have no idea what to say."

Merry lifted her head and squinted at me. "Considering I've seen into your head, do you want to reciprocate those words?"

Oh.

"You know I love you. I've never tried to hide that," I said.

"Yeah, but the words are important, too. Even if I can read your mind."

I kissed her. "Understood."

When I lifted my mouth from hers, Merry said, "For our first fight, this went pretty well."

"I agree."

"Does that mean it's time for make-up sex?"

Every time I thought I had a handle on how her mind worked, she threw another curve ball at me. Merry gave a little hop and wrapped her legs around my waist, which made me laugh. At least until she whipped her shirt over her head.

"Jesus, Merry. We're outside in the middle of the day."

Her bra followed, leaving her naked from the waist up, her pale skin gleaming in the afternoon sunlight.

"So? Your nearest neighbor is over a mile away, right? Unless you're worried about drones and spying humans."

She didn't give me a chance to respond before she kissed me again.

For a few seconds, I waged an internal argument about whether or not I should carry her into the house, but she ground her hips against mine and the decision was made.

I knelt in the grass with Merry astride my thighs. She didn't even hesitate before she yanked my shirt off and unbuckled my belt.

In less than a minute, we were both naked in the grass. Merry pushed me back onto the ground and leaned down to kiss me.

Her skin was warm under the sunlight and soft as water. I skimmed my thumbs over her nipples, loving the way she shivered against me. She arched into my touch as she ran her hands over my chest and shoulders.

Sweat broke out over my skin when her fingers danced over my cock.

Maybe someday her touch wouldn't destroy me, but I didn't antici-
pate that happening for a long, long time.

"We have to hurry," she murmured, positioning my cock so she
could envelope me.

I squeezed her hips. "No, we don't."

"Yes, we do," she argued, taking me in fully with a gasp. "Well,
I do."

Her hips undulated against mine as she leaned down to kiss me
again.

Within minutes, tension seized her muscles and she tightened
around me. Merry tilted her head, offering me her neck in a gesture
that never failed to move me.

I bit her just as her body began to buck against mine, dragging a
cry from her lips.

Our minds connected and I felt what she felt—the pleasure, the
joy. The love.

Her hands cupped my head as her body surged against mine and
drew taut.

I drank from her, each pull of my mouth drawing a trembling gasp
from her lips.

Finally, I released her and licked her neck to seal the wounds.

Merry collapsed against me, her heart thudding against my chest.
Her lips touched the side of my neck, almost in the exact spot where
I'd bitten her.

"Someday, I'll get to take my time," I murmured.

"No one rushed you this time."

I huffed out a tired laugh. "Says the woman who insisted that she
was in a hurry."

Merry nuzzled my throat. "Okay, so you have a point." She sighed.
"There was another reason we needed to hurry."

I stroked a hand over her back. "What was that?"

"I sunburn easily and I estimate we've been naked outside for about
twenty minutes, which means I'll be turning into a lobster in the next
fifteen."

I glanced at her shoulders and back and saw a distinct rosy tint to her pale skin. "Yeah, you're turning pink."

I sat up, taking her with me, and she grunted. It took some maneuvering to get to my feet, but I managed it. I staggered the first couple of steps but had her on the back porch in a few minutes. I opened the back door, carried her inside, and straight to the guest bedroom where we both slept now because the bed was bigger.

She laughed when I dropped her on the bed, leaning back on her elbows. "So chivalrous."

I went to the dresser, pulled a pair of shorts out of the bottom drawer, and tugged them on. "I'll be right back."

I went outside to gather our clothes and found Merry in the shower when I returned. Since I was almost certain I had grass stains on my ass, I stepped in behind her.

And promptly yelled bloody murder.

"What the hell?!" I tried to back out of the spray, but the stall was so cramped there was nowhere to go. "Why is the water cold?"

"It's not cold," Merry informed me, her head beneath the stream as she rinsed the soap out of her hair. "It's lukewarm."

"After being outside in eighty-degree weather, it feels frigid," I complained, climbing out of the shower.

"Exactly. My skin is burning a little, so I thought a cool shower would help."

"Well, I'm going to take a warm one in the other bathroom."

Her laugh followed me as I stalked out.

Ten minutes later, I returned to the bedroom with a towel wrapped around my hips and found Merry dressed in a loose t-shirt, cotton shorts, and barefoot. She was drying her hair with a towel.

As I watched her, I realized this was exactly what I wanted, for the rest of my unnaturally long life. As fraught as the last few weeks had been, they were still the best I'd had since Macgrath turned me.

"Will you marry me, Merry?"

Her hands stopped scrubbing the towel over her hair and she looked up at me. "What?"

"Will you marry me?"

Her mouth fell open but she remained silent.

"Is that a no?" I asked.

She shook her head, closing her mouth with a click.

"So it's a yes?"

She shook her head again.

I cocked my head, trying to understand. "Then, what's your answer?"

"I don't know," she whispered. "This is...a little sudden."

I laughed. "You can accept and forgive that I lied by omission due to selfishness and absentmindedness, but a marriage proposal leaves you speechless?"

"Well, you never mentioned marriage...specifically. Just living together and maybe turning me into a vampire. Marriage is a big deal. I mean, I'm not sure what I really think about God, but if I'm going to make that kind of promise, I want to be positive that I won't change my mind in twenty or forty years. Or a hundred and fifty."

I walked over to her and touched her cheek. "I'll tell you what. I'll ask you again next month and we'll see if your answer is different."

"What if it's not?"

"Then, I'll just keep asking until you give a straight yes or no. I've waited lifetimes for you, Merry. I love you enough to wait a little longer."

"What if it's ten years before I decide?"

"Like I said, a little longer. Ten years is a blink when you're talking about eternity."

"I love you," she whispered, wrapping her arms around my waist and resting her head on my chest.

I returned her embrace. "I love you, too."

"Someday, I'll marry you," she said.

"See? You've already said yes." I squeezed her.

"Not officially."

I laughed. "Like I said, I'll keep asking until the answer's official."

"Good. I'll hold you to it."

I certainly hoped so.

EPILOGUE

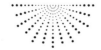

AVA STARED into the crystal orb, desperately trying to see through the thick mists that filled the interior.

There was nothing more frustrating than knowing something dark lurked over the horizon, but not being able to see details.

"You're not a god, you know."

Ava turned toward the source of the drawled words and saw Ewan leaning against the wall with his arms crossed over his chest. It had been more than a year, but her heartbeat still picked up speed every time she saw him again, as though she were seeing him anew.

After thousands of years without each other, they were together once again. It was bliss. But every day, she half-expected something or someone to come and destroy everything they had built. After all, it had happened before.

"I know," she retorted, mirroring his stance.

"Then, why are you so upset that you can't see the future? No one holds you responsible."

"I do," she muttered, looking down at her feet. "It's my job to protect them."

In a blink, Ewan Macgrath stood in front of her, his hands on her hips. "I can assure you that they're fully capable of protecting themselves."

"I know, but I feel like it's my duty to take care of them."

"You do. In so many ways. But you can't keep them safe for eternity. Danger will come and go. We can only be vigilant and face the enemy as it comes. You'll wear yourself down to nothing if you keep this up."

"Something big is coming," Ava said. "I can feel it. I just can't *see* it."

"You will. When the time is right, you will."

"I hope you're right."

He leaned down and kissed her. "I know I am."

"So arrogant." Still, she smiled.

Ava rose up on her toes and pressed her mouth to his. When she released his lips, she whispered, "When should we tell the others?"

He immediately understood what she was talking about. "About the baby?" he asked.

"Yes."

He paused. "I would love to tell them now, but maybe it's best to wait."

Though they were usually in sync, Ava wasn't sure what the expression on his face meant. "Why?"

"As you said, something big is coming. They need to be focused on protecting themselves, not you. That's my job."

Ava shook her head. "I can protect myself pretty well, too, you know."

He pulled her in closer, burying his face against her hair. "I know, but now we have a little boy on the way. It will be a two-person job."

She didn't argue, knowing that he was remembering the child they had lost so very long ago.

"You have given me everything," he murmured. "At this moment, the entire world lives within you."

"Do you think we're well-equipped for raising a child?" she asked, also thinking of the one they'd lost.

"We've put up with Callum for the last year, a baby will be a breeze."

Ava laughed and pulled back, tears sparkling on her lower lashes. "That's true."

Macgrath cupped her cheeks and rested his forehead against hers. "I'm so happy."

"As am I."

Ewan lifted his head and kissed her again. "I'm also afraid."

"Me, too." The tears slipped down her cheeks. "But I have to believe that we're strong enough together to protect our baby now and forever."

"We're not alone anymore," he said. "We have our friends. We have Marcus, Callum, Rhys, Savannah, and so many more."

This time, she kissed him. He was right. They weren't alone. They had friends who would help them if they asked.

"Speaking of Callum," she said when the kiss ended. "Have you heard from him in the past few days?"

"No." His face darkened. "And neither has Marcus. I think we're going to need to track him down."

"Do you think he's in danger?"

"I don't know. He wasn't himself when he left last week. He could just be avoiding us, but I need to be sure."

Ava laid her hands over his. "Want me to look into the crystal?"

Macgrath shook his head. "It won't do any good. He's wearing your amulet."

"Shit."

"Yeah, he's completely hidden from magic. And he turned his cell phone off, so we can't track him that way."

"You need to find him," Ava said, her eyes growing brighter as magic filled her.

"I'm sure he's fine," Ewan started to argue.

Ava shook her head. "No, he's not. Something's happened."

"Fuck."

*****

Callum

. . .

My wrists were bound with metal. I tried to move them, but they were held fast. Chains rattled, their sound heavy.

I cracked open one eye, trying not to moan. My head was splitting. The lights were dim, thank the Goddess. I hadn't felt this way since my time as a human. What in the hell happened?

Thick shackles wrapped around my wrists. A thick chain with five or six links connected them to a metal loop on the floor. It was huge and bolted down to the concrete floor with large screws.

Damn. I could probably pull it free, but it would take a long time and a great deal of strength.

I searched my mind for the memory of how I ended up here and came up empty.

One minute, I'd been lying on the ground near the complex that housed the Fallon Group, watching the comings and goings, and the next I was on a concrete floor, chained.

Somewhere in the distance, I heard a door open and footsteps coming down a long hallway. I kept one eye cracked and waited as the steps stopped. Bolts clicked and turned. Three, four, five of them.

The door in front of me opened, casting a patch of light over my prone body. A lean silhouette stood in the doorway. I could smell pomegranate and apples, a light scent of soap rather than perfume.

A woman, then.

She came into the room, shutting the door behind her. Her steps were light and quiet as she walked over to me. The woman stopped just out of what I estimated my range to be and squatted down.

I know you're awake, vampire. Save your act for someone else.

My eyes opened. I knew that voice. It was one I'd heard before. When Marcus, Merry, and I had been kidnapped by her boss, Edward Channing.

I tilted my head and looked up, into the eyes of the telepath that worked for the Fallon Group.

"Oh, it's you," I said, aiming for nonchalance. I didn't want her to realize how weak I felt. Whatever she'd given me must have been strong enough to knock out a rhino. I'd never before been successfully drugged as a vampire and I now knew that I never wanted to be again.

"Hello, again," she said, resting her elbows on her knees. Her dark hair was pulled back into a long, sleek tail.

I couldn't see her face because of the shadows that surrounded her and my blurry vision courtesy of whatever drugs she'd pumped into me.

"Well, I'd say it was nice, but I'd be lying," I drawled, resting my head on my stacked fists.

"I feel the same."

"Then why am I here?" I asked.

"Because you owe me," she replied.

I laughed, fighting the urge to wince as the sound made my already sore head hurt even more. "Considering you've kidnapped me twice now, I'd say it's the other way around."

"You and your friend outed me to Channing. Now, I'm on the run."

"Poor baby."

She got to her feet with a sound of disgust. "I'm on your side, you idiot. I infiltrated Channing's group so I could keep an eye on his dealings. After your friend called me his pet telepath, he decided he needed to know more about my abilities. Whether I was okay with it or not."

I had to laugh again. "What can I say. It's irony."

She paced back and forth, her arms crossed in front of her. After she thought long enough for me to practically hear the gears turning in her brain, she stopped pacing and faced me.

"We're going to help each other," she stated.

"What makes you think I'll help you?" I asked, lifting my brows as I smirked.

"Because Channing may be half an idiot, but he was smart enough to wear a button cam. He knows about you and your friends and he's trying to put the pieces together. Once he does, he's going to come for you again."

Shit.

"Get me out of these things," I said, shaking the shackles.

"Are you going to help me or strangle me?" she asked.

"I'll help you first, then strangle you when I know that the people I care about are safe."

"Jeez, that's comforting."

Still, she came over and a key appeared in her hand, almost like magic. I watched as she deftly slid the key into the lock and twisted it. When they popped open, she lifted her head to look at me.

Icy green eyes looked out at me, piercing and intelligent. Something inside me clicked, falling into place.

Fuck me. This wasn't the time or place.

And she definitely shouldn't be the one.

The End

If you enjoyed this book, please click here to sign up for my monthly newsletter to get exclusive content and to stay up-to-date on sales and new releases!

ABOUT THE AUTHOR

Born and raised in Texas, C.C. Wood writes saucy paranormal and contemporary romances featuring strong, sassy women and the men that love them. If you ever meet C.C. in person, keep in mind that many of her characters are based on people she knows, so anything you say or do is likely to end up in a book one day.

A self-professed hermit, C.C. loves to stay home, where she reads, writes, cooks, and watches TV. She can usually be found drinking coffee or wine as she spends time with her hubby, daughter, and Jinks the Beagle.

ALSO BY C.C. WOOD

Novellas:

Girl Next Door Series:

Friends with Benefits

Frenemies

Drive Me Crazy

Girl Next Door-The Complete Series

Kiss Series:

A Kiss for Christmas

Kiss Me

Westfall Brothers Series:

Texas with a Twist

Paranormal Romance:

The Witch's Gift

Novels:

Seasons of Sorrow

All or Nothing

Romantic Comedy Series:

Crave Series:

I Crave You

Wild for You

Only for You

NSFW Series:

In Love With Lucy

Earning Yancy

Tempting Tanya

Chasing Chelsea

Paranormal Romance:

Bitten Series:

Bite Me

Once Bitten, Twice Shy

Bewitched, Bothered, and Bitten

One Little Bite

Love Bites

Bite the Bullet

Blood & Bone Series (Bitten spin-off)

Blood & Bone

Souls Unchained

Forevermore (Contains Destined by Blood)

Ensnared in Shadow

Paranormal RomCom:

Mystical Matchmakers:

Rock and Troll (coming 2022)

Paranormal Cozy Romcom:

The Wraith Files:

Don't Wake the Dead

The Dead Come Calling

Raise the Dead

Printed in Great Britain
by Amazon

21808544R00145